In her youth, award-winning author **Ann Lethbridge** reimagined the Regency romances she read—and now she loves writing her own. Although living in Canada, Ann visits Britain every year, where family members understand—or so they say—her need to poke around every antiquity within a hundred miles. Learn more about Ann or contact her at annlethbridge.com. She loves hearing from readers.

Also by Ann Lethbridge

Secrets of the Marriage Bed
An Innocent Maid for the Duke
Rescued by the Earl's Vows

The Widows of Westram miniseries

A Lord for the Wallflower Widow
An Earl for the Shy Widow
A Family for the Widowed Governess
A Shopkeeper for the Earl of Westram

Discover more at millsandboon.co.uk.

THE VISCOUNT'S RECKLESS TEMPTATION

Ann Lethbridge

MILLS & BOON

First Published in Great Britain 2021
by Mills & Boon, an imprint of HarperCollins*Publishers* Ltd,
1 London Bridge Street, London, SE1 9GF

www.harpercollins.co.uk

HarperCollins*Publishers*
1st Floor, Watermarque Building,
Ringsend Road, Dublin 4, Ireland

The Viscount's Reckless Temptation © 2021 Michéle Ann Young

ISBN: 978-0-263-28426-3

09/21

MIX
Paper from
responsible sources
FSC™ C007454

Printed and bound in Spain
by CPI, Barcelona

As I write this, we are coming to the
one-year anniversary of a devastating pandemic.
I would like to dedicate this story
to all the frontline workers who risked their lives
to keep the rest of us safe, and to those who
stayed home, masked up, and did their part
to help make the world healthy again.

Chapter One

October 1818

Marcus James Durst, Viscount Thorne, stood firm, despite the girl sobbing on the lapel of his brand-new coat.

'It is so unfair!' Bess, Marcus's little cousin whom he thought of as a sister and who had turned into a lovely young woman in his absence, burst into another paroxysm of sobs.

Helpless against such misery, he patted her back and sent a look of appeal to her mother, his aunt, who, dressed in deep mourning and seated on the sofa, sent one back.

Marcus had arrived at Thorne Manor some two hours ago after riding up from Portsmouth, where he had disembarked in the early hours of the morning. He'd barely had time to change his clothes and go downstairs to the drawing room, before his cousin Bess and the Viscountess Thorne, his deceased cousin's mother, had journeyed from their new residence at the nearby dower house to welcome him home.

Francis had died more than three months prior. Regrettably, it had taken Marcus all this time to put his affairs in order in Paris because Wellington, while understanding his need to return home, had insisted that Marcus's replacement be fully briefed before his departure. He had certainly not been looking forward to facing the sorrow of his aunt and surviving cousin, and was himself still grieving the unexpected loss of Francis, but he had not expected to be greeted by floods of tears after so many weeks had passed.

He patted Bess's back and made soothing noises. 'It will get better in time, my dear,' he said. 'We all miss him terribly.'

Francis had died in a freak riding accident, leaving the title and his female family members in Marcus's hands. God, the last time he and his younger cousin Francis had been together, they had joked about Marcus being the heir apparent. Marcus had laughed it off and told his cousin to hurry and wed and relieve him of the burden.

Unfortunately, Francis had not taken the advice and as a result Marcus had been forced to leave the career in the diplomatic service that he loved, along with a French mistress whom he liked a great deal, and become head of a household consisting of his aunt Eudora and little Bess, who was not so little any more.

Marcus tucked his handkerchief into Bess's hand where it rested on his chest. 'Come now, darling, Francis would not want to see you so distraught, you know he would not.' Francis was never one to mope about for very long.

'My life is ruined.'

'Not ruined,' he said. He winced. 'I do not profess to be a replacement for Francis, but I assure you that you and your mother will want for nothing as long as you remain my responsibility.'

'It is not that,' Aunt Eudora said. 'Not at all, although heaven knows we miss Francis terribly. I know you will care for us as you ought, Marcus. No, Bess received a letter from a friend this morning and, well, to put it mildly, her marriage hopes were finally and completely dashed.'

Marcus frowned. This he had not expected. He had not heard there was a wedding in the offing. 'Come. Sit down. Explain the whole to me.'

He led her to her mother seated on the sofa. After a moment or two, she blew her nose and offered him his handkerchief back.

'You may keep it.'

Bess leaned against her mother, looking pale and wan. Nothing like the happy girl he'd seen the last time he'd been here.

'What has happened?' he asked.

A flash of anger shone through her tears. 'Lady Cynthia Finch stole the man I love.'

Love. He managed to stop himself from rolling his eyes. He no longer believed in love. 'I see. Please be good enough to explain from the beginning and I will see if there is anything I can do.' He disposed himself in the chair opposite the two women, prepared to lend a sympathetic ear.

'I thought Lady Cynthia liked me. She was very kind and invited me to all sorts of parties. She made me feel special. She is very exclusive, you know.' She shook her head as if confused. 'Algernon said he loved *me*. He was going to ask Francis for my hand, but when Lady Cynthia realised Algernon had fallen for me, she must have been jealous. I don't know how she did it, but she worked her wiles on him. One arch of her famous eyebrow and he ran to her side.

'I felt like such a fool in front of all my friends. The next day Algernon and I had a blazing argument and I told him to choose, her or me...' She waved a hand in a gesture of hopelessness. 'Then we got news about Francis's accident and we came home right away before I could talk to him and—' the tears welled up and she buried her face in her handkerchief '—then Francis—' She took a deep breath around her tears. 'I have not seen Algernon since.'

Aunt Eudora put an arm around her shaking shoulders. 'Hush,' she murmured.

'It is not the end of the world, Bess darling.' Marcus said.

'It is,' Bess replied in muffled tones. 'You are a man. You cannot possibly understand.'

He could and he did. Olga had hurt him badly. He had been blinded by what he thought was love. She had taught him a valuable lesson that winter in St Petersburg by very nearly gulling him into betraying government secrets. Discovering everything she had ever said to him was a lie had made him value the kind of common-sense arrangement he'd had in Paris with Nanette, a lovely widowed aristo of a practical turn of mind, rather than a bent for grand passion.

However, Marcus wanted to strangle this Lady Cynthia for upsetting his little Bess so. A broken heart and a tragic death in the family all at once. No wonder the girl was so upset.

'The letter came this morning,' his aunt said. 'We had been doing quite well, coming to terms with things…' Her voice tailed off. She seemed to shake herself out of a reverie. 'Lady Cynthia is beyond beautiful. They call her the ice goddess. Or her young men do. She is also quite wealthy.'

'She's old,' Bess said, showing a bit of her usual spirit. 'She didn't like it because I was going to be married in my first Season and she's on her way to becoming an old maid.'

'Now, Bess, that is no way to talk,' her mother said, 'nor is it true. Lady Cynthia cannot be more than twenty-four summers. But I am sorry to say, her character does not match her face. Young men fall for her every Season and she seems not to care a snap of her fingers for any of them.'

'I want my Algernon back,' Bess whispered.

This Lady Cynthia woman sounded like a

bully, not with her fists, but in far more subtle ways.

He'd had his share of bullying at school having been small for his age and rather gangly. Boys were notoriously mean to those weaker than themselves and wielded their power both physically and mentally. When he'd finally grown into his overlarge hands and feet, he'd been the biggest boy at school and he'd taught the bullies what it felt like.

The thought of dear little Bess, the child he'd carried on his shoulders when they went on long walks during his summer holiday with Francis, the little girl he'd comforted when she scraped her knee when she fell— well, the thought of her being bullied by this woman ignited his temper. Francis would not have stood for it, he was sure.

'Leave it with me,' he said. Getting her Algernon back might be beyond him, but it seemed as though it was time someone taught this lady to give a little more consideration to others. Perhaps that someone should be him.

'There is something else I must talk to you about,' Aunt Eudora said. 'That horse cost Francis a small fortune and when it fell on my poor son it broke its leg and had to be shot. Now we are left with a stable full of mares eating their heads off and no stud. Why could Francis not stick to farming like his father? If he had…' Heartbreak was written all over her face. 'You are not ruined yet, Marcus, but it will not be long before you are if things are not taken in hand. If I were you, I would abandon this idea of a stud farm.'

Marcus grimaced inwardly. While he had a rudimentary knowledge of the way the Thorne estate worked—having spent most of his summers here as a youth—he knew nothing of the business of a racing stud. Francis had been horse-mad and the moment he inherited he had sunk a great deal into this new enterprise.

Marcus was going to have to learn whether he should try to salvage what was left or do as his aunt suggested and abandon the idea before the estate lost money on the venture.

Not that he was impoverished coming into the title. Quite the opposite. He had made some very shrewd investments over the years. But he was not a man to throw good money after bad.

'On that front, I will need to meet with the bailiff and the stable master and see what is to be done.'

'See!' Bess said, leaping to her feet. 'That

is all you and Francis ever cared about. Stupid horses. What about me?'

She ran from the room.

Her mother sighed and shook her head. 'She does not mean it. Losing Francis has been a terrible blow. I wish I had waited until she was eighteen before I took her out into society, but she twisted Francis around to her way of thinking and a broken heart is the result. But I do think Lady Cynthia Finch acted very badly. Indeed I do.'

'As I said. Leave it with me. I have to go to London to consult with my lawyer and the bankers. I will also have words with this Algernon…?'

'Fortescue,' his aunt supplied.

Only by force of will did Lady Cynthia Finch prevent herself from staring at the strikingly masculine gentleman who strolled into the ballroom as if he owned it. And yet… She risked another brief peek at the tall, dark-haired, dark-eyed man she had never seen before.

A flicker of warmth sprang to life in her belly. A spark of interest she had not experienced for a very long time. Perhaps it was his size, being a man of impressive height and breadth, or the keen eye with which he observed his fellow guests. For a brief moment, she had felt that sharp gaze upon her person with a prickle of awareness.

Or perhaps there was something about the way the slight wry curve of his lips turned his harsh manly features into something bordering on handsome that made him worth a second glance. Although he was not at all good-looking in the accepted sense, he was definitely attractive.

Who was he? She had certainly never seen him before and prided herself on knowing every member of the *ton* worth knowing. Resolutely, she turned away.

'May I request your hand for the next dance?' Lord Vince asked. Slight and sandy haired with pale blue eyes, he'd arrived new on the town a year ago and she found him very young and very intense. 'It is my turn.'

Cynthia ran through her list in her mind. She had discovered that the only way to stop the young men who hung on her every word from coming to fisticuffs over her favours was to ensure that she favoured none of them. Consequently, she had invented the list and, based on this, each man took his turn driving her out, walking with her in the park, dancing with her, and so on. As long as she stuck to the correct order, there was never any squabbling.

'I do believe you are right.' She smiled at him.

He beamed. Inwardly, she sighed. It really was time for him to receive his congé. When he'd first come to town he had become embroiled with a couple of bad apples. He did not seem to have anyone to guide him so she had brought him into her little fold of innocent lambs who, if not kept busy, would easily become trapped and indebted to the unscrupulous rogues who hung about on the fringes of society. She had discovered the way the hells worked because her brother Thomas had nearly taken that path himself. Now, though, Lord Vince was well able to stand on his own two feet. Up to every rig and row in town as the young men liked to say. She certainly didn't want him to harbour dreams about a future with her.

She glanced around at the other four who made up her court. Some were there because they knew gaining her affections was hopeless and being in love with her was the fashion. The idea that they used her to protect themselves from matchmaking mamas amused her greatly.

Fortescue was a different story. He was a man of the world with an eye to the main chance. He made shivers go down her spine whenever he looked at her with what was supposed to be adoration. All he adored was her fortune and he had easily been lured away from the innocent Miss Elizabeth Durst by the thought of landing a bigger fish. Normally she would have had nothing to do with a man like him. A shudder ran down her spine every time she looked at him. Knowing what he did to the women whose services he used… it made her feel ill.

Unfortunately, she had no proof and, being a lady, she was not supposed to know about such things. But she had believed her informant, a woman the men liked to call Covent Garden ware. So… She had done the only thing she could do. She had separated him from Bess. And in so doing had lost the girl's friendship.

Fortescue, standing beside Vince, pulled out a notebook. Being the oldest member of her court, he had taken it upon himself to be official keeper of the list. He referred to it and nodded his assent. Vince's smile broadened.

'I have the supper dance,' Mr Fortescue added, stroking his elegant blond moustache.

Cynthia smiled at him, while her skin crawled. What else could she do but keep him at her side, keep him wondering if she would accept an offer from him, until Bess found a decent man to be her suitor? 'Your turn to take me to supper?' she said. 'How delightful.'

Fortescue preened.

She glanced back at the stranger across the room chatting with Lady Summerfield, their hostess. How interesting. The lovely widow, Mrs Maggie Willow, was openly ogling him over her beautifully painted fan. He must have noticed, because a moment later Lady Summerfield was introducing him to the only woman with more wealth than Cynthia.

He must be poor. How disappointing.

She thought about asking Lord Vince if he knew the gentleman's name, but that would only start rumour and gossip, if not outright jealousy. She had learned that by never appearing interested in any particular male, she could avoid the trap of an offer of marriage.

The one offer of marriage she had accepted from Lord Drax had been a disaster. She had actually liked the man and thought him honourable. She had thought he liked her, too, and had risked everything to tell him right before the wedding about being seduced years before.

Cornelius Hart, the second son of a squire, had described himself a gentleman fallen on hard times. He certainly had the manners of a very engaging young gentleman. When Cynthia was ten, he had become her and Thomas's riding master. He had been so charming, so attentive, so handsome, or so she had thought. By the time she was fifteen, she had been thoroughly smitten. If only she had realised that he saw her as a way to improve his fortunes. She had been so eager to please him, she had not needed a great deal of persuading to tryst with him, to let him snatch little kisses that made her feel all hot and bothered and delightfully feminine.

Oh, he had been very careful, taken his time to lure her into his snare, but by the time she was seventeen, she had been mad for him to take her to his bed, where she'd learned to please him. And then he'd called her minx and wanton and make her feel as if she had led *him* astray.

A year later, she had told her father she wanted to marry Cornelius. In the face of his fury, she had lacked the courage to tell him the full extent of what she and Cornelius had shared and Papa had immediately whisked her off to London for her come out.

She had thought that if she gave her father a bit of time to get used to the idea…if he had come to realise that her feelings were constant… What a fool she had been. Unbeknownst to her, Cornelius, bribed handsomely by her father to cease his attentions, had gone and married her best friend.

Hurt beyond enduring and not knowing what else to do, given that Cornelius was lost to her, Cynthia had kept the secret of their illicit love affair until the honourable Lord Drax made her an offer.

Appalled at the prospect of a wife sullied by another, Drax, to her shock and dismay, had instantly rejected the notion. Her trust in his kindness and understanding had been badly misplaced. Thomas, too, had been appalled, though far more forgiving than she had a right to expect when she refused to tell him the identity of the man who had, in his words, defiled her. Fortunately Drax was not so honourable as to refuse a payment in settlement of disappointed hopes, agreeing to keep her secret and proving it was not her he cared about, but her money. Because of that, she had avoided a ruinous scandal.

As far as the *ton* was concerned, the rich Lady Cynthia had jilted Drax at the altar. Ever since, they'd called her the ice goddess behind her back and sometimes to her face.

To keep herself occupied, she had devoted herself to furthering Thomas's political career as well as her own personal projects. And done her best to keep all marriage proposals at bay, by surrounding herself with young men who were not yet ready to settle down.

Cynthia glanced over at her companion, Mrs Paxton, the grey-haired widow of a distant cousin who suffered from dropsy in her legs and feet. These days, the poor dear found any kind of exertion wearisome and loved nothing better than to talk about her aches and pain. At this moment, she was deep in conversation with a couple Cynthia recognised as Dr Morton and his wife. No doubt the perfect audience as far as Mrs Paxton was concerned. She certainly wouldn't be worrying about Cynthia and which man was leading her out to dance. They had come to the understanding, not long after Mrs Paxton arrived to take up her employment, that Cynthia did not require Mrs Paxton's permission or even her presence.

From that day forward they had got along very well.

Lord Vince escorted her onto the dance floor and they joined the nearest set. To Cynthia's surprise and delight, her mysterious stranger joined the same set with Maggie on his arm. Delight? Surely not? She smiled brightly at Lord Vince as they took their places.

'Did I tell you how ravishing you look this evening?' Vince said eagerly.

'Why, thank you, my lord. Is that a new waistcoat you are wearing? I am almost certain I have not seen it before.'

His chest swelled. 'I hoped you would notice. I knew I had to have it the moment I saw the design.'

The little sprigs on the pale grey fabric were lilies of the valley. Her professed favourite flower. She had chosen them because they were only rarely found in florists' shops and only then for a few weeks in the spring. It meant that there was little opportunity for her court to bury her in floral offerings. Flowers made her sneeze. A red nose and watery eyes were not at all stylish.

As the number one couple, she and Vince had little time for conversation. Besides, an energetic English country dance made one too breathless to engage in chatter. As she moved through the figures, she could not help but notice her stranger did not seem the least out of breath. When the dance brought her hand to rest in that of the stranger during the star formation, tingles raced up her arm. A glance at his expression showed no reaction at all.

Strangely reluctant, she let her hand fall and she returned to her side of the set. The next figure, a hey, sent her weaving through the line ladies, passing Maggie Willow with a bright artificial smile until she arrived at the top of the dance where she and her partner were required to stand out. A chance to catch her breath and to observe her fellow dancers.

The man of mystery was lithe and athletic and his steps were precise and strong. His tailoring was clearly of the best. Each of the London tailors had their own particular style, Weston or Schultz being among the two best known. Except the cut of his coat, the set of the shoulders, so smooth and snug fitting, had a flair she did not recognise.

Perhaps he was French. Or Italian. He was dark enough, certainly, to be from one of those countries. And now that the war was over, travel between the Continent and England had resumed in full force.

'Are you attending the Baldwins' rout on Saturday?' Vince asked. He tugged at the hem of his waistcoat.

So very young and eager. Any day now he was going to try to make her an offer. Likely at or after the Baldwins' rout, which would be one of the highlights of the autumn, attended by all members of the *ton* who had come to town to take part in the business of Parliament.

Inwardly she sighed. How was she to cool his ardour without hurting his feelings too badly? Divesting herself of these young men was always a delicate matter. A diversion was in order. Her eye caught a glimpse of sweet little Miss Caregrew hovering anxiously beside the orchestra. She was the sort of young lady who would suit Lord Vince very well. All she needed was a way to get them together.

She glanced down the set. Would her mysterious stranger attend the Baldwins' rout? 'I have not decided whether to attend or not.' She was surprised at her answer since she had already accepted the invitation. The young men upon whose escort she relied would soon lose interest if they did not have to vie for her attention.

Then why would she consider changing her mind? Certainly not because she wanted to avoid a gentleman she had never met.

Marcus scanned the ballroom, looking for familiar faces. Why his hostess had insisted on him meeting the dashing Mrs Willow, he wasn't sure, but she was certainly not the woman he was seeking. However, he was not going to mention the name of any lady to a woman renowned for her delight in gossip.

Once more his breath caught in his throat as his gaze passed over the extraordinarily lovely blonde at the edge of the dance floor. Exquisitely gowned in silver tissue, she shone like a diamond. Their hands had touched in the course of the country dance a few minutes ago and he'd been shocked at the heat that had raced through his body.

'Marcus, you rogue!'

He swung around to greet the smiling, rather short fair-haired gentleman who had tapped him on the shoulder.

'John Caulfield, you rapscallion.'

They had been best friends at school.

Seeing Caulfield gave Marcus a sense of

homecoming he hadn't felt since arriving in England. Having been a member of Britain's diplomatic corps since his early twenties, Marcus had scarcely set foot on English soil for fifteen years.

In that time, things had changed.

Not the least with regard to his own circumstances, having gone from being the son of a gentleman vicar, to inheriting his title by way of the freak riding accident that had killed his cousin.

He shook Caulfield's hand. 'It is damnably good to see you again.'

'You, too. Finally whipped those Frenchies into shape, did you?'

He shook his head at the simplification of the last three years, during which Wellington had commanded the army of occupation France. Navigating the intricacies of the return of the Bourbon King to his rightful place had been a delicate matter. 'It has been interesting, to say the least.'

'Do you think peace will hold?'

'I do not believe the French will give us any trouble for a long time to come. I must say I wasn't sure who I would find in town ahead of Parliament sitting. I am glad to discover you here. I find I do not recognise anyone at all.'

'There are a few you will know, though company is thin,' John said. 'A couple of matters that will come before Parliament have brought in members of both houses to engage in negotiations during the drafting of legislation. Including me. And you will meet fellows you know at White's of an evening. I will take you there if you like.'

'I shall look forward to it.'

His friend grinned. 'I see you caught Maggie Willow's wandering eye. You'll enjoy her company and no worries about being caught in the parson's mouse trap.'

So that was why he'd been so swiftly introduced to the lady. 'She is charming. And who is the blonde in the silver gown?'

Caulfield made a sound of dismissal. 'If you'll take my advice, you will steer clear of Lady Cynthia Finch. She's as cold as ice and as cruel an incomparable as I have ever come across.'

An odd sense of disappointment filled him. So, this lovely woman was Bess's infamous Lady Cynthia.

He had half expected it and half hoped he was wrong.

So much beauty wasted on a woman who apparently was nothing but a bully. No wonder his little cousin Bess had felt herself completely outmatched.

Lady Cynthia seemed to sense his observation. She glanced his way and their gazes locked. Even from this distance, her eyes were a startlingly bright blue. Her full lips parted a fraction, as if her breath had caught. His heart picked up speed along with the feeling he had caught and held her attention for long enough to give her a start of surprise.

He forced his gaze to move on. 'Does her fortune match her face?' he said idly though he already knew she was wealthy.

Caulfield looked grim. 'She has money.' His voice sharpened. 'Why? Are you hanging out for a rich wife? If so, I would not set your sights on her. She already jilted one fellow, Drax, though he said they had parted by mutual agreement. She keeps a bunch of young idiots handing on a string, until she gets bored and cuts them dead. Broken quite a few hearts, she has. Still, it is rumoured she had her sights set on a wealthier title than poor Drax.'

'Why does society tolerate such behaviour?'

He shrugged. 'Her brother, Earl Norton, is a likeable enough fellow and highly respected.

All the time he turns a blind eye, everyone else does, too. She acts as his hostess when they are in town and I hear she is a worthy conversationalist.'

He watched her from the corner of his eye. Lord Liverpool, whom he knew well, had stopped to speak to her and laughed at something she said. Her smile in return was simply glorious.

'I gather you do not like her?' Marcus said.

'I adore her.' Caulfield's grin was infectious. He winked. 'What man in London does not? She is the fashion and has reigned supreme among the ladies for the past three years. Thankfully, I am happily married.' Caulfield gave him a knowing look. 'Shall I introduce you?'

He had the feeling that this lady would require a different approach to catch her attention. 'Perhaps later. Can we meet at White's tomorrow evening? I want to hear all about what you have been up to these past fifteen years.'

Caulfield's eyes twinkled. 'Most certainly. I shall look forward to it.'

'Good. I am so out of touch with society, I need someone to steer me clear of the pitfalls.'

John laughed. 'I thought diplomats were good at weaselling out of tricky situations.'

He was. And he was good at what he did, which was why John had no idea that another goal of meeting him tomorrow at White's was to gain an introduction to Lord Norton.

'Now if you will excuse me, I promised my hostess I would dance with Miss Hart.' John wandered off.

The orchestra struck up a waltz.

He was surprised to notice that Lady Cynthia did not seem to have a partner. On a whim he did not quite understand, he strode up to her and bowed. 'I do not believe I have had the pleasure. Thorne, at your service. May I have this dance, Lady Cynthia?'

Her bright blue eyes widened. 'Lord Thorne.' She held out a hand and he bowed over it. 'I do not waltz.' Her voice was light and musical and cool in the extreme.

'Is that because you do not know how? Or you prefer not? If the latter, allow me to assure you I shall not step on your feet or crash into any of the other dancers, so you need not fear on that score.'

She chuckled and her gaze warmed for a brief moment. 'Very well, since you come so highly recommended, you may lead me out.'

The foolish fops hanging about her glared

their envy and made him want to laugh. He pretended not to notice.

She placed her hand on his sleeve, a barely there touch that, despite the layers of cloth of his coat and her evening gloves, sent warmth spreading up his arm. Without a doubt, this woman was dangerously attractive.

At least, she would be dangerous to an untried youth, which he was not.

He strolled with her to the dance floor, aware of several pairs of eyes gazing at him in surprise. Wondering about his identity, no doubt.

Likely they thought him another of Lady Cynthia's victims.

He eased her into the dance and discovered he did not have to adjust the length of his steps as much as he did with most women. Their steps seemed to match without effort. He had learned to waltz in Paris and enjoyed the smooth flow of the dance and the closeness it offered.

His aunt, however, on seeing him dance it with his cousin at a local assembly a couple of years before when he had been home on furlough, had mentioned that London society had some rigid ideas about the proper performance of the dance.

He glanced down at his partner, feeling the slight resistance in her body as she put distance between them.

He eased his hold to accommodate. 'Ah, yes, I recall—there are rules about the proper distance between partners.'

Her expression was cold. 'You are new to London, then.'

Everyone seemed to assume he was a Johnny-Raw. Indeed, *she* made him sound like some parochial puppy. He hid his irritation and repeated his history. 'I was last in London while you were yet in the schoolroom, my lady. I have spent many years on the Continent. In Paris this dance has far more *esprit de joie*. Here it seems more like hard work.'

Her eyes widened a fraction. 'You were a soldier?'

'Not I.' He twirled her beneath his arm and guided her past two other couples.

'Thorne,' she mused. 'Family name of Durst. You are Marcus, then, cousin to the last Viscount, who died in an accident.'

She must have learned *Debrett's* by rote.

'His horse fell on him. Broke his back.'

'Yes, I heard. I am sorry.'

'Did you know him?'

'No.'

'Then why are you sorry?'

An expression of uncertainty flickered across her face. Her icy blue gaze narrowed on his face. She gave him a cool smile. 'My brother knew him. He said he was a good man and died too young. I believe one can regret such a passing.'

'One can. But does one?'

Her startled laugh sounded pleasant to his ear. Not less so because she had caught on to the dryness of his humour, which often passed over the heads of society ladies.

'Since my brother does, then so do I.'

'Do you always do as your brother does?'

'I trust his judgement.'

And what did her brother think of the way she lured another woman's fiancé into her clutches? 'As is your duty, since he is the head of your household.'

Her expression remained cool, but he had a sense that his words did not bring her pleasure. 'As you say.'

The woman could not have been more non-committal. Clearly, she was skilled at hiding her feelings. 'I look forward to meeting your brother, if he is as charming as his sister.'

She narrowed her gaze on his face as if

weighing his words very carefully. 'I believe, according to most, he is rather more charming.'

He found himself chuckling at the dryness of her wit. This was a woman with few illusions. And that did not line up with what he knew about her, did it? Against his will, he was thoroughly intrigued.

The orchestra played the closing notes and he led her back to the group of young men who were glowering at him. He left her to explain. He certainly wasn't going to hang about and risk being challenged to a duel or some such nonsense.

For a seemingly intelligent young woman, he was surprised she was happy to keep company with such a troop of nincompoops.

Fortescue among them.

Chapter Two

Cynthia gazed at her plate of scrambled eggs and gammon and for the second day in a row realised she wasn't hungry.

She'd barely slept a wink all night. It was all Thorne's fault. If she hadn't danced with him and then, feeling quite unlike herself, left right afterwards, her court would not have entered into a war over how to reorder the list.

On their walk the previous day, Fortescue had insisted he must have the honour of taking her into supper at the next event they attended. Lord Vince, who had been next on the list in that regard, was refusing to give up his place.

Pleading a headache, she had left them to their negotiations and gone home.

At least, that was the reason she was telling herself she wasn't hungry. The fact that the self-contained Lord Thorne made the clinging young men in her court seem irritating in the extreme was neither here nor there. Was it?

Thomas sauntered in. Cynthia loved her brother dearly. Always he stood by her, no matter what sort of scrape she got into. He had tried to intervene with her father when she had wanted to marry Cornelius. Though fortunately he had not prevailed. And he had been there with a manly shoulder to cry on when Cornelius had proved false.

Upon her father's demise, Thomas had taken up the reins as head of their household with surprising ease. He'd been Cynthia's rock after Drax's scathing words upon receiving her confession that she was no longer a maid.

Recently, Thomas had made it clear he was looking to wed and start his own family. Cynthia did not blame him one bit. It was his duty. However, once he married, Cynthia had no intention of remaining in his household, playing second fiddle to a wife who might treat her as little more than an unpaid servant. Even if the woman her brother chose turned out to be the kindest person in the world, Cynthia would find it difficult to hand over the reins of a household she had been running since she had turned twenty, some four years ago.

As a fallen woman, her prospects of finding her own bridegroom were minuscule. She had no choice but to tell any prospective bridegroom the truth about her past. If her own honour did not preclude her from keeping it a secret, then Cornelius would certainly find a way to bring it to their attention.

And besides, even if there was a man out there who would accept her as she was, why would she want to be married? At one time she had dreamed of a husband and children, but she had lost her right to such happiness with her own foolishness. Besides, the more she learned of men the less she trusted them. Certainly the ones she seemed to attract were either fortune hunters, bachelors hiding from matchmaking mamas or innocents who would be shocked at her past. No, the plan she had devised for her future was a far better option, if only she could convince Thomas she was right. If not, then next year, when she was twenty-five, she would set up her own establishment with her own money without anyone's permission. Although she really would prefer Thomas to see the wisdom of her plan.

'Good morning, Thomas.'

Thomas's hair was a darker shade of blond than hers. He had the look of their Viking ancestors. A big and burly cheerful fellow, who was hard to rouse to anger, but if one did, beware. He looked up from filling his plate at the buffet, a spoonful of scrambled eggs hovering in mid-air, and grunted.

He was not one for conversation before he had downed a cup of coffee.

After adding kidneys to his plate and a couple of rashers of gammon, he sat down. She handed him a cup of coffee exactly as he liked it: a dash of cream and three teaspoonfuls of sugar.

He swallowed it down and held his cup out for a refill. 'I gather you met a chap named Thorne at the Summerfields' ball the other night?'

She stiffened. 'I believe I did.' She spoke casually, but every nerve in her body tingled in anticipation of what he might say. 'We danced.'

'Rather a forward chap for a new title,' he said vaguely and opened his newspaper.

She hated that he read the paper at the table, but if she complained he would tell her to breakfast alone in her room.

That she did not want. Mornings were the only time she had a chance to converse with him privately about anything important. And she was thinking of trying again to convince him to help her with her project.

'Forward because he danced with me?'

Thomas lowered his paper and grinned. 'Lord, no. Every male in London wants to dance with you. No. He introduced himself to me at the club. Said he'd heard about the success of our family stud and wanted to seek my advice about the purchase of a stallion.' He grimaced. 'I can't quite decide if I invited him to dinner next Wednesday or if he invited himself. As I said, forward sort of fellow.'

Her heart picked up speed. He was coming here, to her home? Inside, she was a mixture of trembling excitement tinged with dread. What on earth was the matter with her? What was it about this man that caused her body to tingle and her heart to race? She could recall those same sensations when she had been besotted with Cornelius. Was she about to make a fool of herself again? Certainly not. So what if she found him attractive? She was no innocent young miss with stars in her eyes. But perhaps she wasn't as impervious to an attractive man as she had assumed. Nonsense.

She would never be as stupid as to fall in love again. She had nothing to fear from herself.

She forced herself to be calm. 'We will need additional guests, then. What a bother on such short notice.'

He stared at her, his blue eyes wide, as if he sensed something odd in her reaction. 'Not like you to make a fuss over trivialities.'

Why did men always think women's duties were trivial when they thought nothing of fuming over a wrinkle in a cravat?

Surely he realised that much of the success of his dinner meetings was due to her careful planning. It was she who made sure the right people sat next to each other and she who remembered who hated what sort of food and made sure the wine never ran out. Did he not see how she artfully steered the conversation in the direction Thomas desired when it looked as though it was flagging?

'He does not seem like a good fit with your usual crowd.' Most of the men Thomas mixed with these days cared only for their land and their sheep and the amount of rain they were enduring.

Thorne, on the other hand, seemed to be more a man about town. A charmer of ladies and more likely to lay his blunt down on a horse than a business investment. Which was why he was interested in the stud, no doubt.

A big man, Thomas was always hungry in the mornings and for the next few minutes he ploughed through his breakfast without speaking.

He picked up a slice of fried bread, took a bite and waved it in her direction. 'Why do you think him not a good fit? Admittedly he has been out of the country for years, but he has an estate to run and he's expressed an interest in continuing with the stud his cousin had planned. Run properly, there is a fortune to be made. I don't mind giving the fellow a bit of advice on bloodlines and so on. I hear he's not short of funds.'

The money, of course, was the deciding factor. 'You plan to sell him one of your mares, or a foal?'

'Apparently he's got enough mares. What he needs is a stallion. Rufus Choice might be just what he is looking for.' Rufus had been her selection; her father had promised he would never be sold. He put up a hand when she opened her mouth to object. 'I am not proposing selling him, merely putting him out for stud until he finds the right stallion.'

'For a fine fat fee, I hope.'

'Naturally.'

'I suppose it would be all right, provided he doesn't do anything stupid, like his cousin.'

Thomas's gaze dropped to his plate and he stared at it as if surprised to find it empty.

He got up, refilled it at the buffet and sat down again. 'It was an accident, could have happened to anyone. I doubt something like that would ever happen again. What he should buy is one of our mares, but he has too many already, he tells me. But we can discuss all that over dinner.'

Mentally she sighed. Once Thomas made up his mind, there was no moving him. 'Very well. I will let Bromley know we will be having guests for dinner. I'll invite Caregrew and Gayle. They love nothing better than horse talk. Perhaps it will be as well to seat Thorne beside me so I can keep an eye on him.'

Thomas's fork full of scrambled egg paused in front of his mouth. 'What? Do you expect him to make off with the silver?'

Goodness, surely she had not sounded as critical as that. 'Of course not. But as you say, he is new to town and new to his title. He might not be ready for the sort of political discussions likely to come up during dinner. I might be able to give him a helping hand.'

'He seemed pretty well up to snuff to me,' Thomas said and ate the eggs. 'He was in the diplomatic corps. Surely he ought to be able to carry a decent conversation. And besides, given that the intention is to discuss business, we don't need any other guests. We will dine *en famille*, if you don't mind, old thing. And we aren't going to be talking politics.'

'Really? I for one would like to know where he stands on the employment of children.'

Thomas glared at her. 'Look, Cynthia, I do not say a word about your involvement with this bunch of reformers you are so fond of, but please do not introduce these ideas of yours at my dinner table.'

Cynthia pressed her lips together. Normally, she would never have made so bald a statement. If she had not been envisaging Thorne at her dinner table and wondering what on earth she would converse with him about, she might not have, either.

Unfortunately, she and Thomas did not see eye to eye on the subject of child labour. No, that was not true. He didn't condone cruelty, he simply thought she was wrongheaded and repeatedly pointed out that families relied on the income from their children working in the mines and the factories. He also had no doubt that in time steam engines would replace child workers and their parents. When that happened, those families were going to starve.

The people who were trying to reform the laws about the employment of children were fighting an uphill battle, for all the reasons Thomas ascribed to. In her mind, there was one particular group of children who were worse off than all the rest: climbing boys.

And on this particular group she and Thomas stood on opposite sides of the fence. He was convinced that without the services of those little boys, all the houses in London, and elsewhere in the country, would burn to the ground. Their employment was, in his opinion, a necessary evil.

She was determined to prove him wrong. She might never have children of her own, but at least she could do something to help those who could not help themselves.

'It was a passing thought, Thomas. Of course I will do nothing to divert attention from the important matter of the breeding of horses.' For now, at least.

His lips pursed and his brow furrowed. 'Do your best to make Thorne feel welcome, will you? I don't want to let the chance of good stud fees slip by for the want of effort.'

Startled, she stared at him. A moment ago, he'd been boasting about the success of the stud. A chill of foreboding slid down her back. 'Is there a problem?'

'No. It simply makes good business sense.'

Before she could dig further, he stood and picked up his newspaper. 'I think I will read this in the library.'

In other words, he'd had enough conversation for one morning. She bit her lip. If there was something wrong, now was not the time to press him.

'I'll send Bromley along with a tea tray and some more scones.'

He nodded his satisfaction and left.

Her stomach dipped. Had something gone wrong with the stud? Most of her money was invested there. Her future comfort depended on its success.

Marcus watched his man of business depart from his luxuriously appointed study, half expecting to awake and discover the last few months were nothing but a bad dream. In truth, he knew it was wishful thinking.

The last time Marcus had seen his cousin Francis, they had joked about him being the heir apparent to the viscountcy. And the need for a wedding post haste. He had never imagined he would inherit.

Francis had been ten years younger than Marcus and still sowing his wild oats. He had also been an excellent horseman. It seemed impossible that he was gone. And for such a reason as a fall from a horse.

Marcus felt ill thinking about the loss. It was tragic for his aunt, whose husband had died of an apoplexy five years before. Francis had been the light of her life. And for Marcus. He and Francis were not only cousins, they had been best friends. Marcus had certainly never considered the idea that he would inherit the title. His future had been set, as far as he was concerned.

Indeed, in some ways, giving up his career as a diplomat had come as a bitter blow. An ambassadorship had been very much in his immediate future. He could likely have kept his position, if not for his aunt begging him to come home and take up the reins of the title. She needed him, she had said. How could he deny her appeal for help? His own mother had died when he was just a child and she and Uncle James, his father's brother, had often invited him to stay with them in the school holidays. They were family.

So he had left Paris and all its delights, including his mistress, and returned to England to comfort his aunt and his cousin to regretfully take up the reins of the title.

There wasn't much he could do to mitigate the loss of a son and a brother, except help his family through their loss, but having promised he would do his best with regard to Fortescue, he would do his damnedest to keep his word.

This morning's meeting with his man of business had been exceedingly educational. He stretched his back with a groan and got up from the desk. Not only was he now a titled peer, the estate was in extraordinarily good shape, despite his aunt's dire predictions. The previous Viscounts Thorne had been shrewd with their money. Even Francis, of Corinthian bent, a sporting man who, in spite of purchasing a stable full of horses and who liked to bet on horse races and boxing matches, hadn't managed to make much of a dent in the family coffers.

In addition, both the Viscountess and Bess had been left well off. Indeed, Fortescue must be an idiot to turn down a bride with such a substantial fortune.

Except that Lady Cynthia had a very nice

independence of her own and a great deal more beauty than little Bess, who was quite attractive in her own way. Beauty and fortune. A dangerous combination in a woman.

He pulled the bell and his butler came in answer to the summons.

'Have the stables send round my horse, please, Lister.'

He was now engaged to join Norton for dinner the following Wednesday and, as he understood it, Lady Cynthia would be his hostess. For some strange reason the idea pleased him far more than it should.

Cynthia guided her horses through the Mayfair traffic. Thomas would not be pleased to know she had driven herself into the city, if he ever found out. Ned, her groom, a big taciturn Scot, would never speak of it, provided she brought along him or another groom.

As an unmarried woman well on her way to becoming a spinster, she had a good deal of freedom to pursue her own interests. It was those that had taken her to the city so early in the day.

The Society for Superseding the Necessity of Climbing Boys was finally getting somewhere. Or they would if they could garner more support from men like the one she had met this morning, Master Chimney Sweep Harry Symes.

She turned into Hyde Park. Thomas was sure to ask her where she had driven and she liked always to tell him the truth. Some of it. Besides, Members of Parliament often rode here in the mornings on fine autumn days like today. It was a good time and place to engage them in pointed conversation.

Meeting people at balls and routs was all very well, but gentlemen in their cups or accompanied by their wives were not the best of listeners to serious matters. Also, this early in the day, there were likely to be few carriages on Rotten Row and she could let her team stretch their legs.

She eased her horses into a low canter and enjoyed the cool breeze against her face. In no time at all they reached the end of the Row and she turned her carriage around.

A gentleman rode towards her at a gallop. She recognised him instantly. Her heart picked up speed. My, Thorne looked fine on horseback.

Despite he was not one of the gentlemen she had hoped to meet, she felt a burst of anticipation in her stomach. Occasionally, the members of her court accused her of having a heart of ice. They were wrong. She didn't have a heart. It had been crushed by Cornelius and excised by Drax. But apparently she wasn't yet immune to the prospect of a handsome man on horseback.

But that was all it was. She had no real interest in Thorne or any other man. The only reason she continued to come to London each Season was to help Thomas and to continue her work on the committee.

Thorne slowed when he recognised her and brought his horse to a stop. It was impossible to ignore him.

She pulled up and put her whip in its holder. 'Lord Thorne.' She acknowledged his bow with an incline of her head.

'I did not think ladies drove out so early in the morning.'

She smiled coolly. 'I suppose you hoped you would not find the Row cluttered with carriages.'

'You are putting words in my mouth, Lady Cynthia. I meant only what I said.'

She blinked at his directness. It made a refreshing change from innuendo and flattery. 'I had an early-morning meeting. I was on my way home when I thought to take a turn in the park.'

He raised a brow at the word 'meeting', but did not comment. 'Horses need exercise, no matter where they are.'

'Indeed.'

Her team stirred restlessly.

He gave them a considering glance and then turned that same look on her. A little shiver ran down her spine. It was as if he was looking deep into her soul. Which was nonsense. 'If you were not riding, I would offer to take you up,' she said, feeling stupid the moment the words were out of her mouth. Only the most blessed of her court were ever taken up in her carriage.

And…good heavens, she had sounded almost flirtatious. Not like herself at all.

His dark eyes sparkled with mischief. 'If your groom would ride this fellow to the gate, I would be pleased to take a turn with you.'

Dash it. He was actually taking her up on her offer. And how nicely he had disposed of her groom. She sighed. Thomas would not want her to snub him, not even politely. He wanted this man's money from stud fees.

'Ned, please ride Lord Thorne's horse to the gate.'

Ned jumped down from the seat behind her and took the reins from Lord Thorne, who easily climbed up beside her.

She set the horses in motion.

'They are beautiful steppers,' Thorne said. 'Perfectly matched.'

His praise warmed her. 'I picked them out myself at the start of my first Season.' Oh, and now she sounded as though she was bragging. She felt more like an eager schoolgirl than a woman who had been out for years and who ran a household.

'You know horses, then,' he said. 'It must run in the family.'

'Ah, yes. You have met my brother, Thomas.' She turned her gaze on him. 'You will be wise to take his advice when you go to Tattersall's next Wednesday. That animal of yours is a showy beast, but quite knock-kneed to my eyes.' That should keep him at a distance. No man liked his choice in horses criticised. She waited for the bluster and denial.

He grimaced. 'Any fool can see the animal isn't what it should be, given the cost of it. I do not know what Francis must have been thinking. After hearing of your brother's reputation for judging good horseflesh I am delighted I ran into him at White's.'

A man who actually sought advice. And about horses no less? A rare specimen indeed.

She frowned. 'You were fortunate to obtain your membership so quickly.'

He chuckled. 'I had my introduction to London years ago, before I went abroad on diplomatic service. During that short visit my uncle Thorne kindly put me up for membership, so it would be there for me whenever I returned to England. I never expected or wanted to use it under the circumstances in which I now find myself.'

'One rarely gets what one wants.'

His dark eyebrows rose a fraction. 'What is it you want, that you are not getting?'

'Why?' She sent him an enquiring glance. 'Do you anticipate rectifying the matter?'

She winced. Had she really just made such a gauche invitation? He would think she was encouraging his attentions.

'I know better than to promise anything before I know what it is, Lady Cynthia.'

Most gentlemen would have immediately promised her the moon if she desired it, especially if they thought it to be impossible. Not him. That reply was an outright refusal to be drawn in.

Clearly, he was not like most gentlemen.

And she found that disturbing. And—dash it—interesting. And of all things, a challenge.

Chapter Three

Once more, Marcus was struck by Lady Cynthia's beauty. The chill of the early-morning air gave a tinge of pink to her cheeks. Her blue eyes, the colour of a summer sky, sparkled with what appeared to be genuine amusement, though he knew better than to trust appearances. Her hair, a most unusual pale blonde, almost white, was pulled back severely from her classically beautiful face and hidden beneath her fashionable Leghorn bonnet. A few strands, teased free from the restraint of their pins by the wind, made her all the more intriguing. The curve of her lips when one of her rare smiles touched them enticed him to taste.

His blood stirred at the thought. Would she be as cold as she appeared, or did passion burn beneath the chilly exterior?

He pushed the thought aside. Bess's tear-stained face and pained expression came instantly to mind. This was a woman who had injured a member of his family. A woman who used her beauty like a weapon.

The sparkle died and her face resumed its remote expression. Oddly, he felt the lack. This must be the way she held men enthralled. This desire to bask in her smile. Well, he was too experienced a hand to be caught by such wiles.

When he was younger, Olga had wrapped him around her little finger with her smiles and her subtle promises of more. For a time, he had actually thought she loved him. Fortunately, he had seen through her lies before she ruined his career.

'Did you have some purpose in seeking to converse with me alone?' she asked. 'Or is it merely the pleasure of my company you seek?'

He half turned on the seat the better to watch her expression. She had a lovely profile: a high forehead, a straight small nose, a cheek with a soft curve and a small, well-formed ear. 'Do I need a purpose to seek to be driven by a lovely lady?' he drawled.

She shot him a look askance. 'Now you offer me a false coin, my lord.'

'Come now, Lady Cynthia, you know you are one of the most beautiful women in London.' If not in the world.

She delicately manoeuvred her team around a pair of gentlemen on horseback who had stopped to talk. One of them raised his hat and Lady Cynthia acknowledged him with a wave of her whip. 'Only one of?'

Good Lord, did the woman's vanity know no bounds? 'Indeed.'

She laughed. A light musical sound.

Again, a surge of warmth sped along his veins.

'I gather from Thomas you are interested in learning about the business of owning a stud and you will join us for dinner on Wednesday.'

The change of topic surprised him. He had expected her to continue along the path of flirtation, that her vanity would prompt her to push him to admit she was the most beautiful woman he had ever seen. A truth neither of them doubted. Instead she seemed genuinely amused by him not placing her above all others.

'I have to admit I am a novice when it comes to the breeding of racehorses.'

She turned her head to look at him. There was a considering expression on her face, a look of searching in her gaze. 'A stud is a risky business. And extremely expensive.'

Was she trying to judge his wealth? Expecting him to brag?

'So I understand. My cousin spent a great deal of money on horses in what he considered to be a wise investment. I need to understand the risks before I decide whether or not to go further.'

'You are to be commended for your caution, then.'

Her cold tone made caution sound like a fault. He refused to rise to the bait. 'The stallion he purchased did not survive the fall, so I am at a crossroads. Press forward and invest more or sell off the mares and recoup what I can. And you?' he asked. 'Are you interested in the business of your brother's stud?'

She arched an eyebrow. 'Not in the least.' She brought the carriage to a halt, neatly gathered the reins in her left hand and held out her right. 'Thank you for your company, Lord Thorne, I shall look forward to seeing you at dinner next week.'

Clearly dismissed, he took her hand and bowed. 'Thank you for the drive. I look forward to our next meeting. Do you attend the Baldwins' rout? Perhaps I shall see you there.'

'I do not believe I shall. Good day, Lord Thorne.'

He jumped down, recovered his horse from the groom and watched her drive away. He could not help but admire her skill with her horses as she negotiated her way into the stream traffic.

For some reason, he felt as if he had taken a step backwards in his goal to get closer to the lady.

Politics had taught him that in order to gain what you wanted, you must know exactly what your opponent wanted and why. The latter was always their weakness. Knowing an opponent's weakness was the greatest strength.

He had assumed that her vanity would be her weakness, but she was so confident in her beauty, she did not look for affirmation. Nor was she a silly simpering miss. There had been a purpose to her questions. And she had not spoken the truth when she said she knew nothing of her brother's business Why lie?

Clearly, he needed a different tack if he wanted to achieve his goal of getting close to the lady.

Thoughtful, he rode home.

* * *

When Cynthia told Thomas she intended to forgo the Baldwins' rout, he had not been pleased. And now, sitting here at home, alone, she wished she had gone with him.

How could she, when she had told Thorne she would not?

Really? Why on earth was she letting him dictate her actions? What did it matter if she found him strangely attractive? She might be heartless, but she wasn't dead. She could appreciate a good-looking man. Except he really wasn't that good-looking. He was rugged, rather than handsome, manly rather than elegant and exceedingly self-assured to the point of arrogance.

Dash it. Was she afraid to meet him again for some reason?

The butler scratched on the door and bowed, holding out a silver salver. 'A gentleman to see you, my lady. Lord Thorne.'

She stared at him in shock. Her heart seemed to falter.

'Thorne?'

'Yes, my lady. Shall I advise the gentleman you are not home?'

Well, this was dashed awkward. She had given Mrs Paxton, her lady companion, leave to visit her family this week and could hardly entertain Lord Thorne alone. 'Ask him to come up, please, Bromley, and ask Mrs Merton to send up a tea tray. Perhaps you would not mind pouring for us. Or asking one of the footmen to do so.'

'It will be my pleasure, my lady.'

He left.

Her heart was pounding. She pressed a hand to her chest, willing herself to calm. What was she about? Why had she not sent him away? Because she knew how important his good will was to Thomas? That must be it.

She settled herself on the sofa and picked up her embroidery. It would not do to look too eager. Indeed, she did not want him here. Did she? Surely that was why she felt so unsettled.

Finally, the knock came and Bromley bowed him in before turning to take the tea tray from a footman and taking it to the console on the far side of the room, giving them the appearance of privacy.

My goodness, Thorne looked impressive in his evening clothes. His tailoring was exquisite, but it was the masculine form within the clothes that gave him an aura of power. A visible inner strength.

'I was not expecting to see you this evening, Lord Thorne,' she said once the niceties of greeting were concluded.

'I met your brother at the Baldwins'. He mentioned that you had remained at home. I wondered if you might be unwell.'

What was Thomas doing discussing her with a man who was practically a stranger? 'I am perfectly well, thank you. I was not in the mood for company.' Perhaps a set down would prevent him from making impromptu calls uninvited.

'I am delighted to discover you are in good health.'

Wasn't he listening? Or was he more obtuse than she had supposed?

Bromley delivered her a cup of tea exactly the way she liked it. 'Milk and sugar, my lord?'

'I prefer lemon and sugar, if you have it.'

Bromley looked chagrined.

'Sugar then, no milk.'

How interesting. 'That is the Russian preference, is it not? Lemon in tea.' Cynthia said.

'It is. I was there, before I was posted to Italy.'

'Oh, Italy. What did you think of it?' She had never travelled beyond Britain's shores.

'If you love art and architecture, there is nothing like it. I wish I had spent longer there. These last few years I have been in Paris with Wellington.'

'The Parisienne court has returned to its former glory, I suppose?'

'It depends on one's perspective. The loyalists feel it has gone downhill and the Bonapartists regret the return to the old ways of the *ancien régime*. Wellington has done his best to restore order without treading on too many toes and has made a fair job of it, too. I certainly do not think it is possible for things to go back exactly as they were.'

'Not with most of the nobility dead, you mean. I should like to visit Paris, Rome and St Petersburg, one day.'

He sipped his tea. 'Perhaps when you marry, your husband will take you on a tour.'

'I doubt I shall ever marry.' Now, why had she said that? She had not ever spoken that thought aloud to anyone, apart from Thomas, since the day she had thrown the words at her father upon learning of Cornelius's marriage. Her father had thought her a foolish chit and she had never told him the full truth about her and Cornelius.

Thomas thought that if she found the right

man, her despoiled state would not be an impediment to marriage, but if an honourable, genuinely likeable man like Drax didn't want her, then surely there would have to be something wrong with any man who did. No. She was better off being a spinster than being tied to some sort of blackguard. She certainly didn't want to marry a man who was only after her money or her connections.

And yet...she had, for some reason she did not understand, casually enquired into Thorne's circumstances. The gossip said he did not need to marry for money, so why had he singled her out at the ball? She certainly did not want him joining her court. His presence was far too disturbing for her peace of mind and she could only imagine Thomas's delight if he thought she had captured the notice of such a worthy suitor.

Surprise crossed his face. 'Surely every woman wishes—' He halted and there was an odd look on his face.

'You were saying?'

He shook his head. 'I suppose I should not generalise. Marriage does not appeal to all.'

What an odd remark. 'Is marriage in your near future?'

He smiled briefly. 'One has a duty to the title, as I am sure your brother knows.'

Yes, together they had reviewed several young ladies in this year's crop of debutantes and had identified two or three possible choices. Cynthia's stomach dipped a little as it always did when she thought about the future once Thomas wed. The closeness they had enjoyed these past many years would no doubt be lost, but she was also looking forward to the freedom setting up her own household would bring. She just hoped Thomas would not baulk at her request with regard to her living arrangements.

'It seems that you and Thomas will be rivals for this Season's debutantes.' She spoke dispassionately, as if she did not care about the bride Thomas chose. She did. A sister-in-law who was not a friend made a powerful enemy.

'May the best man win.' His calm assurance that he was the best man annoyed her intensely.

She got up.

He rose to his feet. 'Thank you for the tea, Lady Cynthia. I look forward to meeting you next Wednesday.'

Bromley ushered him out.

* * *

The lady did not expect to marry.

Marcus was still musing on that little nugget of information a couple of days later, as he sauntered along Bond Street, heading to White's. The weather was abysmal. A light drizzle had hung over the city for most of the past two days. He had forgotten how miserably damp London could be at this time of year.

Naturally, it also rained in Paris and Venice and Lisbon, and winter could freeze your cods off in St Petersburg, but English rain, London rain in particular, seeped into every nook and cranny—and it went on for days.

He dodged a lady, travelling in the other direction head-down, wielding her umbrella like a battering ram.

Why, if Lady Cynthia did not want to marry, did she gather some of London's most eligible bachelors around her and keep them dancing in attendance?

He'd made enquiries about those young men. Oddly, most were too young to think of settling down. Their fathers, whom he had met at this club or that, remained sanguine about their sons' adoration of the unattainable lady. Indeed, they seemed to see it either as completely harmless youthful nonsense or as the perfect way to keep them out of other sorts of mischief, like gambling hells or bits of muslin.

Fortescue was a slightly different prospect. He was older than most of them and from a good family that was clearly in need of an infusion of funds.

Charming was the word most used to describe the man. Elegant and with excellent manners, lauded another. An esteemed guest, always willing to oblige his hostess by dancing with any wallflower pointed out to him, one lady had said.

All in all, a paragon.

And the moment he met Bess, according to her mother, he hadn't as much as glanced at another woman. Until Lady Cynthia had beckoned.

If Fortescue was such a paragon, why would he let another woman divert his attention from a girl he had professed to love? And who clearly loved him.

Romantic love. It was rather a lot of nonsense as far as Marcus could tell. He much preferred respect and companionship, much like his relationship with Nanette.

There had been nothing but complete honesty between them and no long-term commitment. Certainly, no jealousy or drama had ensued. They had enjoyed each other's company when it suited them and had respected each other's privacy when it did not.

The so-called romance he'd experienced with Olga had been torrid and unbelievably exciting. It had also been uncomfortable in the extreme. While he had been cut to the quick by her betrayal, he had also been relieved when the affair finally came to an end.

But Fortescue was a different kettle of fish, altogether. If Bess's happiness depended on this man Fortescue, then so be it. None of his enquiries had revealed anything bad about the man. Everyone he spoke to simply assumed that like so many he had been dazzled by the attention of a diamond of the first water. Lady Cynthia.

He paused at the kerb, waiting for a gap in the traffic to cross the road.

Was that...? Surely not?

A willowy figure hesitated on the threshold of an inn while struggling to raise her umbrella. There wasn't a footman or a maid in sight.

Marcus threaded his way through the slow-moving carts and carriages and reached her side before she had it open.

He snapped his own umbrella shut. 'Allow me.'

Startled, she stared up at him. The expression that flashed across her face seemed almost guilty. As if she was doing something untoward. Her gaze held him. A sense of drowning in a pool of bright blue held him captive.

Her lips parted on a breath. As if she, too, felt the strange sensation. She blinked and the moment was gone.

'Lord Thorne.' She held the umbrella handle towards him. 'I seem to have caught my glove in the mechanism.'

He took a deep breath, bringing himself back to earth and to her conundrum. Her York tan glove was indeed caught beneath the slide. He gave it a tug. It was jammed tight.

He shifted his angle of attack, jerked it free and accidentally jabbed her with his elbow. She staggered back. He caught her, steadied her.

The umbrella fell.

They both reached for it at the same moment and he scraped his forehead against the brim of her bonnet.

She stepped back.

A gentleman leaving the inn squeezed past them. He raised his hat. 'Excuse me.'

Lady Cynthia let out a sigh of irritation and gestured to the umbrella at her feet. 'If you wouldn't mind, Lord Thorne.'

She had no reason to sound so stuffy. He had come to her rescue, after all. He bent and picked up the brolly. He glanced behind her, into the public bar a few feet inside the entrance. What on earth had she been doing in such a place. 'Where is your footman?'

She raised her chin. 'I didn't bring one.'

That was it? No explanation? No fluster? Just a make-of-it-what-you-will challenge in her gaze.

She had to be meeting someone. A lover? A twinge of jealousy caught him by surprise.

Why would he be surprised? She was a beautiful woman. A man would have to be dead not to find her attractive.

But if she was meeting a lover in a place like this, what sort of man—? His thoughts paused—could she be meeting a woman? It was possible. The lady did not want to marry, after all. But given his own reaction to her, he would be surprised if her lover was female.

In either case, if there was a secret lover,

he was going to have to work a little harder to claim her interest.

'Allow me to escort you to your next port of call,' he said, holding out his arm.

'I am going home. I have finished my errands for now.'

'Then allow me to escort you there. A young and beautiful lady such as yourself should not be wandering the streets of London alone.'

Her cheeks took on a faint tinge of pink.

Not as indifferent to him as she made out, then. Perhaps it was evidence that her affections were not firmly fixed.

Indeed, if such an outwardly chilly woman was capable of taking a lover, then clearly her armour of coldness had its chinks. He was looking forward to tearing them open in more ways than one.

Chapter Four

Cynthia stared into the pier glass in her chamber with a frown. Had she perhaps made too much of an effort?

'You do not like it, my lady?' Millie, her maid, asked.

Millie was excessively sensitive regarding any sort of criticism.

'It is lovely.' Indeed, the cascade of ringlets falling to her left shoulder and the feather-soft curls framing her face were perhaps one of the prettiest hairstyles she had ever worn. Usually, on the advice of a leader of fashion, she stuck to plain and simple. After all, as he had said, her type of beauty needed no adornment.

She smoothed a hand down the blue satin of her modestly cut gown. At least she had enough sense not to agree to the pink silk dress festooned with roses around the neck and the hem. While the gown was in the latest style, it was far too ornate for a dinner at home. As was this hairstyle. And the diamonds at her throat and wrist.

She glanced at the clock. Almost nine.

Thomas's guest would be arriving at any moment. There was nothing she could do about her hair now. 'That will be all, thank you, Millie.'

The woman dipped a curtsy and left.

Cynthia removed the necklace, replacing it with a choker of pearls and exchanged the bracelet for a plain gold bangle. She took a deep breath and headed downstairs. Thomas would expect her to be at his side when Thorne arrived.

She would miss these duties when Thomas married. They had given her life a purpose, but she had her interest in the fate of climbing boys to keep her busy. And when she was settled in her own home she would be able to give her committee and its aims her full attention.

She ran lightly downstairs to the first floor. The sound of voices had her peeking over the balustrade to the ground-floor entrance.

Bromley was assisting a gentleman out of his greatcoat in the hall.

Recognising the masculine form even though he had his back to her, an impulse made her continue on down.

'Lord Thorne. Good evening!'

His swung around, his eyes widening a fraction as his gaze took her in. 'Lady Cynthia. Good evening.' He bowed. 'Excuse my dampness, it is pouring yet again.' He sounded thoroughly irritated as he handed over his dripping wet hat. Bromley gave it a little shake. 'There was no sign of rain when I left home.'

'So, you walked instead of taking your carriage.' She swallowed a chuckle of amusement. 'I will see Lord Thorne to the withdrawing room, Bromley, while you deal with His Lordship's wet articles.'

'You are too kind, my lady.' Thorne held out his arm and she led him back upstairs to the first floor.

'Look who I found on my way down to join you, Thomas,' she announced upon entering the drawing room.

'It is not often one is greeted at the door by the lady of the house,' Thorne said. 'I consider myself honoured.'

The man was certainly a charmer.

Thomas looked startled, then beamed. 'Glad you made it, Thorne. The weather has been the very devil these past few days.'

The two men greeted each other and Thomas provided his guest with a brandy and Cynthia a sherry.

'How are you settling into the viscountcy?' Thomas asked.

Thorne took a ruminative sip from his glass. 'I am familiar with much of it, since Thorne Manor was a second home to me growing up. But I cannot say it is an easy fit.'

'I felt the same way when my father died. It took me a long time not to look around for my father every time someone addressed me by the title. My sister was a great help during that time. And still is.'

Cynthia smiled at her brother. 'Losing Papa so young was a great shock to both of us.'

'Francis was barely twenty-five,' Thorne said. 'His mother and sister are devastated.'

'I can imagine,' Thomas said.

Cynthia felt Thorne's gaze upon her face. She glanced his way and saw he was watching her intently.

'You know Elizabeth, my cousin, I believe, Lady Cynthia?' he added.

And, of course, his cousin would have mentioned Fortescue's switch of affections. Naturally, Cynthia had been described as the villain of the piece. And now she could not help but wonder about Thorne's motives for accosting her brother at White's. She retreated behind her usual chilly demeanour. 'Of course I know Miss Elizabeth. A dear sweet girl. We are the best of friends.'

Not any longer. And the tightening of Thorne's mouth said he did not believe a word of it.

Bromley scratched on the door and entered. 'Dinner is ready, my lord.'

'We are dining *en famille* this evening, Thorne. I hope you don't mind the informality, but we can be comfortable and I have gathered up a good deal of information to show you.'

'Why don't I leave you two to your discussions and take dinner in my apartments?' she said, suddenly unnerved by Thorne's disapproval.

'You would have us make you eat alone?' Thorne said with raised eyebrows. 'We will not hear of it, will we, Norton?'

Thomas's jaw dropped a fraction. He glanced at Cynthia, then back to Thorne. His blue eyes took on a calculating look Cynthia did not like before he beamed at Thorne. 'Absolutely not. I find the ladies keep us rude fellows civil. Besides, Cynthia knows almost as much about the stud as I do.'

'Nonsense,' Cynthia said. 'I have hardly set foot in the stables since Papa died.' The stables held too many embarrassing recollections of the way she had thrown herself at Cornelius for her to want to be there. If her father had guessed how besotted she had become over her riding master, he would have dismissed him out of hand. But Cornelius had been careful to observe all the necessary formalities when anyone was near. Only when they were alone had he turned on the charm, teasing her, flattering her and making her feel so very special.

Thoroughly entranced, she had found every opportunity to get him alone and receive the bounty of his attention. She would sneak into the stables when she knew the stable lads were busy exercising the horses and she knew Cornelius would be tacking up in preparation for their lesson. There had been all too brief stolen kisses in dark corners. His caressing touches when he corrected her form during their lessons had sent fire racing along her veins. But it had been late one night in the stable loft where they had made love. A rather hasty fumbling event that had confused her as much as it had excited her.

Of course, he had proposed marriage at once. As honour required, he had said, begging her not to reveal how far their love had taken them, in case her father challenged him to a duel. Fearing for his life, she had done as he asked, simply telling her father that she had fallen in love with him and begging him to let them be married.

Her father had point blank refused and had ignored her insistence that she would have Cornelius or no one.

Before she could catch a breath, she was whisked off to her first London Season and Cornelius married the local squire's daughter. Cynthia had felt so betrayed. Now, every time she went to Harrowglen she was sure to see Cornelius or his wife and had to act as if nothing had happened. To avoid a scandal, Cynthia had let Thomas think she had been swept off her feet by one of the many young officers she had danced with in her first Season, who had subsequently fallen in battle.

If only Cornelius didn't smirk at her in that

unpleasant way every time she saw him, she might be able to ignore her past. Unfortunately, since they were neighbours and since Thomas had no idea they had been lovers, she had to mingle with him socially.

How could a man who said he loved you marry another? But they could and they did. Take her grandfather, for instance. He had been madly in love with his mistress, but he'd sired several children with his wife. Indeed, it was quite normal practice among the *ton*. But a nobleman expected his wife to come to him as pure as the driven snow. And while Thomas might hope for a different outcome, she had no illusions left.

'Let us go,' Thomas said, 'before chef starts complaining that we are ruining his dinner by letting it get cold.'

This intimate dinner with Norton and his sister would allow Marcus to form his own opinion of the characters of the pair, particularly Lady Cynthia.

When she had met him at the front door, her beauty had left him short of breath. She looked different tonight, as if she had made some sort of special effort. Was it for him?

Something about her hairstyle gave her face a softer expression. But at the mention of Bess, she had definitely cooled. As for her description of them being dear friends, well, that beggared belief. Did she take him for a fool? If so, she would find out she was wrong.

'How much longer will we need to keep our troops in France, d'you think?' Norton asked once they were seated. 'Hasn't this war cost us enough, that we have to keep the army eating its head off in France?'

'Firstly,' Lady Cynthia said, 'the British government is not paying the cost of maintaining the army of occupation. The French are, as set out in the terms of the peace after Waterloo. You would know this, Thomas, if you took any interest at all in foreign affairs. Once the French have reimbursed the allies for the cost of remobilising against Napoleon, our soldiers will return home.'

Marcus hid his surprise at the lady's detailed knowledge. 'Lady Cynthia is correct. And believe it or not, the French are making very good progress. I should not be surprised if the debt is not paid up before the end of this year.'

'Which likely means we did not ask for enough,' Norton said.

Marcus chuckled at the dryness of the other man's tone. 'In hindsight, you may well be right. Unfortunately, I do not know what this country will do with all the demobilised soldiers when they return home. I doubt there is enough employment for all of them.'

'Are you recommending that Britain start a war elsewhere?' Lady Cynthia asked.

He stiffened against the edge to her voice. 'Not at all. Simply an observation. And a concern. Among them are the dregs of England's prisons for the most part. A set of villains, who without the discipline of the army are likely to run amok.'

The butler entered and dishes were delivered to the table *à l'anglais*, which made sense given there were only three of them. It reminded Marcus of family dinners at the kitchen table in the rectory with his father, who either read or prepared his Sunday service. Marcus had taken to reading at the table, too. When he had mentioned this to his aunt, she had been horrified. Dinner at Thorne was always in grand style, with everyone dressing elaborately and always served in the dining room.

'I hope you do not object to our informality,' Lady Cynthia said as if reading his mind. 'This is our custom when it is only Thomas and I for dinner.'

Norton grinned cheerily. 'The dining room is full of portraits of my ancestors looking down their noses in disapproval. Or at least that is the way it seems to me. Quite puts me off my feed to be honest.'

'I know the feeling,' Marcus said. He'd always preferred the kitchen at home to the stiffness of his aunt's dining room, but the lessons in manners and conversation had served him well in his career.

Lady Cynthia served consommé into bowls and handed them across the table.

She picked up her spoon and sipped. With a glance at the butler, she nodded her satisfaction.

The soup and all the other dishes placed on the table at intervals were delicious and while they ate he and Norton talked about stable designs, equine diseases and inherited faults.

A sideways glance at Lady Cynthia informed him she was listening intently to the discussions when he had half expected her to be bored.

'The thing is,' Norton was saying, 'one can

either invest in a stallion of one's own, breed one, which takes years, or hire out a stud with a known history.'

Marcus leaned back in his chair. 'My cousin decided to buy.'

'I have nothing negative to say about your cousin's decision, but to be honest, I never saw the horse. It came from France by way of Ireland, I gather.'

'Are any of the mares in foal?' Lady Cynthia asked.

Marcus shook his head. 'None. I understood from the head groom, that the stallion wasn't all that interested in the mares. Francis was pushing him to get the job done when he met his untimely death.'

Norton nodded. 'The stallion might have been too young.'

'That was what my groom thought. He had a feeling the horse was younger than the dealer said. Apparently, Francis got him for a song.'

'Beware of horse dealers offering good prices,' Lady Cynthia said. 'I can recall my father saying that on more than one occasion.'

'Well, there is nothing to be done about it,' Marcus said. 'Now I have to figure out whether to move on or cut my losses.'

'I would say it depends on the quality of the mares he bought,' Norton said. 'Perhaps one of these days I can visit and take a look.'

'That is an extraordinarily good offer.'

Lady Cynthia shifted in her seat, a subtle movement, but it seemed to catch her brother's attention.

He cleared his throat. 'To be absolutely forthcoming, I am really hoping you will take up the offer of one of my stallions to breed with your mares. I'll charge you a fair fee and I'll want a good price on any foal that I purchase later, but the rent won't be cheap. Rufus Choice is in his prime and he's thrown a couple of Newmarket winners in the past, so I am confident you won't be disappointed.'

The reason for Norton's generosity in his offer to give advice was now on the table. Marcus liked the lack of subterfuge. It was going to be a business deal. A friendly one, but business none the less. Except...would Norton have been quite so forthcoming if he hadn't been prodded by Lady Cynthia? And... well...he hadn't quite expected her to be the one with ethics.

Intriguing. 'I look forward to learning more about this stallion. I would also like to take a look at him myself.' His stable master had already given him some pointers as to what to look for in a stud. Indeed, the man had seemed quite nervous about Marcus's visit to Harrowglen, as if he feared his employer might purchase something he did not approve of.

'Don't you trust me to do right by you?' Norton asked.

The man seemed insulted. 'Are you telling me you would put your mares to stud without as much as a glance at the sire?'

'You know you would not, Thomas,' Lady Cynthia said.

Norton flashed an easy grin. 'I would not, indeed. Very well. Come to Harrowglen and take a look for yourself. Stay for a couple of days.'

Lady Cynthia frowned. 'The servants are not expecting our return until the Christmas season, Thomas. Sheets must be aired and a guest room prepared.'

Norton looked down his nose. 'I am not proposing we drive up tomorrow, Sister. I will write and let the household know they can expect us next week, if that suits you, Thorne. Cynthia, you will accompany us to manage the household.'

'In the middle of November with the Season well under way? I—' She ceased speaking, clearly seeing irritation on her brother's face. 'Certainly, Thomas. As you wish.'

Her submission surprised Marcus. 'I would not take you away from your pleasures—'

'Nonsense,' Norton said. 'M'sister is not a girl just out of the schoolroom. This is her third or is it fourth Season? She is not going to care about missing the odd ball or drum.'

He made Lady Cynthia sound positively ancient, whereas Marcus judged her not to be older than three-and-twenty. Yes, a little older than the usual debutante, but certainly not old enough be classified as an old maid as Bess had labelled her.

Lady Cynthia's mouth tightened, but her expression remained remote.

Perhaps her displeasure was nothing to do with balls, but rather to do with her reason for being in Cheapside. Not something he would raise in front of her brother, of course.

After a short pause, she arched an eyebrow. 'You make me sound as if I am in my dotage, Thomas. I shall be delighted to join you at Harrowglen.'

'Good,' Norton said. 'We will get up a

party and introduce Lord Thorne to our neighbours.'

'There is no need to create a fuss,' Marcus said. 'I will not be with you above a day or two.'

Norton grimaced. 'Our neighbours will view it dimly if they are not regaled with the doings in town. Cynthia also likes to check up on all the local gossip.'

Lady Cynthia's smile would freeze a pond in July. 'No trouble at all.'

'Then dinner with your neighbours would be a pleasure, I am sure,' Marcus said, ignoring her lack of warmth.

Norton looked pleased. 'Then it is settled.'

Lady Cynthia gestured for the servants to clear the table and deliver the dessert. 'Let me know when you have the date fixed, so I can let Mrs Paxton know the good news.'

'Mrs Paxton?' Lord Thorne asked.

'My lady companion. Naturally, she will accompany us.'

'Impress on her the importance of the visit.' Thomas said sternly. 'For once, don't let her duck out of her responsibilities.'

Marcus sensed there was something behind that statement.

Lady Cynthia must have seen his curiosity. 'Mrs Paxton hates to travel.'

'Mrs Paxton hates to bestir herself at all,' Norton said. 'She is as overpaid as she is lazy. I believe I serve as your escort more than she serves as your companion.'

Lady Cynthia smiled serenely. 'Mrs Paxton suits me very well.'

'Speaking of escorts, Lady Cynthia,' Thorne said, 'I was wondering if you would drive out with me one afternoon this week. Perhaps Friday, provided it is fine? I will drive you in my carriage this time. My cousin's phaeton is the first stare of fashion, so I am told. More importantly I would like to put his horses through their paces.'

Norton rolled his eyes. 'Don't say you are going to make up one of Cynthia's pack of hounds? I should warn you that there is some sort of list and you will have to wait your turn.'

Cynthia lifted her chin 'That is no way to speak of Lord Vince and the others, Thomas. They are all amiable young men. The list is merely a way of keeping things fair. And since I have no engagements set for Friday afternoon, I would be pleased to drive out with you, Lord Thorne.'

Norton cast her a surprised glance. 'No engagements? How unusual.'

'None that I cannot reschedule.'

'Then I shall hope for fine weather,' Marcus said. Now why was she prepared to reorganise her schedule for him? Was this a way to curry favour on her brother's behalf? Or was she actually interested in his company? Likely the former.

Cynthia nodded. 'And so shall I. Now if you gentlemen will excuse me, I will retire to my drawing room for tea and leave you to your port and your breeding programmes and lineages.' Marcus rose to his feet and watched her depart.

'Let us get down to business,' Thomas said. He crossed to a sideboard and drew out several rolls of paper. 'Look at this.' He unrolled one of them and spread it flat on the table. 'Rufus Choice's lineage. He has many top-notch ancestors. You would not believe how many people have offered to purchase him. I rarely let him out for stud. Why help my competitors?'

'Then why help me?'

Norton rubbed at his chin. 'Not that I would say anything to Cynthia, but I had some unexpected expenses recently. If we can come to an agreement on the stud fee that suits me, it will save me some embarrassment.'

'Losses at table?'

'A stupid bet.'

Friday rolled around a lot quicker than Cynthia wanted or expected, but here she was riding out of London towards Hampstead in one of the flashiest curricles she had ever seen. The body was a bright blue with dark red accents. The Thorne crest in gold on the doors proudly announced its owner.

'I hope I am not going to be called out by any of the young fools who follow you around,' Marcus said as he tooled his team of chestnut horses along the road in prime style.

'These beasts of yours are as showy as the carriage. I hope they will make it up the hill to Hampstead. The leader looks as if he is short of breath.'

He laughed. It was a warm pleasant sound. It made her toes curl inside her half-boots and her heart beat faster.

Something like the way Cornelius made her feel all those years ago?

And why was she even thinking about Cornelius after all this time? The recollection of her naivety sent her stomach sliding away. A welcome dash of cold water to her wayward thoughts.

'Are you saying my cousin Francis was a poor judge of horses?' he asked with a teasing note in his voice.

Generally, men did not like criticism of their selection of horses. 'That is up to you to judge.'

He sighed. 'You are right. The team is beautifully matched in looks, but two of them are not at all sound. I'll have to put them out to grass.'

'Or sell them on to some unsuspecting soul.'

'Now, now, Lady Cynthia, that would not be at all sporting. Or honourable.'

'You are right. And I am glad to hear you say it.' She was glad. More pleased than she should have been, in fact.

'I have the feeling you are as knowledgeable about horses as is your brother.'

'Does that surprise you?'

He looked thoughtful. 'I find that ladies have a great deal of knowledge, but often they don't care to share it. Perhaps they fear appearing bookish, or mannish. These are admonitions I have heard my aunt repeat to my cousin Elizabeth.'

She chuckled. 'My governess said much the same thing. But my father loved to share his knowledge of horses. It was his passion. One could not be around him and not learn something useful. With regard to horses, he encouraged me to observe things for myself and have opinions. Occasionally, he was forced to admit I was right, which he did with very good grace, I might add. But I would not say I know more than Thomas.'

It had been galling acknowledging her father had been right about Cornelius. But she had done it, recalling all the times when he had been persuaded by her logic that she had spotted something he had missed in dealing with a sick horse.

'Well, I shall be grateful for both your opinions.'

'You are not suggesting I accompany you when you and Thomas go to take a look at your mares.'

'Why not? You have an instinct for what is wrong with an animal. Francis's stable master must not have noticed the lead horse's laboured breathing or Francis would not have purchased him, I am sure. It appears they both were dazzled by his looks.'

'I do not think it would be a good idea.'

She could just imagine Miss Elizabeth's face if she were to arrive on her doorstep.

'You are thinking of my cousin?'

Her jaw dropped. 'For a diplomat, you are very blunt.'

'I believe in speaking the truth. My aunt and my cousin have removed to the dower house. It is unlikely that we will run into them if we are only there for a few hours.'

She was sorely tempted. For some reason she wanted to see his home. 'If Thomas would like me to go with him, I will come.'

'Do you like keeping house for your brother? Is that why you said you would never marry?'

It appeared he had remembered that ill-considered remark. 'I am happy to help Thomas until he finds a wife. Then I shall set up my own establishment.'

'I see.' He sounded puzzled, but did not press her further.

While they chatted, they left the crowded buildings and houses of London behind them and the road climbed slowly. The countryside changed with each mile and soon they reached the village of Hampstead, and beyond it, open heathland with patches of golden sand among stretches of rough grass and wild gorse.

'One can imagine how dark it must be here at night,' Cynthia remarked. 'I have passed through here many times, but always in daylight.'

'You are thinking of highwaymen,' Thorne replied. 'Nothing to worry about these days, I assure you.'

'You are right. Most of the crime occurs in the cities these days.' She pursed her lips. 'And not all of it committed by common criminals.'

He frowned at her. 'I do not take your meaning.'

She shook her head. She had promised Thomas not to bore Thorne with talk of climbing boys and her work with the committee.

'It is of no consequence. What a beautiful view.' The wilderness of the heath surrounded them. Dotted with stands of trees, vivid green swards carved by ribbons of yellow sandy footpaths, vistas were endless and varied in whichever direction one looked. 'The air is so clean…it seems almost impossible that we have driven such a short distance from town.'

He drew off the road. 'It is lovely. My uncle introduced me to the place the first time I was in London.' He pressed his lips together as if he felt he had said too much.

She did not press him to continue. Gentlemen did many things they thought unsuitable to bring to a lady's ear.

'To appreciate the true beauty of this place,' he continued, 'one needs to walk. Are you of a mind to take a stroll?'

'Most certainly.' She enjoyed walking.

He helped her down from the carriage and he took her arm. 'The ground is rough, so I suggest you watch your step.'

He guided her along well-trodden paths where the sand had been compressed. Here and there sheep grazed on the short rough grass watched over by a child. A little girl in a ragged grey dress and grimy apron met them on the path with a gaggle of geese waddling behind.

Thorne and Cynthia stepped aside to give them a wide birth.

The little girl stared at them curiously as she went by and the geese hissed and flapped their wings.

The child waved her stick and scolded them loudly and the geese stretched their necks in a most aggressive manner, but kept on walking.

Cynthia remained watching the little girl

until she disappeared from view. 'If a child must work, that is a healthy occupation.'

He took her arm. 'She made a charming picture, did she not?'

Around the next turn the ground dropped away.

'Oh, my goodness,' Cynthia said. 'How pretty.'

'I know,' Thorne said. 'This was why I was so pleased the weather was clear today.'

From here, nestled in the valley below, one overlooked a body of water and beyond it, through the haze of smoke, the spires of London's churches poked upwards.

'We are fortunate indeed. I wish I had brought my sketchbook, though I doubt I could do it justice.'

'You have an artist's eye for beauty, then,' Thorne said. 'Turner's studies of the Heath have been much admired.'

'I do not profess to compete with his sort of talent, but one has the urge to somehow capture the beauty of such a scene.'

They wandered a little way down the hill towards the pond. Not far off a couple of men were filling a donkey cart with sand. 'Quarrying,' Thorne remarked. 'The reason the ground is pockmarked. The sand here is of the finest quality for building.' He glanced up at the sky. 'I am not sure I like the look of that cloud heading our way. We might need to find shelter. Have you ever been to the Vale of Health?'

'Health? Is it some sort of spa?'

'Not at all. A small picturesque village with an inn where we can take tea.'

While it was perfectly fine to go for a drive in an open carriage, taking tea tête-à-tête in a secluded inn was sure to lead to trouble. She recalled bumping into him in Cheapside. Oh, goodness, had he formed some sort of unsavoury impression from that meeting?

'Without my maid or Mrs Paxton to accompany us, I must regretfully decline.' She sounded stiff and rather accusatory, but he really should not have put her in such a position.

He turned the carriage onto the main road. 'They have tables outside in the courtyard. Not at all private.'

'Why did you not say so?'

'Because you are a lady and I am a gentleman, therefore I assumed it would be obvious I would not endanger your reputation.'

She stared at him open-mouthed.

He laughed, his eyes twinkling with mischief, like a naughty boy. He was teasing.

No one, except Thomas and Cornelius, had ever teased her—most men were all too anxious to gain her favour.

She resisted the urge to grab his arm and give him a shake, the way one did with naughty lads, but did not hold back her chuckle. 'Very well, let us take tea in the Vale of Health.' She glanced upwards. 'And hope it does not rain.'

Chapter Five

⁓⁓⁓⁓⁓

To reach the village, Marcus turned off the main road and followed a rutted track of hard-packed sand. His passenger was required to cling to the handle on her side, to stop herself being thrown around.

He noticed that she was very careful to make sure their bodies did not come into contact, which made him pick some of the bigger ruts to see if he could give himself an excuse to put a protective arm around her. It did not work.

The inn he was seeking stood in the middle of a village that consisted of a few cottages along the single track. As promised by his friend Caulfield when they had met for lunch the previous day, it provided a magnificent view of this part of the Heath.

An ostler ran out to take care of the horses.

No other patrons graced any of the small round tables set alongside the inn where the view was at its best. As Caulfield had suggested, they were likely to be quite private, without seeming to be engaged in anything clandestine.

Of course, he had not told Caulfield which lady he planned to escort here and nor had his friend asked. Those were things a gentleman did not gossip about.

'What do you think?' he asked Lady Cynthia, quite willing to let her change her mind about stopping for tea if she had any concerns.

'How clever of you to find such a pretty place.'

Her obvious delight pleased him. 'A friend mentioned it as a lovely spot. I think it lives up to his description.'

He jumped down and helped her out of the carriage. A waiter guided them to a table beneath an awning and he ordered tea and cakes.

While the waiter bustled about with napkins and trays of cakes and freshly brewed tea, Marcus kept the conversation to innocuous topics like the view, the weather, and whether or not they planned to attend Almack's the following Wednesday.

'If you are looking for a bride,' Lady Cynthia was saying, 'you really cannot do better than show your face there at every opportunity. While the company is quite thin at this time of year, there are always a few hopeful young ladies in attendance who are worthy of any man's consideration.'

He leaned back in his chair. Did she plan to give him a hand finding a wife, or was she also talking to fill in what would have otherwise been an awkward silence? 'Actually, I am in no rush to find a bride, although I do thank you for your advice.'

The waiter finished delivering items to their table, bowed and left. Lady Cynthia poured him a cup of tea. 'You might well be wise to wait for next year's crop of young ladies.'

'It would suit me better. My cousin Francis left quite a few loose ends that need to be tied off.' One of those being Elizabeth. If he didn't get Fortescue sorted out, he'd be squiring her and her mother about, husband-hunting, in the spring and putting his own plans on hold until the matter was settled.

It was not a role he particularly cared for, though if duty required it, then it would be done.

Her thoughtful gaze gave him the feeling

she knew he was thinking about his cousin. He leaned forward and offered her the scones. She delicately picked two and placed them on her plate. For a moment or two, they busily added butter and jam to the flaky little pastries.

'Now, Lady Cynthia, tell me about this meeting of yours in Cheapside. I am concerned that a woman who is as careful of her reputation as you so clearly are would allow herself to be seen in such an unsavoury location.'

Her eyes widened. Had she thought he would not ask? 'You sound like Thomas.'

'I take that as a compliment to both of us.'

She pressed her lips together. 'I shall not tell you because it is none of your business what I do and, if you think to tattle-tale to Thomas, I can assure you he will not care.'

'I do not believe your brother would be so careless about his family's reputation. Very well, if you do not wish to tell me your reason for being there, I will commit to saying nothing further about it, if you will promise not to repeat your recklessness. The City of London is rife with cutpurses and other unsavoury characters—a lady alone is not safe.'

'I thank you for your concern, but I will make no such promise.'

He took a bite of scone. 'Delicious. You should try yours.'

She made a sound of impatience. 'Very well, if you must know, I met a group of like-minded people about a matter I consider important. Continue to feel is important.

It sounded like one of those groups that ladies formed to do good works, but why on earth would they meet in such an unsavoury location?

'You are interested in making the world a better place?'

'Why do you look so surprised?' she asked.

'To be honest, I am surprised that you of all people would expose yourself to scandal for the good of others.'

She stiffened. 'Me of all—' Her eyes narrowed. 'If you have such a low impression of my character, sir, I wonder that you seek out my company at all.'

Well, that had not been exactly diplomatic, had it? 'I beg your pardon, that was poorly phrased. And why, if the matter is so important and worthy, will you not say what it is?'

'Why would I need to satisfy your curiosity? Unless you are interested in offering assistance?'

'I can hardly offer assistance if I do not know what it is about.'

Her gaze sharpened. 'If you must know, I was meeting with The Society for Superseding the Necessity of Climbing Boys. We meet in Cheapside because several of the members are sweeps themselves.'

Surprise filled him. 'Climbing boys?'

'Yes. The little lads who clean our chimneys. Some of them are not more than five years old. The sweeps light fires beneath them to force them upwards, you know. And I have even heard of them getting stuck and—' She closed her eyes for a moment. 'Poor little fellows. It is inhumane.'

The outrage in her voice gave him pause.

'How could I be of assistance?'

'You want to help?'

'I would know more about it.'

'We need a law passed in Parliament, protecting the children. It is really the only way to stop it. Thomas does not agree that we can stop it.'

Her brother would likely know more about it than Marcus. 'I cannot promise help, but I do promise to look into the matter.'

She looked disappointed and he had an urge to jump into the fray with both feet. But he knew better than to make promises he could not keep. 'In the meantime, I would have your word that you will not go alone to Cheapside for these meetings or any other reason.'

'Very well.' Her tone was begrudging. 'I will engage to take a footman with me, next time.'

'Thank you.'

Whether she could be trusted to keep her word, he wasn't sure, but he had done his duty and he was in no position to force her to do his will.

Her expression became frosty. 'Was this why you sought me out today? To chastise me for what you see as a transgression? It was not to make use of my expertise with horses at all, was it?'

'Certainly not.'

Understanding dawned on her face. 'Then it was because of your cousin, Elizabeth. You are trying to make me give Fortescue up.'

There was no point in denying it. 'Her heart is broken, so she tells me. Why do you not give Fortescue his congé? It does not appear to me that you favour him above any of the others in your court. Elizabeth loves him. Why keep him hanging on a string? It is unkind.'

Her gaze remained hard, though her voice

was light, almost playful. 'I would not like to limit my options.'

How could she feel so strongly about the plight of climbing boys, yet behave with such callousness to a young woman she had not long ago called friend?

He had been right in his judgement of character. She really was a cold-hearted woman. Regret filled him. It was as if he had really hoped she was not as she appeared, not the woman Caulfield had described. His hope was groundless.

He looked down at the plate of scones. He had lost his appetite.

He glanced over at her. She was staring at the view as if transfixed. As if sensing his gaze upon her, she turned her head and gave him her usual cool smile. 'What a pleasant afternoon we have had, but I think it is time you took me home, don't you?'

Damn it, he had handled her badly. If Wellington would have seen him floundering around, he would have laughed his head off at the clumsiness of his approach. But the truth was in the open now and what was said could not be unsaid.

He paid their tab and sent for his carriage to be brought around.

* * *

The silence between them was palpable as they turned onto the London road.

Cynthia folded her arms across her chest and then forced herself to uncross them. She would not let him see that she was upset. Not for a moment.

What a nerve for him to think he could use her presence in Cheapside to get her to give up Fortescue. And for him to lecture her on her behaviour to boot. Who did he think he was?

And besides, what sort of person would she be if she allowed the likes of Fortescue to prey on an innocent young thing like Miss Elizabeth Durst?

No. That she would not do. She did not give a fig for Thorne's opinion of her character. She liked Elizabeth. She was a sweet young woman who did not deserve to marry a man like Fortescue. No one did. If there was some way to prevent him from marrying anyone at all—she would do it.

Clearly Thorne had an exceedingly low opinion of her intentions. It would not occur to him that she was trying to help his cousin. Damn him. It did not matter what he thought. There was no reason she should feel so…

disappointed...sad...hurt. Hurt? What nonsense.

'By the way, I have decided not to go with you to Harrowglen, after all,' she said calmly. 'My presence is superfluous. As it happens, I had forgotten an appointment with my dressmaker. I need a new winter wardrobe. The fashions this year are so different I feel quite the dowd.'

'I doubt that your presence is ever superfluous, Lady Cynthia. Or that anyone would ever think you dowdy.'

Two compliments in a row after such a scathing assessment of her as a person? How like a man to think he could say whatever he pleased, then return to one's good graces by way of outrageous and insincere flattery. On the other hand, what was it about that deep voice that caused shivers of delight to run down her spine when he spoke? It was as if her body had awoken from a long sleep and now demanded attention. Not from her, but from him.

She pushed aside the unwelcome thought and the little dip it caused in her stomach. 'Do not think to butter me up, my lord. Having invited me to go driving under false pretences, there is nothing you can say that will redeem you in my eyes.'

'False pretences? I have no conception of what you mean.'

'Really? You make me think you wished to seek my advice, when it was really an excuse to plead your cousin's cause.'

He gave her a hard look. 'I sought your advice. And I should have known better than to hope that a woman as cold as you would feel the slightest sympathy for a rival.'

Shocked, not only by the words, but the cuttingly cold way in which they were delivered, she stared at him. Her heart contracted painfully. The hurt that she had felt at his earlier assessment of her character increased fourfold.

It had been a long time since any man had been able to hurt her feelings. So why did this man have the ability to cause her pain? She scarcely knew him. He meant nothing. None of them did. Cornelius had taught her the truth about men. They were selfish, cruel creatures.

Including her brother, Thomas. And he was one of the very best men she knew. And she had thought, for some odd reason, Thorne might be another of the better ones.

Clearly, when a man was attractive as he was, a woman forgot the lessons of the past.

Damn him.

She stiffened her spine. 'How fortunate that we have come to a common understanding.'

'Have we, now?'

'Oh, I believe we can both say without reservation that we hold each other in contempt.'

His mouth set in a grim line. He did not disagree, however.

They passed through the bustling Hampstead village without a word.

Good. She did not care if he never spoke to her again.

A yard or two beyond the village he pulled the carriage off onto the verge and turned to face her.

'Why have you stopped?'

'Naturally, I am wondering whether I should leave you to walk home by yourself.' There was a dry note to his voice she did not trust.

Surely he could not be serious. Could he? 'You would not dare leave me in the middle of nowhere.'

'It is but three miles to London. You could walk it in an hour.'

Aghast, she stared at him. Visions of highwaymen and ruffians sent cold shivers down her spine. Damn him, she was not going to show him that she was afraid. 'Very well.'

He sighed and shook his head. 'You actually believe that of me. I presume your state of high dudgeon prevented you from noticing that one of my horses threw a shoe.'

She almost collapsed with relief. She had been so busy with her own thoughts, her anger, she indeed had not noticed.

He climbed down and lifted the foreleg of the offside horse.

'Your stable master should have checked him before you left,' she said.

He gave her an impatient glance. 'He did. There will be a blacksmith in the village.' He turned the carriage around.

She jumped down.

'What are you doing?'

'Relieving him of my weight.'

He said something under his breath.

'What did you say?'

'I said, the woman never ceases to surprise.'

'What did I do now?'

'It really doesn't matter.' He started walking. While the horse's gait was a little awkward, it did not seem to be in any pain.

She had no option but to walk alongside him. 'It is a good thing it happened here and not another mile down the road. You would have had to ride back and leave me with the carriage.'

'Yes. It was a good thing,' he said drily. 'Excellent.'

She repressed the urge to chuckle at his wry expression. 'You know what I mean.'

The blacksmith's shop was at the end of an ally of the main road. He was busy shaping some sort of farm implement. He looked up at their approach and stepped away from his anvil.

'Good day to you, sir, madam.' He touched his forelock.

Thorne nodded an acknowledgement. 'Can you shoe my horse?'

'My son be the farrier here, sir, but he do be off at Plank's farm for a foaling.'

'When do you expect him back.'

'All depends, sir. No rushing nature, like.'

'No indeed.' Thorne glanced over at her. 'We have no choice but to wait.'

'Perhaps we can rent a carriage and you can return for yours later. Thomas will worry if I am not home in time for dinner.'

The blacksmith scratched his head. 'Livery is one street over. Old Sam might have something you can rent. If not, you might catch a ride with a carter. Old Sam could put you in the way of it.'

Thorne looked unconvinced. 'How long has your son been gone?'

'Called for him at midnight they did. I must say I thought he'd be home afore now.'

'Very well.' He pulled out some coins and agreed on a price with the blacksmith, then held his arm out to Cynthia. 'Let us see if the livery stable can be of assistance.'

The man who met them in the livery stable courtyard was bent over and had a large hump on one shoulder. He looked up at them sideways. With a start, Cynthia realised he was in fact quite young. Her stupid heart went out to him, though he seemed quite cheerful. Thorne explained their predicament.

'I am right sorry, sir. I don't have a single vehicle in the yard suitable for you and the lady.'

'What do you have?' Lady Cynthia asked.

'Nought but that there donkey cart of Miss Denby's and I ain't finished fixing it.'

There was indeed a cart laid on its side with

tools all around it and a donkey munching on some hay in a nearby stall.

'How long before it is ready and how much will you charge me to use it?' Thorne asked.

'I can have it ready in a couple of hours, sir. In the meantime, I'll ask Mrs Denby if she'll let you use her cart and how much she wants. I don't s'pose she'll argue at making a bit of coin, you being a gennelman and all.'

'She will have the security of my carriage at the blacksmith's if she has concerns of that nature,' Thorne said. 'We may not need it, if the blacksmith's son returns in time to shoe my horse.'

'Ah, then I will hope he does, sir, but I will get the cart ready in case you needs it.'

'Is there an inn where I can rent a private parlour until the work is done?'

'The Black Sheep has a nice private parlour, sir. Very clean, so I am told. I was never in it.'

'I know the place. Thank you. We will return in an hour.'

Thorne held out his arm. She could hardly refuse. 'Bother,' she said. 'We are having the worst of luck.'

'Indeed,' he replied.

On their way to the inn, they once more

passed by the blacksmith's shop. Since there was no sign of the blacksmith's son having returned, they continued on their way.

This inn did not have an outside garden.

'I do not think anyone can censure our use of a private parlour under the circumstances,' Thorne said flatly as if expecting her to baulk at his offer.

She cast him a look of aggravation. 'They would censure you if you did not, provided the waiter remains on hand at all times.'

The innkeeper greeted them warmly and saw them settled in a table by the window after asking their preference. Cynthia was glad Thorne had enough sense to realise they should not skulk in a corner as if they had something to hide.

The waiter brought a pot of tea and, at Thorne's request, remained on hand in case they needed anything.

There was likely nothing more daunting than taking tea with a lady who had baldly stated that she held one in contempt. And for the second time in less than an hour. This afternoon really was not turning out at all as he had planned.

The light from the window spilled across

the table, but left her face in shadow. The impenetrable air of cool mystery kept him at bay. Like armour or a shield. And yet several times today he thought he had glimpsed what lay beneath. The occasional chuckle that had seemed genuinely warm. Her obvious pleasure at the surrounding scenery.

And then there was her unmatched beauty. The soft curve of her cheek. The perfect arch of her eyebrow. The ever-changing blue of her eyes, sometimes the colour of bright summer skies and sometimes the soft hazy blue of shimmering water. And then the times, like now, when they were as hard as chips of glass.

Also, she called to him on a visceral level he preferred not to admit.

How could she be so cold as to ruin the happiness of a sweet young woman like Bess?

'I do not hold you in contempt,' he said. The words were out of his mouth and sitting on the table between them before they had fully formed in his mind.

As she returned her cup to its saucer, the smooth silky skin of her hand seemed almost translucent. A trick of the light, but fascinating.

'I see.' Her words held no emotion at all.

'Elizabeth is more like a sister to me than

a cousin. My instincts are to do all I can to make her happy. She is as dear to me as your brother is to you.'

The elegant hand curled into a fist and disappeared beneath the table to rest on her lap.

Now what had he said? 'Your brother is dear to you, I assume?'

'Very dear. Yes.' She drew in a breath. 'And you think Fortescue will make Elizabeth happy.'

Was there a hint of incredulity in her voice? 'She believes so and I have no reason to think otherwise. The only negative aspect of his suit is his lack of funds.'

'Does that not trouble you?'

'Not in the least as long as the man is honourable enough to admit it. Which he has done.'

'Honour counts more than anything among gentlemen, does it not?'

'Naturally. Is it not so for you ladies also? A true friend would do anything to ensure a friend's happiness?'

'I suppose a true friend might.'

Damn it, why did she have to be so bloody enigmatic?

'I see. You do not consider yourself Elizabeth's friend.'

'We move in the same circles. I suppose we were friends for a time. I wonder that she still hankers after a man who transferred his affections so easily.'

He had wondered the same thing. 'Perhaps she is not as confident in her allure as you are in yours.'

She leaned back and because of the angle of the sun, a bright bar of light fell across her face. There was a small smile on her face. As if something he had said had amused her.

'Your beauty is unparalleled,' he said pressing for an answer. 'We already agreed on this.'

'Nevertheless, if his heart had been true...'

'He may have felt compelled by duty to his family to seek the richest prize offered. Let us be honest, if you had discouraged him, made it clear he stood no chance with you, he would not have switched his allegiance.'

She nodded. 'I do not disagree. Let us hope she finds another eligible suitor waiting in the wings.'

He huffed out a breath. 'Perhaps she might have, if Francis had not died, thus requiring Bess to go into mourning. She has had nothing but losses. She is devastated.'

'You call her Bess?'

'It was her sobriquet when she was small, but she prefers Elizabeth now she is a grown woman. Still, I do think of her as little Bess, having not seen her for fifteen years. Blast it. How in heaven's name is she to fall for someone else when she never leaves the house? She won't even go on calls with her mother.'

'The pain of losing one's first love.' The longing in her voice took him by surprise. Then she laughed lightly. 'Or so I have heard.'

'Do you intend to marry Fortescue, then?'

Her expression eyes widened. 'Really, Lord Thorne. Is that any business of yours?'

'It is, if it affects Elizabeth's happiness.'

'I haven't made up my mind. When I do, I shall be sure to let you know.'

For a moment, Cynthia considered telling Thorne what she had heard about Fortescue. The whole sordid tale, as told by one of the chimney sweep's wives, who had heard it from a less than respectable friend.

She had tried to tell Thomas, thinking she could somehow get him to force Fortescue to leave London. Thomas had refused, saying he wasn't going to ruin a man's reputation based on a bit of overheard gossip. If she didn't have proof, he would not do it.

Even so, Thomas had enquired of others of his acquaintance if they had heard of anything to the detriment of Fortescue. Nothing had been reported. He had dismissed her accusations as nothing but malicious hearsay. Thorne clearly wasn't going to believe anything bad about the man, either.

'In the meantime, since you are her guardian, it behoves you along with her mother to find a replacement.'

The truth of her statement registered on his face in a look of horror. She almost laughed, but somehow managed to keep a straight face.

'Her mother will be tasked with that duty. It will have to wait until spring now, since she will not be out of mourning until then.'

'A great deal can occur in the space of six months. They do say time is a great healer.'

His expression was grim. 'How very trite.'

She looked at her teacup. She had barely taken a mouthful, but she really did not want any more. 'Do you think there is any hope of the horse being shod by now?'

'I have no idea, to be honest.'

'If we do not head for home now, we will not be home until after dark and Thomas does not like to be kept waiting for his dinner.'

'Do you keep country hours, then?' He ges-

tured to the waiter that they were finished and
settled the bill.

'No but we are engaged to attend the Fields'
masquerade this evening and dressing in costume always takes an age, so we agreed on
an early dinner.'

She rose and he escorted her out into the
street. The sun was already dipping down towards the horizon.

'I shall see you there, then. What is your
costume?'

'That is for you to discover.' This time she
really hoped she could keep her identity secret. 'You?'

'Let us see if you can identify me and I will
try to find you.'

She stared at him in surprise. 'Is that a
dare?'

'It is.'

Did he really think she would not know
him immediately? And yet... The others in
her court had all whispered to her what they
were wearing, so she could be sure to recognise them. Their desperation made her want to
yawn. Whereas Thorne's challenge gave her
a tickle of excitement in the pit of her belly.

'I wager I shall find you out first,' she said.
There was absolutely no disguise she would

not be able to see through. 'And when I win,' she said, emboldened by her feeling that he was a man she could trust, despite their differences of opinion, 'as forfeit, you will promise not to pursue the matter of Miss Elizabeth and Lord Fortescue.'

And then she wouldn't be tempted to seek Thorne's good opinion and let him have his way in the matter. To do so would be a great disservice to his cousin.

Their gazes met at the same moment. He was looking at her as if to assure himself she was serious. 'And if I win?'

There was no hope of him winning.

But there was a teasing note in his voice and there was a naughty twinkle in his eye.

Her heart tumbled over.

Oh, dear, she liked him. Too much. She steeled herself against the sensations roiling in the pit of her stomach. Except she didn't want to deny those sensations. For the first time in years she felt as if she was truly alive. She let her feelings overwhelm good sense.

'Why, then, I shall grant you all my time for the rest of the week.' Something she never did, in case a gentleman got the wrong idea. She was, after all, the ice goddess. A week of his constant company ought to be enough to make her as bored with him as she was with the others in her court.

Unfortunately, it would also make her young men redouble their efforts to get her attention, particularly Fortescue. The thought left her feeling weary. How she looked forward to the time when she could retire from London society.

He shook his head. 'While I cannot deny I enjoy spending time with you, I am not interested in being your lapdog accompanied by footmen and maids and jealous young men.'

Her jaw dropped. Then reality hit. He was not some foolish romantic boy making calf love. He was a man of the world for whom such games would have palled long ago. 'Then what prize do you seek? If you want me to give up Fortescue to Miss Elizabeth, the wager is off.' It was the one thing she dare not put at risk.

'Very well.' He gave her a long look. 'You will kiss me.'

Her heart leapt. Her pulse raced. What on earth was the matter with her. 'Certainly not.'

He laughed. 'I did not think you were a coward. What do you fear?'

'I fear for my reputation, sirrah.'

'Your reputation for being cold-hearted and cruel?'

She glared at him, hoping he would not see his words cut deep. Yet it was true. Despite that her intentions were good, the *ton* believed she had cruelly ended her engagement with Drax and saw the way she kept her court guessing as to her intentions as unkind. Unfortunately, there was no possible way to explain it was done out of the best of intentions without creating a scandal. 'I mean my reputation as a lady.'

'I promise you I do not kiss and tell. Besides, it is a masquerade. No one will take any notice.'

'You will kiss me, right there, at the masquerade? With everyone looking on?'

'Or in private if you prefer.'

He gestured for her to continue walking.

If she refused his terms, then he would certainly refuse hers and he might actually be able to convince Fortescue that Elizabeth was a better option as a wife. Enough money would do it.

Besides, she could not lose. She would make sure of it. There would be no kissing. A pang of regret twisted in her chest.

No, no. Kissing was out of the question.

She took a deep breath. She didn't want to hear about Elizabeth's hurt feelings any more. 'We have a wager, then.'

'Excellent.'

Dash it. He sounded far too confident for her peace of mind.

At the blacksmith's they were delighted to discover that Thorne's horse was in the process of being shod and their carriage would be ready in less than half an hour.

Chapter Six

Looking in the mirror, Cynthia could not contain her excitement, or her certainty she would win her wager. Not for years had she felt this young or this silly. She should not do this. Really, she should not. She really ought to send a note around to Thorne, calling the whole thing off, and go in the first costume she had ordered, a perfectly acceptable Viking goddess.

Her maid was looking at her in dismay. 'Are you sure Your Ladyship wants to look so…?' She winced.

'So what?'

'So manly. And that wig! No one will know it is you.'

Cynthia laughed. 'That is the whole point. No one is supposed to guess your identity.'

'But when they do the unmasking at midnight and everyone sees...I think Lord Norton will be displeased.'

'Do not worry, I will tell him you had nothing to do with it.'

The maid did not look reassured.

While it was true that dressing as a male was a bit on the scandalous side, she intended to leave before the unmasking, and ensure that no one, including Thomas, would ever know. Which was why she had delayed her departure and told him to go on ahead. He would be looking for the Viking costume, if he bothered to look at all.

The only person there who would know the truth was Thorne, whom she was sure to spot first. She was sure she could rely on him not to give her away. Nearly sure. The fact that she trusted him that much was a bit of a surprise.

It was a long time since she had trusted any man, apart from her brother. And she didn't trust him with all of her secrets. So why would she feel comfortable about trusting Thorne? Was it because he had always been truthful and had not flattered or tried to wheedle her in any way? That must be it.

The odd feeling of warmth in her chest she felt when she was around him was nothing but the appreciation of a woman for an attractive man and had nothing to do with softer emotions.

Cynthia twisted this way and that as she stared into the mirror. Her legs were encased in dark green padded breeches tied below the knee and she had also added padding to her calves and shoulders to make them seem manlier.

'You think it is easy to guess I am a woman?' she asked the maid.

'No, Your Ladyship. I do not.'

The poor girl was clearly scandalised.

'Good.'

She sat down and the girl laced the soft leather boots specially made for her, then tied the quiver across her back. She had decided not to bother with a bow, it would get in the way for dancing. Naturally, all her dance partners would be female, to ensure she remained wholly in her disguise.

Thorne would never guess, not in a million years.

She could not wait to see his surprise when she revealed her identity to him and him alone, then she would leave before everyone unmasked. Would Thorne be scandalised? Thomas certainly would be if he ever found her out.

* * *

It wanted an hour to midnight and Cynthia had not seen hide nor hair of Thorne. The wretch had backed out of their wager, while she'd been forced to cavort around as a man, dancing with one lady after another since not one person had guessed she was a woman.

It was likely the moustache that had them fooled, because despite being above average height for a woman, she wasn't particularly tall and certainly below average height for a man.

Across the room, a very tall woman with flashing dark eyes dressed as a Spanish beauty caught her eye. The woman gave her a come-hither glance, clearly hoping to be asked to dance. It was so freeing to be the one who decided whether or not to step onto the dance floor, instead of having to wait to be asked. The poor dear was rather tall and Cynthia had noticed a couple of gentlemen avoid her hopeful glances.

She felt sorry for the poor soul. She sauntered over to her and bowed, holding out her hand.

'What a delightful Robin Hood you make, Lady Cynthia,' the woman murmured in familiar tones. 'Have you enjoyed dancing with all the lovely ladies?'

'I guessed first,' she said, hoping he would believe her.

'When?'

'The moment I saw you.'

'Ah, but I knew it was you the moment you walked into the room.'

Her jaw dropped. 'You have been here all the time?' Even as she spoke she recalled seeing the top of that mantilla flitting here and there, though she had never quite managed to get a good look at the lady it adorned until now.

She giggled. She couldn't help it. 'I thought by dressing as a man I would fool you completely, but you fooled me instead.'

He tittered behind his fan in a most ridiculous manner. She covered her mouth with a hand to stop herself from laughing too hard.

'To be honest,' he whispered, 'I wasn't absolutely sure it was you, but when I saw the way you were peering at everyone and hunting around the room, I knew I had you. When I took a closer look a few minutes ago, it was obvious you were no man.' He pointed to her throat. 'No Adam's apple.'

A small detail she could do nothing about

apart from the high collar. Apparently not enough.

She grinned. 'You win. I'll not argue the toss with a lady.'

He made an odd sound as if he had swallowed a laugh and a groan.

A naughty idea popped into her head. 'May I have this next dance? A waltz, I believe.'

He flapped his fan madly. 'Certainly not. I've been dodging amorous fellows all evening. I'd make a perfect cake of myself.'

'Coward. Come along. Follow my lead.'

She held out her arm in the courtliest of manners and with a groan he laid his hand on her arm. An enormous hand in white gloves. She should have spotted it immediately. But then the blackguard had made sure to keep out of her way, hadn't he? Making him dance with her would salve her wounded pride— somewhat.

What a strange-looking couple they must make, the Spanish lady towering over Robin Hood, and she was in awe when he twirled beneath her arm, albeit a little awkwardly. Surprisingly, no one seemed to take any notice. Perhaps because there was an alligator dancing with a swan and a knight clanking about in armour with a woman dressed as a beheaded Queen Anne. Taking pity on his plight, she kept the steps simple and they managed a good five or six minutes without a stumble.

'Who on earth made your gown?' she asked. 'The poor seamstress must have had quite a shock.'

'I had it made in Venice. No one is shocked by anything in that city. I bought it to play a practical joke on a friend.'

Men and their practical jokes. Thomas had been evil as a lad. 'Did it work?'

He narrowly missed stepping on a lion's tail. 'It did. He had been mooning about all week over a very tall lady and thought I was her. At the unmasking I thought he was going to call me out.'

'Oh, dear.'

'Yes, indeed. He didn't speak to me for a couple of weeks.'

'And you kept the gown?'

'It was in the bottom of one of my trunks that travelled all over Europe with me. I had forgotten it was there until we made our wager.'

Oh, yes, the wager. 'I am feeling a little warm, let us see if we can find somewhere cooler and quieter to talk.'

'Talk?' He chuckled. 'I shall expect more than talk.'

She could not ignore the heat that the low-voiced sensual murmur sent racing through her body. Tonight, she was not herself. She was the rogue Robin Hood having an assignation with a lady. As long as no one ever found out…

They peeked out onto the balcony but there were a number of gentlemen who had stepped outside to smoke. 'Perhaps the hallway?' he said.

Out in the entrance hall surrounding the grand staircase, costumed ladies and gentlemen were chatting and mingling, likely also looking for somewhere to cool off.

They ducked down a side hallway when they thought no one was looking. He found a hidden door between two portraits and, before she could catch a breath, he pulled her inside and closed the door behind them. It was the servants' staircase, lit by a few meagre lamps.

'What are you doing?' she whispered. 'What if someone saw?'

'No one knows who we are. This is a masquerade, after all.'

There was a certain amount of licence that

was allowed at masquerades, mostly for married people, though. Unmarried women always had to be careful of their reputations and she more than most. Still, not a soul had recognised her beneath her costume, although she had seen and spoken with many who knew her well.

And if she had been unable to recognise Thorne she doubted that anyone else would, either.

'Come on,' he said, taking her hand.

'Where are we going? Surely this landing is quiet enough for you?'

'Someone may have seen us enter and come to discover who we are.'

She did not like the sound of that. 'I think you have done this sort of thing before,' she muttered.

He chuckled low, causing soft little flutters deep inside her body. 'Of course I have.'

They climbed upwards past the second floor to the third floor. He opened the door on the landing and peered out.

'The third floor,' he said softly. 'Perfect.'

Nannies, governesses and children were usually the only occupants of third floors. Servants would be housed one floor above.

They stepped out into a corridor that was

narrower than the one they had left, but decorated with wall hangings and a lush carpet underfoot. The first door they opened was a large room which had clearly been used as a school room, but the furniture was pushed to one corner as if it was no longer in use. It made sense. This family's children were all grown up.

He moved on until they found a little sitting room with a chamber leading off it. In the hearth a fire had been lit. 'I wonder who uses this room.'

'Perhaps a lady's maid. Or a companion. Whoever it is, it will do for us.' He closed the door and turned the key.

Over and over again, Marcus had told himself, the reason for his impulsive wager was to teach Lady Cynthia a little lesson in humility. He had absolutely no intention of collecting his reward. Indeed, that was the whole point of it. To not kiss her. To let her see that to a sensible man, she wasn't the most irresistible woman in London.

Unfortunately, now the moment had arrived, the attraction he sensed between them made him want to claim his prize. Could a woman this lovely really be as cold as she would have everyone believe? Every instinct within him said she was not. Could he be so misled by his very real desire to kiss those lovely lips and feel her melt in his arms? He wished he knew.

He glanced around the small parlour. The small room boasted one armchair beside the hearth, a desk and an upright chair with a worn workbasket and a pile of what looked like stockings no doubt set there for mending.

The room had an air of functionality, rather than luxury, and was no doubt the chamber of an upper servant.

Lady Cynthia glided across the room to the window and peeked out. 'It looks down on the mews.' How had anyone missed her femininity beneath her disguise? For him, knowing that feminine curves lay beneath the male attire made her seem all the more tempting. He could not help but admire her pluck. His body warmed.

She turned back to face him. 'Very well. You won fair and square. Take your kiss.'

She closed her eyes as if preparing to take some unpleasant-tasting medicine. He couldn't believe it. Had she ever been kissed? Properly? By a man who knew what he was doing?

From where he stood, she looked thoroughly uncomfortable with the whole idea. And the moustache—well, that would have to go. If…

No. It was not going to happen. On the other hand, she looked like the idea of kissing him was worse than the idea of going to the gallows. As if she saw it as a penalty. And perhaps it would be if a kiss would chip away at the ice around her heart.

Although… He recalled his first thoughts about her, when he had met her in Cheapside. Could she really be one of those women who preferred those of her own sex to the male of the species?

Or perhaps she was just nervous. Perhaps she had never been kissed before. The nobility guarded their women very carefully. Perhaps she needed to relax a bit.

'We do not need to rush,' he said. 'Please, sit down.'

She opened her eyes and frowned. 'Why?'

'You seem a little tense. Did you think I would fall upon you like a hungry wolf?'

She relaxed a little. 'I wasn't sure what to expect.'

He gestured to the sofa. 'Make yourself comfortable.' He dove a hand into his skirts into the pocket cleverly secreted there and pulled out his flask. 'Perhaps a sip of brandy would not go amiss.'

She sat down and put her hands on her knees and then, as if realising they were practically naked knees, she folded them in her lap. 'No, thank you.'

The demure reply was at odds with her risqué costume.

He had not meant for her to feel vulnerable. Getting her alone had been about preserving her reputation, for as angry with her as he was, he had no intention of ruining her in the eyes of society. That would be cruel and, despite his assurances downstairs about them being incognito, if he had recognised her, then someone else might well have also.

He took a swig from his flask and passed it over. 'Go on. A small sip will bolster your courage.'

With a sigh she took the flask. After a delicate sip, she leaned back against the cushions. 'I really did not think you would win.'

'So you were prepared to snap your fingers in my face at the end of the evening and walk away.'

She took a deep breath. 'Yes.'

'It is all right. I won't insist on taking my

due.' He certainly wasn't going to force himself on an unwilling woman.

'I would have insisted on my prize.'

'I am not you.'

She shook her head. 'It would not be right for me to renege on a bet.'

'You are not reneging. I simply do not intend to collect.'

'You don't want to kiss me?' The lady was exceedingly quick-witted.

'Not particularly. No.'

She looked stunned. 'Then why did you make such a wager in the first place?' Her gaze narrowed. 'What sort of game are you playing?'

'The sort of game you play with young men who are new to the town. How many hearts have you broken in all these many Seasons?'

She glared at him. 'None at all as far as I know.'

'You broke my cousin's.'

'Oh, Elizabeth. We are back to that.' She bounced up from the chair and went back to the window and stared down.

Out of habit, he got up, though given their role reversals, he could just as easily have remained sitting. He could not help but notice the round swells of her buttocks as she leaned forward to look down into the street.

She spun around. 'I should go, before someone misses me. A kiss in a corridor where people can see you and pretend they don't know you is one thing, but being here alone with you—' she flung out a hand '—is quite another. Or is that your intention, to ruin me, out of revenge?'

Anger rose in his gorge. 'Do not ascribe your sordid motives to me, my lady.'

'My sordid motives?'

'Why else would you snap your fingers in Fortescue's direction if not because you were jealous of Bess's youth and beauty? She was about to receive an offer of marriage, whereas you are heading for spinsterhood. I don't suppose you can see it, but most of the young men who hang about you are not looking for wives. They profess love because it is fashionable to be in love with you. The only real prospect to wed you have is Fortescue, as far as I can tell. And I wish you well of him. As you said yourself, Bess can easily find someone else. You *need* a man who needs a fortune.'

As he let his annoyance get the better of him, she had leaned against the windowsill with her arms folded over her chest in a most boyish posture. And yet it was also supremely feminine.

His throat dried.

And strangely, she didn't seem the slightest bit distressed by what he had to say. She was as cold as ice, then. With not a bit of human kindness in her character.

'I wish her the very best of luck,' she muttered. 'Now, let us get this kiss over and done and return to the ballroom.'

Now she was giving him orders. He smiled. 'If you recall the terms of our wager, you are to kiss me.'

She frowned. 'No such thing.'

He raised an eyebrow.

She made a face. 'You did that on purpose.'

'Did what?'

'Worded it that way. You said, you will kiss me. But I didn't think you meant I was the one who would... I mean that is not the way it is done.'

He shrugged. 'It is completely up to you. I cannot say I care one way or the other.'

She gasped. 'Is that so?'

'It is.' Not exactly true—he would be disappointed if she did not follow through and on more than one front. Despite his very real reservations about her, he had thought she had courage and honesty. Two traits he very much admired.

Perhaps he was wrong.

A determined expression filled her face. 'I see.' She took a step forward. And another and hesitated, looking up at him. Then she flung her arms around his neck and kissed him quickly on the lips. The hair on her upper lip tickled his. She drew back.

He gave her a wry look. 'Is that the best you can do?'

She froze. 'It was a kiss.'

'It was a peck.' He gazed into her face and she stared back at him. A clock on the mantel he had not noticed before ticked loudly into the silence.

Slowly, carefully, he reached up and tugged at one end of the moustache. It peeled away from her upper lip, leaving a red mark on her pale skin.

She touched it briefly with one finger.

'Perhaps you would like to try again?'

He lowered his head a fraction, quite ready to withdraw at the first sign of denial, yet hoping she would not baulk.

Cynthia had forgotten all about the moustache. She had been staring at Thorne like a hungry puppy expecting a treat and was quite shocked when he had removed it.

Her breathing became shallow, her pulse raced. Was he going to kiss her properly, or not? And what would she do if he did?

The glow from the fire danced in his dark eyes. Even in a dress, with a touch of rouge on his cheek and lips, he was the most masculine man she knew. The boys in her court did not come close to his commanding presence and Fortescue always reminded her of a weasel.

Thorne was not a pretty man and certainly did not make a pretty woman with those heavy eyebrows and the square jaw that was already beginning to shadow with a new growth of beard, but he was lovely none the less.

He took her hands in his and guided them around the back of his neck, holding them there for a brief moment. His warmth permeated through her skin and sent tingles racing up her arm.

She closed her eyes. Their lips met. A soft brush. A gentle nuzzle. It felt lovely.

Her heart pounded in her chest. She had forgotten what it was like to desire and be desired in this carnal way.

Forgotten the way blood would rush hot in

her veins and how her feminine places would tighten and ache for more. She had not expected to feel anything at all.

Startled, she froze and drew back.

His eyelids were heavy and his expression sensual when he smiled and he stroked her bottom lip with his thumb. 'I have left some of my lip rouge behind.'

She licked her lip. 'I must go. I do not think I will return to the party. I cannot risk being recognised, having been gone for such a long time. I assume our wager is satisfied?'

'If there is more to be had, I am certainly ready for it,' he murmured, leaning forward again.

His arms went around her back and he drew her flush with his body, her breasts even tightly laced aching at the pressure. This time the kiss was fiercer, more demanding and she, without thinking, parted her lips to welcome the questing of his tongue.

It felt so good. So right. And her body begged for more.

He deepened the kiss. Pleasure and heat raced upwards from her belly and the feel of his strong muscled thighs beneath hers gave her chills down her spine.

His tongue swept her mouth, touching and tasting and wooing.

Giddying sensations made it hard to think. Her body wanted to melt and give in to his touch.

She stiffened. Pulled away. Sat there frozen by the knowledge that with this man she could easily repeat all of her earlier mistakes.

He lifted his head. 'I beg your pardon. I became a little carried away.'

Her heartbeat stumbled. If only Cornelius had said those words, she might not be facing the future as a spinster. An old maid, some would no doubt call her, in due course, but she would never be that. Not now.

And if she let things go any further, he would learn that truth also.

Thomas had paid dearly to allow her to keep her secret, she was not going to undo all his good work.

She gave a terse nod.

'May I escort you to your carriage?'

'I do not think we should be seen together, do you?' She picked up the moustache from the sofa arm and got up to look in the mirror. Her hat was askew, her lips rosy red. She pressed the strip of hair against her skin.

Hopefully it would hold long enough to get outside.

'Where is it? Your carriage?'

'Around the corner. I did not want anyone to recognise it when I got out.'

'Very wise of you.'

The laugh she gave was shaky. Her lack of control appalling. She had the awful feeling that had he continued to kiss her, she would have succumbed to her desires and the devil take the hindmost.

She drew in a steadying breath and appraised him coolly. 'I think it is you who need the escort, dressed as you are. No one is likely to trouble me.'

'Oh, good Lord. You are likely right. I had quite the task defending myself from one very amorous gentleman in the ballroom. Heaven help me if he catches sight of me again. I will need your protection.'

They laughed at the ridiculousness of it all and the tension in her body faded away, leaving her feeling happy, almost contented.

How strange. There was something floating at the back of her mind. Some sort of idea that she could not quite seem to grasp. Or perhaps was afraid to examine too closely.

'We can take the back stairs. That way I

can be sure I will not run into Thomas and you can see me safely aboard my carriage, if you must.'

He grinned. 'Thank you, kind sir. I shall be most glad of your company.'

As they made their way down the narrow stairs to the street the heat of embarrassment rolled over her. How would she ever look him in the face again? And yet she must. When she told Thomas she had decided not to go to Harrowglen after all, he had put his foot down and insisted, asking her what the devil sort of game she was playing. At the time, she had expected to win the wager and had thought it wouldn't matter. Now, it was going to be exceedingly embarrassing. Well, like all the other things in her life that were embarrassing, she would simply have to act as if it affected her not at all.

A servant eyed them askance as he passed them on the staircase, but said nothing and hurried on his way.

They slipped out of the door at the bottom of the stairs and made their way through the courtyard and out into the street.

Her carriage was waiting as ordered. She stepped inside and dropped the window, suddenly fearful of what she had done. After years of never putting a foot wrong where gentlemen were concerned, she had let herself relax her guard with a man who didn't like her or trust her.

Was the whole reason for her problems that she was attracted to men who could cause her harm? 'You have taken your prize. Our wager is honoured. That is an end to it. I rely on your word to say nothing of this to anyone.'

His expression darkened. 'I have no more wish to have this known than you do.'

His obvious distaste was a slap in the face. She sank back against the squabs as the carriage moved off. What on earth had she been thinking when she agreed to wager a kiss?

A wager he had contrived. To what end?

To prove to her she was no better than she should be, as a way of paying her back for hurting his cousin? If so, he had entirely missed the mark. She already knew that about herself.

She blinked against the sting of moisture in her eyes. She didn't need anyone to tell her she had made a mess of her life. Least of all him.

Blast being attracted to the man. Thomas hadn't accepted her proposal that she stay in London rather than accompanying him to the country. Her hand forced, she felt it her duty to travel as originally planned. But Thorne's visit to Harrowglen was definitely going to be awkward. Hopefully Thomas would notice nothing amiss.

Chapter Seven

Hungry and damp from the rain, Marcus pulled into the inn courtyard twenty miles from his journey's end. There was no help for it but to call a halt. The rain showed no signs of abating and it was at least another three hours' drive from here to the Norton estate in good conditions. Given the weather, Norton would no doubt forgive him for arriving a day late.

An ostler dashed out to take the horses' heads and Marcus climbed down. His coachman, who had sounded heartily relieved when Marcus had suggested they stop at an inn for the night, set about arranging for their care.

Marcus grabbed his valise and strode into the inn. He handed the innkeeper, a stout balding gentleman in his fifties, his calling card. 'Do you have a room with a private parlour for one night?'

He read the name and bowed. 'A room I do have, my lord, but no private parlour. You are welcome to use the dining room for dinner. You will be quite private. All my other guests have dined.'

'Thank you. I will be down to make good on your offer as soon as I have changed my clothes.'

'Very good, my lord. Joe, take His Lordship up and give him a hand with his things, please. I'll go and speak to cook and see what he might have in the pantry.'

'Cold meat and a mug of ale will go down very well,' Marcus said and followed the elderly footman up the stairs.

He had been at the head of a long queue of traffic waiting for the mail coach that had turned over on a bend in the road to be cleared away. Those behind him would have to find a room elsewhere.

The chamber was small but clean and it wasn't long before, with the help of Joe, he was dry and comfortable and heading downstairs.

'Not one single room?' a light female voice was saying as he descended the last few steps.

A voice he instantly recognised with a pang of surprise.

He hesitated. Should he reveal his presence? They had parted with harsh words and she had told him she would not be at Harrowglen when he visited her brother. What had made her change her mind? Whatever it was, he was strangely pleased to know she had decided better of it.

If he revealed himself to her here, would it cause her embarrassment?

'No, my lady. Not a single room left. I just let the last one go to a…to this gentleman.'

And the decision was no longer his to make.

Lady Cynthia turned towards him. She was looking rather wet and bedraggled as if she had been travelling in an open carriage. She could not have been. She must have leaned out of the window to see what had caused the hold-up. 'Lord Thorne?'

He bowed. 'My lady. I did not expect to meet you on the road?'

'I was supposed to leave yesterday, with Thomas, but my companion, Mrs Paxton, came down with a megrim after a day of packing and had to lie down. So I decided to wait until today. Then she decided she could not possibly travel, at all, so I had to find a replacement.' Mrs Paxton, the widow of a distant cousin, who had been left in straitened circumstances, had proved to be an excellent companion—from Cynthia's perspective. The dear lady was more concerned about the state of her own health than she was about protecting Cynthia's reputation. The thought of attending large gatherings sent her to bed with a headache. It left Cynthia with more freedom of movement than she might otherwise have experienced with a more diligent woman.

She gestured to a young woman standing quietly off to one side. 'This is Millie, my maid.'

He acknowledged the girl with a smile and a brief bow. 'Miss Millie.'

The girl blushed and dipped a curtsy.

Marcus noticed she did not address the matter of her telling him she had no intention of travelling to Harrowglen. He decided to let it pass. She was here and what more was there to say?

Lady Cynthia gestured to the innkeeper. 'It seems we must continue on since my idea of taking a room here has not borne fruit, but I would like to bespeak a hot cup of tea and a bowl of soup if that is possible?'

The innkeeper looked at Marcus. 'If Your Lordship will permit Lady Cynthia to join you in the dining room, I will make arrangements.'

'Of course.' Marcus frowned. 'But the roads are appalling. I cannot hear of you travelling on, Lady Cynthia. Take my room.'

'Oh, it is very generous of you, my lord, but I would not feel right about putting you out into the storm.'

She must think ill of him indeed if she thought he would even consider letting her leave. 'Nonsense. I can manage very well in the commons. No need for either of us to go anywhere. And we can set off together in the morning.'

The innkeeper, who had been looking troubled, beamed. 'As to that, my lord. I had been thinking as how I might be able to offer the lady use of the snug to rest in 'til morning. There is only a sofa in there and it is not very private, but—'

'It will do for me,' Marcus said.

He turned to Lady Cynthia. 'It is decided. Go and warm yourself by the fire in the dining room while they remove my things from the chamber and, once you have things settled to your liking up there, you can join me for dinner in the dining room.'

She narrowed her eyes as if trying to see some ulterior motive in his offer, then nodded briskly. 'Thank you. I am most grateful.'

Oddly, he had the feeling that it went against the grain with her to accept his offer of help. Likely because of their wager and that extraordinary kiss.

A kiss he had not been able to forget.

His gaze focused on her mouth at the pleasant reminder.

Her lips parted as if she, too, was recalling the sensations they had enjoyed together.

He forced his gaze back to the innkeeper. 'Let me know when the room has been prepared and please send a decanter of sherry to the dining room. Something to warm us, while we wait.'

He escorted her into the dining room and led her to the merrily blazing hearth. She put out her hands to warm them. In the light from the candelabra around the room he could see clearly that she was positively dripping and her hems were mired almost to the knee.

'You are soaked through. Let me help you

out of that wet coat. Good lord, what happened?'

'The road was a quagmire and the carriage wheels got lodged in a rut where some fool had gone off the road. I had to go to the horses' heads while my coachman and a couple of other men worked it free.'

'You cannot have been all that far behind me. I wish I had known. I would have assisted you.'

'You are assisting me by giving up your room, my lord.'

He hung her coat over the back of a chair.

She stripped off her gloves and removed her bonnet. Strands of fine damp hair stuck to her cheeks and forehead, but most of it was in its usual severe knot at her nape.

She rubbed her arms. 'That is much better. My coat kept out the worst of it, except at the bottom of my skirts.'

'You will need to get out of those wet things as soon as possible. You will not want to come down with an ague. Let me bring you a chair.'

He moved a chair closer to the fire and she sank into it wearily. The first sign she had shown of fatigue. She was no doubt as hungry as he was.

The waiter bustled in with a decanter and glasses on a tray.

'I'll take care of it. Please go and see if Her Ladyship's room is ready.'

'Yes, my lord.'

Marcus poured her a drink and he wasn't at all surprised when she downed it swiftly.

She took a deep breath. 'Thank you. You are very thoughtful.'

'What is Norton about, letting you travel alone, particularly at this time of year when the weather can change in an instant?'

She bristled.

And he wished he had kept his mouth shut. The air of growing ease between them was replaced by a chill.

'Thomas hates travelling by carriage or dawdling around behind one. He always goes on ahead and leaves me to bring the luggage. I certainly prefer it that way.'

Her tone said she wondered why it was any of his business. 'I presume that, like most men, you think women are delicate incapable creatures, who need a male guardian at every turn.'

He laughed. 'Not at all. Some of the cleverest people I have known have been women.'

'Thomas says I should be a little less clever

or I will be considered a bluestocking and a threat to the rightful order of things.'

'I know men who feel blessed to have a clever woman at their side.' His father had been one. He had been quite lost after Marcus's mother had died.

'The room is prepared, my lady,' the innkeeper said from the doorway. 'Your maid is up there unpacking.'

Marcus brought her to her feet. 'Take as long as you need. Dinner will await your arrival.'

Cynthia had not packed much, since she had a clothes press full at Harrowglen and she tended to wear quite different clothes in the country. Things more suited for the draughty old mansion that she loved dearly.

What she had brought along was the celestial-blue gown she had intended to wear when they entertained their neighbours. A gown designed to show that she and Thomas deemed their guests important and valued. A gown much too grand for an ad hoc dinner in the middle of nowhere. Unfortunately, there was little she could do. The mud on the hem of her travelling dress would take a great deal of time to clean and she would need it for the morning.

She grimaced at her reflection. 'I think a fichu is in order, Millie.' There was far too much bosom on display for dinner alone with a gentleman who was little more than an acquaintance. And one she had kissed in the most shameless manner.

One she would like to kiss again. And more. Oh, dear, her thoughts kept going back to that kiss. To the pleasurable sensations that had burned through her body. This awakened desire of hers was most unseemly, when she had thought she would never feel desire again. Had not wanted to feel desire, given the future she planned.

She had told herself that one kiss could likely be forgiven, if it was ever discovered. But this longing for closeness was unacceptable for a woman in her position. It was all very well for a man to take a lover, but for a single lady to do the same would be scandalous.

Only if she was discovered.

The man would have to be completely trustworthy.

Could she ever trust a man that much that she would risk her future happiness for the sake of a sensual adventure? Especially when she had risked it once before with disastrous results.

She trusted Thorne.

What would it be like to make love to him? She guessed he would be an excellent lover. A man who, in the right circumstances and not constrained by the fear of discovery at any moment, would be considerate as well as generous in attending to his partner's desires. Unlike Cornelius, who most of the time had been in a terrible hurry in case someone came upon them.

And while she had enjoyed the kisses and the excitement of his touches, she had always been left feeling as if there ought to be more. As if something was missing.

Cornelius had noticed nothing amiss.

She must not think of him, of it, any more. It was positively wicked and likely to get her into trouble—more trouble than it was worth.

The girl tucked the delicate fabric into the neckline and folded it artfully. 'I think this is what you mean, my lady. Will you wear any jewels?'

'No jewels tonight. Hide them at the bottom of the trunk and lock the door to the room when you leave.' No sense in flaunting diamonds and pearls in a small roadside inn. One never knew who might take notice.

'Yes, my lady. The landlord gave me two keys. Would you like the other one?'

'Good idea.' She tucked it in her reticule. 'Do not wait up for me, you must be exhausted, and you still have to deal with the results of my trekking about in the road.'

Millie looked doubtful. 'The ties at the back will be difficult.'

'I have done it before and can do it again. Do not double knot the tapes and I will manage very well.' She had learned to manage very well after her trysts with Cornelius. Shame rippled through her in a hot tide. Ugh. She hated that sensation. Would she ever forget what an idiot she had been?

Likely not, since her actions had ruined her future.

She left Millie tidying up and went downstairs. The glass of sherry earlier had warmed her for a time, but now the effect had worn off and she felt chilled again.

Fortunately, the dining room was at the bottom of the stairs and she only passed one footman who had stared at her agog and backed up against the wall as if he'd seen an apparition.

In the dining room, Thorne was standing beside the hearth, one foot resting upon its edge as he contemplated the flames.

With the glow from the fire casting the strong lines of his face into planes and valleys he looked almost brutal. As if he was the sort of man who would stop at nothing to get what he wanted.

And yet he had been nothing but gentlemanly. Even when they were kissing.

Oh, she really did have to put that kiss out of her mind. A bit of flirting at a masquerade was one thing, it was playacting, but at any other time, it led down the road to ruin.

She was already ruined. She hesitated. Startled. What on earth could she be thinking?

She lifted her chin. 'Good evening, again, Lord Thorne.'

He must have been deep in thought because it was clear she had taken him by surprise by the sharp turn of his head. From the way he cleared the frown from his expression his thoughts had not been happy ones.

'Lady Cynthia.' His eyes widened as he took in her gown. 'I beg your pardon. I did not realise our dinner would be quite such a formal affair. I will change.'

She shook her head with a chuckle. 'Please do not. This is the only dry item of clothing I have in my luggage. I was not expecting to dine on the road, though in future I shall always make sure I have more than an evening gown in my valise.'

'You look delightful. I am happy to be the recipient of the product of your misfortune.' His smile was genuine and perfectly sweet. For all his appearance of strength and manliness, there was an underlying quality of kindness.

A pang tugged at her heart strings. This man would make some woman a lovely husband. Loss darkened her mood. The pain of what might have been, had she not been such a youthful fool.

'My lack of alternative clothing, you mean.' She chuckled. 'My lord, you flatter me well.'

'I blame my diplomatic training,' he said, trying to look modest and deliberately failing.

She laughed out loud. 'What a humbug you are.'

He gave her a cheeky grin. 'You must be famished.' He pulled the cord beside the hearth. 'I told them I would ring to let them know we are ready. Let me escort you to the table.'

She held out her gloved hand and he took it with such an air of delight, her toes curled inside her shoes. And he spared her no attention when he seated her at the table and poured her a glass of the wine waiting in a decanter.

She lifted her glass. 'To our fortunate chance encounter.'

'To my very good fortune indeed.'

Now, what did he mean by that? Or was he simply pretending that he was glad to be of service? Likely the latter given his bad opinion of the meanness she had shown to his cousin.

If she tried to tell him the real truth, would he believe her, or would he assume she was making excuses? And she certainly could not prove her suspicions about Fortescue.

Three waiters entered bearing trays and soon the table was filled with enough food to feed an army. In addition to a cold roast of beef, there were oysters, a game pie and assortment of vegetables, some in sauces, some not, along with a trifle and an apple tart.

'No need to serve us,' he said as one of the waiters picked up the carving knife.

The man stepped back. 'Will that be all, then, my lord?'

'It will.'

The waiters left them alone.

She should object.

Now.

But she did not want to object. Always, she guarded her reputation for Thomas's sake. But she was tired of placing her own wishes behind his. This evening she wanted to enjoy the company of this man for her own sake.

When they reached Harrowglen would be time enough for formality and propriety. It wasn't as if they were completely alone. A bevy of servants were a mere tug of the bell away.

And besides, who was here to see them? And if they were seen, they had a perfectly reasonable explanation.

Then she would accept this evening as fate.

He carved her slices of roast beef and she helped him to a serving of pie. They passed dishes back and forth until their plates were full.

'It is rare to see a lady with such a good appetite,' he said.

'Oh, you mean the way fashionable women pick at their food as if they are not the slightest bit hungry when in company. That it is merely an affectation. You do know that they eat before they leave home. A way of perpetuating the myth that we females are creatures not of this world and that the mere thought of food causes a case of ennui.'

She cut a small piece of meat from the slice on her plate and popped it in her mouth.

He chewed thoughtfully for a moment, then swallowed. 'You do this also?'

'One must, if one is not to be talked of behind's one's back.'

'A subject of the scathing tongues of gossips.'

'Indeed.'

'Well, I am glad to see you eating well tonight.'

'The food is surprisingly good for such an out-of-the-way place. Try the pie. The pastry is wonderfully light and the flavour quite lovely.'

'The landlord told me his wife was trained in one of the great houses hereabouts and he was quick to inform me that we would not be disappointed.'

'He was right.'

They ate in silence for quite a few moments, but it was the easy silence of old friends. The sort of silence she enjoyed with Thomas, when they were alone. No need to fill the empty pauses with chatter or search for a topic of interest. How had she come to feel so comfortable around this man, so quickly?

'More wine?' he asked, picking up the decanter.

She probably should not, if she wanted to maintain some shred of control.

She nodded her acceptance.

He filled her glass then filled his own. 'To good food and good company,' he toasted.

'How are you finding your duties as the new Viscount?' she asked. 'It must be a great change from your former occupation.'

'In some respects, it is a great deal easier.' He tried a forkful of pie. 'You are right, this is delicious. As a diplomat, and a junior one at that, there are a great many pitfalls when dealing with the politics of other countries. Like a game of chess there are rules and expected moves, but nothing is as it appears on the surface.'

'It sounds fascinating. You do not find being a viscount equally interesting?'

'While the responsibilities are equally important, I do not find my bailiff secretly plotting with the gamekeeper to alter the boundaries of my estate. And I can actually come to a conclusion and make a decision and have it set in motion without reference to another soul. That in itself is refreshing.'

'But still you miss it,' she hazarded, because while there was humour in his tone there was also a sense of regret. Something she had not expected to hear, given that his position in life had been elevated by his inheritance.

How surprising that she would be the first person to guess he might have preferred his former life to taking up the title.

'Likely I miss it, the way one misses a toothache after the tooth is drawn.'

She laughed as he'd expected, but her eyes showed disbelief a fraction before her face became expressionless.

Was he so easy to read? He had not thought so.

He cut the apple tart into slices and offered her one.

'No, thank you. I will take a spoonful of Charlotte Russe, though.'

After serving her some of the custard pudding, he took a slice of the tart.

'The Russe is delicious. And your tart?'

'Excellent.'

He sat back in his chair. 'I suppose we should make an early start in the morning.'

'I plan on it. Depending on the state of the road, the journey from here can take anywhere from two to four hours.'

'I suggest we set off together. If you run into any difficulties, I will be there to offer assistance.'

'How kind of you.'

He frowned. Her words were gracious, but cold.

'It is simply common courtesy to the lady who will be my hostess once we reach our destination.'

She smiled coolly. 'As you wish. I shall retire now. Thank you for dinner and for giving up your chamber.'

Exasperated by her lack of warmth, he raised an eyebrow. 'As a gentleman, I believe I had little choice.'

Her eyes widened a fraction. If he had surprised her by not fawning all over her, it might be a good lesson.

When they rose to their feet, he offered his arm. 'Allow me to escort you.'

'Please do not trouble yourself. I can find my way.'

'It is no trouble at all. Indeed, it is my duty to see you safe to your door.'

She huffed out a little breath, but took his

arm and they climbed the stairs to the first floor.

He leaned close as they neared the top. 'Not much like our last adventure on a staircase, is it?'

He heard her breath catch. Had she also been thinking about their last meeting?

'I would not have expected a gentleman to refer to the goings-on at a masquerade.'

Goings-on. They'd kissed. Briefly. She made it sound as if they had made love on the stairs. It would be like making love to an icicle.

He watched while she dug around in her reticule for the key and took it and opened the door.

She swung around to face him. 'Thank you for a very pleasant evening, my lord.'

In the light from the candle guttering in a lamp on the wall, he had trouble making out her expression, but she seemed vulnerable in that moment and almost lost.

'You are welcome, my lady.'

She hesitated on the threshold, looking up at him. 'Would you care for a brandy before you retire?'

He hesitated. Oh, what the hell? He had the feeling she had something she wanted to say to him. 'Yes. I would like that very much.' He followed her inside and closed the door.

The fire glowed in the hearth and she lit a spill and lit the candelabra standing on the mantel and another on the table.

No maid? That he had not expected. Then, he had not expected her to invite him in for a drink, either. She always seemed so concerned with the proprieties, so careful of her reputation.

She gestured to a small table near the bed upon which sat a decanter and two glasses. 'If you would care to pour. I can assure you it is very good brandy, I brought it from home. I often find it difficult to settle down to sleep and the brandy helps.'

Really? It was hard to imagine her having trouble doing anything. He poured them both a glass and joined her on the small sofa beside the hearth.

'To sleeping well,' he said, lifting his glass.

'And to a safe journey in the morning.'

She swallowed her drink in one. Surprised, he followed suit.

She inhaled a deep breath, then seemed to tremble. 'May I ask you something?'

There was an anxious note in her voice. An

intensity in her gaze that struck him viscerally. He braced. 'Anything.'

'Have you ever taken a mistress?' A blush rose slowly up to her hairline, clearly visible despite the dim lighting. He found it enchanting. It was as if she had offered him a glimpse of something deeply personal. And yet…

'That is not something a gentleman would usually discuss with a lady.'

She stiffened, peered down into her empty glass, hiding her expression. 'Never mind. I should not have asked.'

He frowned. What did it matter if she knew? 'I have had several mistresses.'

'What was it like?'

'Like?' What a strange question. He shrugged. 'It was fine.'

The hand holding the glass shook slightly. 'Merely fine?'

Blast it. For some reason he had a sense this was important. 'Delightful, if you must know. At least, one or two of them were. One ended badly.'

'I see.' She turned slightly and gazed into his face. 'And did these ladies also find it delightful?'

What the devil was she asking him? Whether he was able to satisfy a woman? Really? 'I never had any complaints.' Bloody hell, now he sounded like a braggart.

She tilted her head like a curious bird, a very pretty exotic bird. 'While married ladies do not disclose a great deal to us single ladies, I understand that not all men are created equal. Some wives seem more satisfied with their husbands than others.'

Could she possibly be asking him what he thought she was asking? Surely not. He repressed the urge to brag that no woman had ever found him lacking in that particular department. 'It is every man's responsibility to make sure his lady receives the greatest possible pleasure from their congress, I assure you.'

She glanced up at his face swiftly and looked away. 'How does a man know that is in fact the case?'

'Believe me, a man knows.' He could not take the dryness from his voice. 'As your husband will know once you marry.'

'I have no intention of marrying.'

'What?'

'I have not met a man to whom I would wish to be tied for the whole of my life. Indeed, the thought of it is quite abhorrent to me.'

He got up and poured them both another

brandy. When she reached up to take her glass, he held on to it, gazing down into her face. 'It is very good brandy. Savour it, rather than gulping it down.' He released the glass.

He settled down beside her and sipped his drink. She did the same.

'So,' he said slowly, 'you are curious about lovemaking, but have no intention of taking a husband.' He recalled how rigid she had been when he kissed her. 'Perhaps the male of the species is not your cup of tea.' He'd had that thought more than once before about her. As it occurred to him again that he was filled with disappointment.

She looked at him blankly.

'Perhaps you find women more to your taste and inclination.'

Her eyes widened. 'Goodness me, no!'

'I see. Then perhaps, despite all those young men who hang about your skirts, you have not found a man to whom you are attracted?'

Her lips parted. She licked them. 'I find you attractive.'

His body tightened. But he was not a man to be led around by the male parts of his anatomy.

Was this how she lured all these men to her

side? This innuendo and playing of games. If so, she was playing with the wrong man.

'Do you, now.' He kept his voice light and uninterested.

'Your kiss, the other evening. At the masquerade. It was nice.'

It had been like kissing a rock. 'You did not seem to enjoy it at the time.'

'I didn't expect it to be nice.'

'Merely nice is not what I intended.'

She blinked.

Cynthia gripped the stem of her glass. What was she doing? It was like with Cornelius all over again. She was letting her emotions get the better of her good sense.

Too much wine at dinner. Too much brandy. And she knew why she had drunk it, too. She had been building up to this. And now she wished she had never started down this path.

She raised her glass to her lips.

A large warm hand covered hers. His eyes, dark and mysterious in the low light, gazed into hers. 'Slowly, remember.'

She took a little sip and he took the glass from her. He put it, along with his, on the little table beside the arm of the sofa.

'Perhaps we should try that kiss again?'

There was a smile in his voice and dancing in his eyes and a small quirk to his lovely mouth. A hint of a naughty-boy grin.

She wasn't sure she was breathing. It was as if all the air had been sucked from her lungs. A recollection of the moment when she had finally given in to the heat of desire Cornelius had so carefully stoked over the course of the summer she'd turned seventeen. The little posies he fashioned out of wildflowers picked on their rides. The stolen kisses. The intimate touches when no one was looking. She had felt so grown up and feminine when she was with him, while her father and Thomas still treated her like a schoolroom miss.

When Cornelius finally made love to her in the barn loft, it had seemed like the culmination of all her daydreams. Constrained by the fear of discovery, they didn't dare disrobe and, after some truly passionate kisses that left her breathless and giddy, the rest had happened so quickly, she wasn't sure exactly what had occurred. Cornelius must have seen her disappointment, for he had assured her it would better when they were husband and wife and could take their time.

The thought that he loved her and wanted

to marry her had thrilled her to pieces. But it was all a lie. He had only wanted her for her wealth and position. Over the years her heartache had disappeared and reason had returned. She had been fortunate in many ways. Cornelius might have got her with child—indeed, she often wondered if that had been his intention.

She also had been fortunate that her father had not given in to her demand that she be allowed to wed him. If he had known they had made love, perhaps he would have relented, but something had held her back from delivering that piece of information. After seeing his reaction to her request, she had the feeling that it might have been a bitter blow and not one she wanted to deliver. Yes, she had been lucky that Cornelius had not got her with child.

While she was saddened by the thought that because of her foolishness that summer, she would never have children of her own, she now knew marrying Cornelius would have been a disaster. The man treated his wife abominably.

Surely she had learned her lesson after her experience with Cornelius. Surely she could never be that mad again. But then she recalled that she did want to know if this man, this very attractive man, could make good on his claim that in his arms a woman would find pleasure.

He withdrew a little. 'If you would like to, that is?'

She gave a swift nod. 'Why not?'

He huffed out a little sigh. 'Is that why you drank so much wine at dinner? Plucking up the courage, were you?'

How did he manage to see what she thought she had hidden so well?

He shook his head. 'Come along, then.'

To her shock, he lifted her effortlessly to sit sideways on his lap and tipped her face up to him.

She tensed.

But he did not immediately mash his mouth down on hers, he stroked his finger along her jaw, across her cheek, around the whorls in her ear. She shivered at the soft caressing sensation.

He toyed with a fine tendril of hair floating free of her pins. And the sensations of being stroked and petted made her want to purr like a cat.

One hand, almost as if by its own volition, for surely she had not guided it, crept up to rest curled up on his chest. He stopped stroking and took her hand in his. He kissed it. A light pressure of warm dry lips upon the ends of her fingers, before replacing it to lie flat upon his chest, his hand covering hers, holding it in place, yet she did not feel trapped.

'Even through my coat, I suspect you can feel how fast my heart is beating,' he murmured. 'You lovely little siren. You have me in your spell.'

She did feel the strong steady beat of his heart, but he was not the one enthralled. As he lowered his head, the room receded, and she waited with bated breath for his mouth on hers.

At first, the touch of his lips was little more than a gentle brush, but it sent a riot of longing storming through her body. Her breathing shallowed. Her heart picked up speed. He moved his mouth over hers, his lips warm and dry and infinitely tender. The tension went out of her body.

And almost before it had begun, the kiss ended. He gazed down into her face. 'You have had rather more to drink than is wise, my lady. And as a gentleman, it is time I put a halt to proceedings that could quickly get

out of hand and lead to events we will regret
for the rest of our lives.'

Stop? Regret?

The room, the circumstance, her past, all
came back into focus. Oh, good Lord, what
had she been thinking? He was right. If they
were caught in such a compromising position, there would be no end to the complica-
tions that would arise. If only Cornelius had
developed such gentlemanly scruples, how
different her life and her future might have
been. For a moment, the unfairness of it all
swept through her, filling her with longings
and sadness. But life was never fair. And she
was perfectly accepting of the consequences
of her youthful folly.

She moved to climb off his lap.

Without effort he lifted her and set her back
on the cushion. He stood up, looking down at
her with an odd expression. 'I do not know
why you have seen fit to grace me with such
favours, my lady, but I think that in future we
should avoid finding ourselves alone.'

'I could not agree more,' she said coldly.

His expression darkened. 'Then I will bid
you goodnight. We will depart for your home
at nine tomorrow morning.' After a perfunc-
tory bow, he left.

She touched a finger to lips that retained an impression of his touch, a shadowy feeling of tenderness and warmth. A kiss she would likely never forget.

How could she have let him kiss her? If he spoke of it, the power she held over her little court of bachelors would evaporate like morning mist. Was that his plan? His way to set Fortescue free to prey upon that innocent girl. Would Thorne now bandy her name about as a woman of easy virtue?

Thomas would be so angry if such a thing happened yet again. He, the best of brothers, would likely disown her. Not that she would blame him one bit.

What on earth had got into her? Was there something wrong with her that she could be so easily led astray? Why, oh, why had she let her guard down with this man, after all the years she had spent keeping every one of them at distance?

She would not let it happen again.

Once Marcus realised she had absolutely no interest in him, he would begin to think he had imagined the whole. Or simply blame it on the wine she had drunk. Wine he had poured in her glass.

Oh, why had she encouraged him in that

kiss? Why had her curiosity got the better of her with him, when she had never been the slightest bit interested in any man for years?

What a horrible mistake. She searched for her anger at Cornelius, seeking its protection from men like Fortescue and men like Thorne.

Chapter Eight

By the time morning arrived and the carriages were in the yard awaiting their departure, Marcus had decided to act as if the previous evening had not occurred. He had the feeling that would be her preference also, since she had not joined him at breakfast, preferring to take a tray in her room according to the innkeeper.

He glanced at his pocket watch. Would she be ready by nine, or would she keep him waiting?

But no. Here she was, looking as beautiful and remote as ever as, followed by her maid, she walked into the courtyard. Rain-washed cobblestones and the grass sparkling with dew promised as pretty an autumn day as one could wish.

When her glance rested on him, her gaze

froze him to the bone. Her straight back and arrogantly tilted head dared him to presume to take any liberties.

Guilt sat uncomfortably in his gut and he could not help but admire her bravery. A lesser female might have been embarrassed by such wayward behaviour the evening before and scuttled into her carriage with her head down.

He bowed. 'Good morning, Lady Cynthia.'

She nodded and tugged at her gloves. 'Thorne. Are we ready for the off?'

'We are indeed.'

'Good. My coachman knows the way. Please follow us.'

He had intended to suggest her coach go ahead in case any accident should befall it, but her imperious manner raised his hackles. He forced himself not to insist her carriage follow his and instead helped her and her maid in and closed the door.

Her coachman climbed onto his box. Marcus looked up at him. 'If you run into difficulties, pull over to the verge. I will do what I can to assist.'

'Yes, my lord,' the man said.

Marcus climbed up into his phaeton and,

once the carriage was out of the courtyard, set off after it.

Fortunately, they were early enough that the traffic on the road was relatively light and they encountered no mishaps along the way apart from the odd patch of mud. The Norton coachman was a good man with the ribbons and took great care that his passengers were not discomforted, Marcus noted.

Once, they had been forced to wait for a flock of sheep to move aside for them to pass and it had taken some time to overtake a slow-moving carter with what looked like a house full of furniture piled in the back of his ve-hicle, but not long after midday they pulled up at the front of Harrowglen.

The house was built of golden-hued sand-stone with two wings wrapping around the central block with its elegant porte cochère.

Someone must have seen them coming up the drive and gone to warn Norton, because he was already standing on the step up to the front door, beaming.

A footman ran to his horses' heads while another helped the ladies out of their carriage.

'If you had not arrived within the next two hours I had decided to come and look for you,' Norton said as the servants scurried to take their luggage around to the back of the house and the butler stood waiting to take their coats.

'How are you, Lock?' Lady Cynthia said as the butler handed her coat to one of the maids standing by.

'Very well, my lady,' Lock replied. 'Will luncheon in the breakfast room in a half-hour suit you?'

'Most certainly, I am famished. Will you gentlemen join me? Or are you too anxious to be off to the stables and will simply grab bread and cheese and take it with you?'

'We will take a proper lunch, Cynthia,' Norton said. 'The horses are not going anywhere. Don't take too long titivating, either.'

He seemed a little tetchy.

His sister smiled. 'Ate early, did you? Well, I am sure Lord Thorne will not keep you waiting a moment longer than need be.' She turned to her brother. 'By the way, Lord Thorne was most helpful in securing me a room last night. We owe him a debt of gratitude.'

Norton's brow cleared a little. 'Thank you, Thorne. I have to admit I was worried when the storm went through yesterday and I had no word from my sister.'

'Word would have arrived at the same time we did, Thomas. And you know that bad news travels much faster than good.'

'Well, you are here now, so hurry along.'

She nodded and, followed by the maid holding her coat, went upstairs. 'Lock will show you to your room,' Norton said. 'One of the footmen is tasked as valet and will be waiting for you. He'll direct you to the breakfast room.'

Harrowglen, it seemed was a well-ordered household, despite its owner's lack of a wife. Was that down to Lady Cynthia?

Brother and sister were waiting for him when he arrived in the breakfast room less than half an hour later. It was a pleasant room overlooking a formal garden, which at this time of year looked rather drab though well kept.

Luncheon was a help-yourself sort of affair, but the dishes presented were plentiful and delicious.

They each filled their plates and sat down.

'Thomas, did you have Styles send out invitations for our dinner party, or shall I arrange it this afternoon while you visit the stables?' Lady Cynthia asked after Norton had demolished a good portion of what was on his plate.

Norton picked up his tankard and took a long draught. 'Home farm ale,' he said. 'You won't find any better in the whole county.'

Marcus took a sip. It was indeed very good.

'The dinner is all arranged,' Norton said. 'Styles can go over the guest list with you and then Lock the arrangements we agreed upon. I believe he has one or two questions from cook he would like answered. But otherwise everything is in place.'

'Excellent, Thomas. Thank you.'

He frowned. 'You really need to get rid of Paxton, the woman is a liability. If she had not let you down at the last moment, you would have arrived here ahead of the storm as I did.'

'Mrs Paxton would be hard put to it to survive without her position. And we get along very well.'

'You get along very well because she is completely and utterly useless.'

She smiled cheerfully. 'Finish your lunch, my dear, you will feel a lot less bearish once you have eaten your fill. Is the roast beef to your taste, Lord Thorne?' She glanced over at the buffet and signalled to the butler, who sent a footman scurrying off, only to return to replace a game pie that was more than three quarters gone. A very delicious game pie.

The woman was clearly in her element running this establishment. A man would be glad to have a wife like her even if she was untrained to the bit.

Another man.

He was looking for a much more amenable lady.

'Everything is delicious, thank you,' Marcus said. 'How many guests are you expecting at your dinner?'

'Half the county,' Norton said morosely.

'No more than ten,' Lady Cynthia said, shaking her head at her brother. 'They are good neighbours and deserve to be treated as such.'

It seemed odd that she would be so considerate of these people after what she had done to Bess. He could not help but feel that much of the time she was putting on an act. But which was the real her: the caring lady or the cold-hearted beauty?

He was beginning to wonder if he had misjudged her completely.

If so, why would she hurt Bess in such a manner?

He shook his head at himself. Had that kiss

affected his brain? Did he now want to see her in a different light, so he could follow the dictates of his passions, instead of using his reason?

Olga had enflamed his passions and he'd acted against all reason and very nearly brought ruin raining down on his head. He was no longer a greenhorn to be caught like that again. Clearly Lady Cynthia was playing her own game and he was not going to be her pawn.

Cynthia would be glad when luncheon was over. She could barely stop herself from squirming beneath Lord Thorne's intense scrutiny each time he glanced her way. She felt like an insect under a magnifying glass. It was as if he was trying to see her innermost thoughts.

She really should not have let him kiss her. Heavens, she had encouraged him to do so, in a most wanton way.

In some sort of gentlemanly show of honour, he had put it down to the amount of wine she had imbibed. She had the feeling that she might have done exactly the same if she had not had any wine at all. And that was what was so mortifying. It was exactly the way she had been with Cornelius. Out of control. Humming with passion. Unable to think of anything else but him.

Thomas put down his knife and fork with a sigh of a man who is replete. 'Sister, why don't you join us in the stables once you have finished checking up on me with Lock? You know more about the historic bloodlines than I do.'

'I am not checking up on you. Or Lock for that matter.'

Her brother grunted. 'Then leave him to do his work and come with us.'

A prickle of awareness across her shoulders. Thomas was not looking at her, but rather he was watching Thorne as if judging the other man's response to the idea of her presence. She pretended not to notice. Thomas would soon give up, provided she showed no interest. Unfortunately, for some reason, her gaze wandered in Thorne's direction more often than she would have liked. Perhaps Thomas had noticed. Clearly she would have to be more careful.

For some reason, recently, there seemed to be more urgency about his ploys to *get her off his hands*, as he was wont to say. Was it possible he had chosen a bride and was simply wanting Cynthia to be settled before setting a wedding date?

What she had to do now was convince her brother to approve the place she wanted to live. She knew she could be happy there and having her own establishment would give her the freedom to engage in the pursuits she considered important without interference. In the meantime, it would be best to keep Thomas happy.

'If you really think you need me, Thomas, of course I will be glad to accompany you gentlemen to the stables.'

They paused only to put on their coats and walked together over to the stables set off to one side at the back of the house. The low red-brick building nestled in a natural indentation in the land, which, with a few strategically planted trees, was invisible from the house.

'It is unusual to find the stable so far away,' Thorne said.

'It can be inconvenient at times, especially in bad weather,' she said. 'But it works better for the horses to be closer to pasture and for turning the carriages around and so forth. To be honest I do not know if it happened by design or by mistake. While these stables are new, they were built in the same place as those that were here for centuries.'

They entered the stable block and the next hour was spent inspecting the stallion and the mares and some of the yearlings. While Thomas extolled their qualities, she provided the bloodlines and history when requested. Thomas loved his horses. He had a feel for them, whereas she had a very good memory.

Every time she spoke, Thorne's gaze homed in on her face. An awareness of him skittered across her skin. Her lips felt numb and her body tingled with life. She became almost breathless, making it difficult to speak. She knew she was talking, but half the time her mind had no clue what she was saying.

Fortunately, Thomas seemed to notice nothing wrong and was moving along the line of mares with a great deal of well-deserved pride.

Was it the associations with the past in these stables that were causing her to lose her balance? Memories of hurried, uncomfortable stolen kisses and fumbling caresses? This was where she and Cornelius had trysted those many years ago. Or was Thorne the culprit, the kiss they had shared being far too much at the forefront of her thoughts? Such a delightful sensation of two mouths fitting perfectly for a brief magical moment.

Stop!

'There is more stock in the pasture on the other side of the estate,' Thomas said when they reached the last stall. He looked at his watch. 'I will take you there tomorrow. It is too late now. We will lose the light before we get there. How about we inspect the feed schedules and talk to my stable master about training?'

'Thank you. I would find that most valuable,' Thorne said.

'If you don't mind,' Cynthia said, 'I will leave you to it, from this point. I need to check the arrangements for dinner tonight and have words with the housekeeper. Unless you needed me for something else, Thomas?'

'No, no. Run along. I am sure I can manage the rest of it quite well, but do not worry about dinner this evening, I am taking Thorne to the Rose and Crown. There are a couple of jockeys there I would like him to meet.'

'I shall look forward to seeing you at breakfast tomorrow, then, Lord Thorne.' She made her curtsy and with a sigh of relief made her escape.

Outside she took a deep, steadying breath

of cool autumn air. She would only have to put up with three days of him being in the house and hopefully Thomas would keep him busy most of that time. She could not have been more grateful when he said they would not eat at home this evening.

What she had felt on hearing his words had definitely not been a pang of disappointment.

An impatient knocking forced its way into Cynthia's awareness and forced her awake. It came again. Thorne? She shook off the dregs of sleep. Surely not Thorne. Fire? Oh, God.

She tumbled from the bed, throwing on her robe.

'Cynthia, it is me, Thomas.' The door swung back and the light from the hallway made it difficult to see his expression, but she had no doubt as to the urgency in his voice.

'Thomas. What is it?'

'Mallock's cow is in calf. They need my help.'

She rolled her eyes. 'I thought the house must be on fire at the very least. I am surprised Thorne isn't coming along to see what is going on.' Though it was unlikely he would hear anything in the other wing.

'I have to go. If I'm not back in time, will

you take Thorne out to the river pasture in the morning? There's a foal I would like him to look at. I think she could be a big winner and, well, I was thinking I might convince him to buy her. He has agreed to use Rufus for his stud, but after our chat this evening, I have a feeling these mares he has are not up to much. He needs to invest in the future of his stud if it is going to be any good.'

Horses. It was all he ever thought about. 'If she is going to be a big winner, why sell her?'

He grimaced. 'Remember, I have a debt I must pay right away.'

Men and their debts of honour. 'If you are going to start gambling away the family fortune—'

'You know me better than that, Sister.'

'I do, which is why I am surprised.'

'The horse should have won by a mile, but it caught a foot in a rabbit hole. Just bad luck. And I would have had the ready money to hand, if I had not paid to have a new roof put on the village hall which I assume you recall was exceedingly expensive.'

It was she who had suggested that it was his civic duty to do so.

'Anyway, none of this matters except that I must get on or Mallock's cow will not last the night and I need to know that you will take Thorne out to the pasture if I am not home in time.'

'Very well, Thomas, I shall do my best to stand in your stead.'

'Be your usual charming self and convince him to buy the filly.' He stomped off.

She took a deep breath. So much for avoiding Thorne during his visit.

As Marcus approached the stables the next morning, he was greeted not by his host, but by Lady Cynthia, clearly dressed for riding. Her riding habit was dark blue with very little ornamentation and worn over a plain white shirt with a high ruffled neck. Her hat in the style of a curly beaver was very like his own and not a feather or a plume to be seen. But despite the plainness of her garb she looked stunning. Perhaps more stunning than usual since there was no ornamentation to draw the eye away from that lovely face. 'You decided to join us after all.'

'Not us, I am afraid. You. Thomas got called away in the early hours of this morning and requested that I ride out with you instead of him. It was unexpected and I apologise on his behalf. I hope you do not mind?'

When he found himself alone at breakfast, he had been told by a footman that his host had breakfasted earlier and that Lady Cynthia always took her breakfast in her room. Since the first meal of the day was usually an informal meal in the country, a catch-as-catch-can sort of affair, he had thought nothing odd about eating alone.

But his host's absence at this juncture was odd. 'Called away where?'

She made a face. 'One of the tenants. A cow is having a difficult labour and they needed Thomas to pull. He is the only one strong enough. He's done it before and they always call on him if he is here. He left at about four this morning. Calves always come at the most awkward of times.'

'I see.'

'It would be a terrible loss to our tenant if the cow and the calf are lost.' She sounded defensive and gave a gesture of helplessness. 'Thomas would never say no. I am sorry.'

'No need to apologise. It makes perfect sense to me. So, you have been given the chore of showing me the surprise Norton had planned.'

'It will not be a chore, I assure you.'

A couple of grooms brought their horses

out. His, a big-boned grey gelding, and hers, a delicate little mare with soft brown eyes and a shining chestnut coat.

Lady Cynthia glanced at his horse. 'Good choice for you. Hercules is definitely up to your weight.'

She fed her horse a carrot and stroked its nose before having it led to the mounting block. 'What do you think of Pepper?' she asked once mounted.

'She looks like a real lady. Very pretty, too.'

She patted Pepper's neck. 'Appearances can be deceiving.'

Wasn't that the truth.

They rode down the drive side by side and out into the lane. He saw she was having to keep the little mare under strict control, which she did without difficulty. 'She's hot like her name, then?' he remarked.

'She hasn't been ridden out for ages. They exercise her, of course, but it's not the same. It is one reason why I prefer to live here than in town.'

He stared at her. 'I would never have guessed that.'

'Well, it isn't done, is it?' she drawled. 'Preferring the country to the city. Now I have admitted it to you, no doubt everyone will be talking about my strange behaviour behind my back.' She did not seem to care if they did.

'I do not gossip,' he said sternly.

She laughed and he joined in.

'Which way are we headed?' he asked.

'East. It is about two miles as the crow flies. We can go by way of the lanes or straight across country if you prefer. It will be quicker.'

'Across country would suit me. I assume there will be places where we can gallop?'

'Oh, yes. And a couple of jumps, too, if you have a mind.' She urged the horse into a canter and they took a footpath across a field left fallow.

He rode by her side. She was an excellent horsewoman and looked fine on a horse.

They skirted a wood, crossed a small pasture with a brook running through it, which they jumped.

'Five-bar gate ahead,' she said and he realised she was smiling. His heart clenched at that smile. It was bright, happy and completely honest. Clearly, for the moment, she had forgotten about their differences.

'Did you want me to open it?' he asked.

'Not on my account,' she said. 'But if you prefer to walk through, you may.'

'Lead the way, my lady,' he said.

She glanced at him and there was a gleam of mischief in her eyes. 'Be careful of the drop-off on the other side.'

Was she hoping to show him up, or make him look a fool? Olga had tried that and had failed miserably.

Lady Cynthia flew over the fence and he watched with his heart in his mouth as her horse's head went dangerously low on the other side of the jump. Clearly the drop-off was considerable. The horse recovered and they were galloping onwards.

Marcus gave his animal its head, but at the last moment offered it a little encouragement and shifted his weight to ease the landing. It was an exhilarating jump. No wonder she had looked at him with that challenge in her gaze.

Even as his horse recovered, he noticed her backward glance—was it in relief or disappointment? From this distance, he could not tell.

Whichever it was, the lady was a challenge. In more ways than one.

Good lord, what was he thinking?

Thorne was as good a horseman as she had hoped. Her match. No. Not in that way, she scolded, startled by the little flutter low in her abdomen. Simply the sort of man she would like to have as a friend. He didn't waffle on about beauty or write sonnets to her eyes or describe her hair as some sort of freak of nature. His conversation was sensible and his riding impeccable. Father had always said one could tell a great deal about a man from the way he sat on his horse.

She slowed Pepper to a trot, then a walk. Thorne caught up.

He gave her a narrowed-eye glance. 'Nice jump, my lady.'

She smiled at him. 'I thought you would enjoy it.'

For some reason he looked relieved. Then he shook his head at her. 'To be honest, are you not being a little reckless making that jump in a ladies' saddle?'

'Now you sound like my father.' She gave him a sideways glance and saw his expression of dismay. Oh, he definitely didn't want her to compare him to her father. A small smile teased her lips. 'Don't worry, I have been over it many times.' She laughed. 'And taken a couple of tumbles. I have great respect for that gate.'

He grunted as if he did not agree, but said nothing further.

They skirted the edges of several ploughed fields at a walk and then arrived at their destination—a meadow sloping down to a swiftly flowing brook.

In the far corner of the field, a group of horses were grazing placidly. They looked in their direction and instantly went on the alert, ears pricked forward.

'We will leave our horses here and walk down.' She gave her head a rueful shake. 'Why is it animals always huddle at the furthest point from the gate?'

He opened the gate for her and offered his arm as if she was some delicate flower unable to walk more than a step or two without aid. She strode down the hill.

She heard his huff of annoyance and ignored it, exactly the way she had ignored his arm.

The mares stirred restlessly at their approach and in their midst revealed the reason for Thomas's desire to bring Thorne out here.

'What a little beauty,' she said. 'A filly.' She looked at the mother and recalled the bloodlines. 'If she is anything like her mama, she will be a winner and make an excellent breeder.'

She sat down on the grass. 'Let us give them time to get used to us being here.'

Thorne sat down beside her without a murmur about grass stains or damp.

Gradually, the mares relaxed their watchful stance and the little foal kicked her heels and ran back and forth, never straying far from her mother, until suddenly she folded her skinny legs under her and took a nap.

'Why are you showing this to me? I am not in the market for any more horses.'

'You told Thomas you had some doubts about your mares. He wanted to show you this one, in case you were interested. However, I should warn you, it will not come cheap.'

He looked grim. 'Perhaps I should do as my aunt requested and give up the idea of a stud farm.'

'You would give up without a fight?'

He helped her to her feet and she brushed off her skirts. 'A wise man knows when to cut his losses.' He rubbed his chin with his gloved hand. 'I would be interested to know whether you think the foal would be a good investment.'

Surprised, she stared at him. 'You would trust my opinion?'

'I know nothing about what makes a good racehorse. Or how one may guess at it in the attributes of a foal. It is my impression that you do. If I am wrong, then I apologise.

'You are not wrong. But most men would defer to Thomas. I suppose since Thomas is not here, I am the next best thing.'

'I don't think I would put it quite like that.'

Warmth spread outwards from her chest at his compliment. She controlled the urge to sigh like a schoolgirl. 'Very well. I would say that she is an excellent prospect, not only from her breeding, which is indeed fine, but from the look of her and the spirit I see in her. And you are right, not only does she not have any obvious faults, but everything about her looks very promising. One cannot be sure until they are two years old, however.' She hesitated. 'It is a long-term commitment and I probably should not say this, but you might be better to offer Thomas a retainer for first refusal and leave her here with us. Once she is weaned, look at her again and make a final decision.'

He narrowed his eyes. 'That is what you would do?'

She met his gaze, penetrating, curious

and—warm. Something seemed to crackle in the air between them. The hairs on her arms stood up. She forced herself to hold his gaze. 'That is what Thomas would do.'

He nodded briskly. 'I will take your advice, then.'

It seemed he noticed nothing of the heat swirling in the air around them. She looked back at the foal, its knobby legs looking too long for its body, and smiled. 'If you have seen enough, then...'

'I have.'

She liked a man who did not dither. She liked too much about this man.

They walked up the hill and remounted, heading home the way they had come.

Thorne pointed to Bellavista Place, whose chimney could be seen above the trees a little further along the river. 'What is that? The dower house?'

She laughed. 'Far from it. The dower house is far grander. My grandmother made sure of that. No, that is a dark family secret. My grandfather kept his mistress there.'

He looked puzzled. 'A dark secret?'

'Apparently he loathed my grandmother, having been required to wed her, and loved a woman named Lucy Bedford to the point of desperation. He spent outrageous sums of money on her and spent more time at Bella-vista than he did at home. My father said she was the love of his life. His legitimate family resented her to the depths of their being. Would you mind awfully if we dropped in? I would like a word with the housekeeper. I left instructions for some repairs before I left to come to London. I would like to see if they were completed.'

Why was she asking him to go with her? She could easily come over another time. Or perhaps not. Thomas had plans to return to London as soon as Thorne left so he could get his Parliamentary business done and get back to Harrowglen in time for Christmas. She might not be able to visit Bellavista until December. There was something about it that made her feel calm inside. It was why she wanted to convince Thomas to let her live there once he married. For some strange reason she wanted to see Thorne's reaction to the house and its sordid past.

He hesitated. 'Will Norton be expecting us?'

'I expect he will go to bed as soon as he gets home—besides, it is almost lunch time. I am sure the housekeeper would be able to find us a bite to eat. I don't know about you, but I am starving.'

He smiled.

Something in her chest pulled painfully tight at the sweetness of his smile.

'You are right,' he said cheerfully. 'Luncheon would not go amiss. And I have to admit I am intrigued by your description of the house as a dark secret.'

She had the feeling he had agreed only because she had said she was hungry. But he had agreed and she felt happier than she had for a long time.

Hopefully, the housekeeper would have something on hand to feed to her unexpected guests.

They rode down to the riverside lane and were soon approaching Bellavista. Without a doubt, the house had one of the most beautiful views on the estate. Her grandfather had chosen very carefully.

The house had been built new for his love on the site of a folly once used by members of the family for picnics in the summer.

Chapter Nine

Marcus had not been quite sure what to expect, after Cynthia's explanation of what the house had been used for in the past, but he could not help his exclamation of surprise. 'My word, what a charming place!'

Lying inside a brick wall encompassing what he judged to be about three acres was a miniature Palladian two-storey mansion. Doric columns supported the porch at the centred front door, with identical sets of light airy windows on each side. A balcony with a delicate tracery of wrought iron graced each upper-floor window and the rustic foundation was surrounded by beautifully kept gardens.

'Wait until you see the view at the rear.'

At their approach, a young lad ran out to see to their horses. 'Jack,' Lady Cynthia said to him, 'this is Lord Thorne.'

The lad touched his forelock. 'We heard as how a lord was visiting the pasture to look at the new filly.' The boy squinted sideways at Thorne. 'Will you be buying it?'

Lady Cynthia shook her head at him. 'Have you been making a friend of our new baby? You know better than to get attached to them.'

'I was there when she was born, me lady. Be you, me lord?'

'Possibly,' Marcus replied, surprised by the lad's informality and his London accent.

The lad's shoulders slumped, but he said no more and led the horses away.

Lady Cynthia strode ahead. The front door opened before they reached it. A short, plump, elderly woman with straggly grey hair and a well-worn apron leaning heavily on a stick limped out to greet them.

'My lady,' the woman said. 'I was not expecting you. I think you will find everything in order.'

'I did not plan to come today, but we were visiting the filly and decided to drop in.'

Her gaze shifted to Marcus. 'Lord Norton is not with you?'

'Unfortunately, no. Lord Norton had to help out at Mallock's, so I am leading our expedition. This is Lord Thorne.' She turned to him. 'Mrs Frost has been here at Bellavista for many years. She was a scullery maid in my grandfather's time.'

The woman dipped a knee and almost fell over.

Marcus smile. 'Good day, ma'am.'

'Is there any hope you can provide us with a spot of lunch?' Cynthia asked. 'Anything you have on hand will do. We would not want to put you to any trouble.'

The housekeeper drew herself up to her full height in silent admonishment. 'No trouble at all, my lady. I will be delighted to prepare something for you. Will you take it in the dining room or…?'

Cynthia inhaled a breath. 'It smells a little musty in here, so on the veranda, if you please. It is such a lovely sunny day and I want to show off the view to Lord Thorne. Though it is much prettier in spring and summer.'

'Certainly, my lady. I will send Annie to put out the cushions.'

'Do not worry, Mrs Frost. We can do it.'

'Oh, no. What would His Lordship think? Annie can do it.'

The housekeeper limped ahead of them into the house.

'Poor old thing. She won't admit she should be retiring,' Cynthia said.

'Is it not a bit cool to be eating outside?' Marcus asked.

'If it is not too chilly to sit in a meadow, then certainly we will be perfectly fine on the veranda. It is very sheltered.'

She sounded quite light-hearted, almost excited, which made her seem younger, somehow.

He held out his arm and this time she took it and guided him through the entrance hall which, while nowhere near as large as that at Harrowglen, showed that someone had spent a great deal of money to make it every bit as luxurious. A lovely, intricately decorated staircase wound to the upper floor.

The entrance hall split the house in two and enormous French doors opposite the front door let in sunlight and offered a teasing glimpse of the countryside beyond.

A young woman in a cap and apron, Annie, Marcus guessed, dodged in front of them and threw open a set of the doors.

They stepped out onto a veranda which reminded him very much of the covered terraces he had encountered at some of the houses he had visited in Italy. Columns supported the roof, but there were no walls or windows to ruin what was indeed a magnificent view of the valley and the rolling countryside beyond it. A low wrought-iron railing ran between the outer columns except in the opening where a few marble steps led down to the lawn and gardens beyond.

Lady Cynthia strolled to the railing, looking out at the view while the maid set out cushions on the chairs.

Marcus joined Cynthia. 'You are right, the back of the house is impressive. I do not know when I have seen a finer view.'

She looked up at him in genuine delight. 'I am glad you agree. Thomas refuses to come here. He says it caused too much trouble in the family and he would sell it if he could. But I love it here. It is so peaceful.'

'It seems rather expensive to keep it up, when no one lives here. I am surprised you do not rent it out. It would surely command a good price.'

That was what she had told Thomas, when she had told him she wanted to live here. She was prepared to pay a fair rent for the place, but Thomas had not yet become resigned to the fact that she was quite happy living alone. 'There is only a skeleton staff to keep the place clean and the gardens tended, but you are right, it is a burden on the estate. Fortunately, it is part of the entail or I think Father would have sold it off the moment he inherited.' She chuckled. 'When he realised he was stuck with it, he decided to make use of it. All our foals are born in the stables here, away from the stallions and younger horses, until they are old enough to be weaned. In that way, he decided that the place could earn its keep.'

'What happened to her, Lucy, after your grandfather died?'

Her face became remote. 'She was forced to leave. I gather that while my grandfather had prepared for that eventuality, my grandmother finally had her revenge for what she considered her humiliation. She contested the disbursement of monies and other items she said rightfully belonged to my grandfather's heir. When she won her case, she had Lucy thrown into the street with nothing but the clothes on her back.'

'Revenge indeed.'

'It was unnecessarily cruel. My grandmother did it to spite my grandfather after his death. They truly despised each other, so my aunt told me. She said, though she would never have said it to my father, that Lucy gave Grandfather what he never got in his real home: love and support.' She gave a dismissive laugh as if she thought it all nonsense. 'Oh, look, lunch is ready.'

Rather than the picnic of bread and cheese he had been expecting, the luncheon that appeared almost by magic made his mouth water. Fresh crispy rolls, shaved ham, a variety of cheeses and fruits spread before them.

He seated Lady Cynthia and looked at the open bottle of champagne. 'May I pour you a glass of champagne?'

'Oh, yes, indeed,' Lady Cynthia said. 'Thank you. I would highly recommend it. It was laid down by my grandfather and was not discovered until after my grandmother's death or no doubt she would have had it poured into the river.'

He poured them each a glass and they chinked their glasses.

'To the filly growing up strong and as fast as the wind,' she said with a bright smile.

Marcus had the urge to drink to her beautiful eyes. 'To the filly.'

He tucked into the feast before him until he could eat no more. Lady Cynthia did likewise.

She put down her knife and fork and picked up her wine glass. She leaned back in her chair, with an expression of hunger in her gaze. If she was hungry, it could not be for food. His body heated.

Surely he was imagining things. And if so, was it wishful thinking? Certainly not. He refused to fall under her spell like the sort of green-as-grass youths that followed her around.

'Would you care for a tour of the house, if you are finished eating?' She rose to her feet. He followed suit. 'There was one thing here that always infuriated my father that you might find amusing.' The laughter in her voice intrigued him.

'Why not? We have time and will still be home in time for dinner.'

She took his arm and they wandered back into the house.

The formal rooms were in the east wing and the cosier family rooms in the west, Lady Cynthia explained. The difference was immediately noticeable. The east-wing rooms displayed fine works of art and were ornately decorated. The west-wing rooms were cluttered with little objets d'art and miniatures of assorted family members. A sewing basket nestled beside a comfy-looking chair and there was a chess board set up and a card table between two upright chairs presented an inviting picture. The walls were covered in beautiful handmade hangings.

'*She* made all of the wall coverings,' Lady Cynthia said. 'While Grandfather spent a great deal of time here, he could not be here always and was away in London for long stretches of time. Apparently, she used the time to ply her needle. There are also a number of unfinished projects in the attics.'

She led the way upstairs and flung open the first door they came to. 'This was their bedroom.'

Sumptuous. There was no other word to describe the room. The walls were lined in silk decorated with gloriously embroidered birds and flowers. The bedspread was similarly embroidered. The upholstery on the deep armchairs and the *chaise longe* was exquisite and definitely of Chinese origin. French doors led out onto a balcony with the same view as that from the veranda below.

'They spent a great deal of their time together in this room according to the diaries that were found after his death. Or so Thomas tells me. Father burned the diaries so I never saw them.'

Marcus had visited bordellos in his youth

that attempted this style of decoration and had failed utterly. This room on the other hand appealed to every hedonistic sense in his body. What would it be like to sink into that feather bed with the beautiful Lady Cynthia naked in his arms?

His body warmed at the vision that his mind conjured up. As if pulled by some invisible force, they turned to face each other.

Her gaze was wide and shining with some emotion he wanted to know more of. Her lips parted. Her chest rose and fell as if she were under some sort of stress. His body tightened and the urge to place his hands on her hips and pull her close tingled in his palms.

She jerked away and threw open the French doors and stepped outside. Unlike below, up here the balcony turned the corner of the house and that was where she headed. She flung out an arm and pointed. 'There.'

In the distance, he had a clear view of Harrowglen.

She pointed to the house. 'Do you see the cupola?'

He nodded. In the centre of Harrowglen's roof was a dome. It looked as if it was centred over the grand hall, but he had seen no sign of it when he had glanced upward upon his arrival there.

She turned and pointed to a small ladder affixed to the wall behind them. 'There is a matching one up there. It is how they messaged back and forth when he was in residence at Harrowglen. If Lucy wanted him, she would raise a certain flag, or light a lamp. They messaged back and forth in code. Whenever he left Harrowglen to go to her, according to what my father told Thomas, my grandmother would say to him, *Hoisted your flag, did she?* Apparently she wasn't talking about a banner.'

She giggled at the naughtiness of the implication.

'And Grandfather would say yes and leave. After a while Grandmother used to use the same method to tell him to come home because there was some business that needed his attention. So much so, that both houses kept boys on permanent watch here and at Harrowglen. It was a very unusual arrangement and it infuriated my father because he was the one who had to trek up the stairs to tell the boy to put up the flag or light the lantern and what message to send. Not to mention that he would have preferred to be in ignorance of what his dear papa was up to.'

'He didn't like the disrespect to his mother.'

'Exactly. But in some bizarre way it worked for Grandfather and Grandmother.

Father burnt all the flags and disposed of all the lanterns. But the cupolas could not be torn down without costing a great deal of money in repairs to the main structures of the houses. So he was forced to leave them in place. What do you think of that arrangement?'

'I think your grandfather could have been a little more caring of your grandmother's feelings and have been a little more discreet.'

'Sneaked around behind her back, you mean.' She spoke with distaste.

'More in the way of not flaunting it in her face so that all and sundry knew what he was up to.' Her grandmother sounded like a sterling character. Someone who stuck up for herself in a difficult situation. Though he did not approve of having the paramour tossed out into the street.

'Is that what you will do?' she asked.

'We are not talking about me. It is what your grandfather should have done.'

'Perhaps you are right,' she said, grudgingly rubbing her arms. The sun was already past its zenith and up here there was no shelter from the breeze.

'You are cold. Let us go inside.'

He followed her back into the bedroom.

'One more thing,' she said softly and drew aside one of the draped curtains at the head of the bed, revealing a picture. 'This is a portrait of them. My grandfather and Lucy.'

The picture was similar to many from the eighteenth century, the subjects attired in whimsical costumes of mythical characters, with white painted skin and extraordinarily large powdered wigs. But it wasn't the sensual costumes or the beauty of the scene that drew the eye, it was the expression on the faces of the couple as they gazed at each other.

The adoration on their faces was unmistakable. Something twisted painfully in his chest. 'They look like besotted fools,' he said. To his ears it sounded dismissive.

She seemed to flinch at the harshness in his tone and gave a tight smile. 'Yes. I suppose they do. There is a great deal of sentimentality about it. I have wondered if those looks on their faces are true to life or simply an artistic impression.'

'No doubt the latter, unless the picture was painted in the first few weeks they met.'

She tilted her head, staring at the picture. 'It was painted after they had been together for twenty years. She was nearly forty and he was over seventy. Her youth annoyed his wife greatly.'

'I can imagine.' He looked closer. 'He looks his seventy summers, true, but the artist has made her look a great deal younger than her years. I expect their expressions were also doctored.'

She sighed and turned away. 'Thomas was going to burn it. I managed to rescue it from the fire and keep it hidden.'

Looking at that picture, seeing those expressions, if it came even a fraction close to what those two people felt for each other, the resentment of his children was not surprising. But more surprising was Cynthia's obvious admiration of the illicit couple.

Disappointed by his obvious disapproval of a portrait she had always thought captured a moment of honesty in a dishonest world, Cynthia gazed up into Thorne's face. Was he really so unfeeling? And if so, would he not be the perfect partner for a woman as cold-hearted as her?

The look he returned was equally searching. A warmth entered the depth of those dark eyes, pinpricks of gold that flickered like flames in mysterious depths. Her body warmed. Excitement trickled along her veins, sending prickles of awareness across her skin and flutters low in her belly.

What was it about this man that she found so irresistible that she wanted to stroke her palms over those wide shoulders, run her fingers through the dark waves at the nape of his neck?

The question turned into action, even as the thought formed in her mind, one hand moving to rest on his chest and slide upwards to shape the strong curve of his shoulder.

He stilled. She wasn't even sure he was breathing. When he did not move away or speak, her other hand slid around his neck and she speared the tips of her fingers into the silky strands of his thick dark hair.

Their gazes remained fixed as if locked together.

Slowly, he lowered his head. She rose on her toes and as their lips touched, her eyes drifted closed.

Every sense in her body focused on the touch of their lips, the hard beating of her heart and the delicious trembling in her limbs.

Their lips moved upon each other. The sheer headiness of the feel of his mouth made it a necessity that her hands clung to him and her body arched into him.

Strong but gentle hands closed around her waist and supported her as the kiss deepened and their tongues met in a delicate exploration of lips and hot sweet darkness.

How long they remained embraced in each other's arms she did not know. Time seemed to have no meaning, while her body flared to life, yearning for his touch, his warmth, his caresses.

His harsh breaths heated her cheek. His large hands kneaded her back while holding her firmly against his lithe body. His heart thundered against her ribcage in harmony with her own rapid pulse. This was the sort of kiss she had been missing. This sense of fusion fulfilled a long-repressed yearning.

With a soft sort of groan, he broke the kiss and shifted slightly, putting distance between them. Only a little. Far too much for the desire pounding along her veins.

She let her hands drop.

He took a step back.

'Lady Cynthia—'

'Surely we are beyond the formality of lord and lady in private. And if you are going to apologise…' She inhaled deeply to stop herself saying too much. 'Do not dare apologise.'

A faint smile curved his lips. 'You are right. I am not the least bit sorry.'

He ran one finger along her jaw, a tingle following in the wake of his touch. A shiver ran down her back. 'I am glad to learn you are nowhere near as cold as appearances would suggest.'

Cold. If people knew what she was like beneath the veneer of civility, she would be outcast from society. 'Nor are you as in control as you would have others believe.'

He frowned.

Had she said something wrong? Missed her mark? Or had he simply not recognised this trait in his character? 'You would deny that you prefer to be in command?'

Slowly, he shook his head. 'It is true. I tend to prepare for every eventuality. It is a skill one learns in the diplomatic corps. Be nimble of mind. Expect the unexpected. I am not sure it means I prefer to take control. However…' he drew himself up tall '…while the attraction between us meant I was not surprised by our kiss, the response to it, yours and mine, lit a fire far hotter than I anticipated.'

A fire. Yes. Flames had burned bright during the few moments their mouths had melded, but now, denied oxygen and banked beneath the strictures of society, the heat became unbearable.

Unable to resist, she glanced towards the bed and swallowed. Had the thought of kissing him, and more, been at the back of her mind when she brought him up here? She had touched him first. Kissed him. And while he had not been passive, he had been a perfect gentleman. And it was he who had stopped things from moving too far.

She had tried to fight the attraction between her and Thorne and she had the feeling he had been similarly afflicted. The idea made her smile. 'If flames are fanned, this is certainly the place for it.'

He glanced at the picture and back to her face. 'Cynthia, do you have any idea what you are implying? You cannot—you are a lady.'

Frustration filled her, years of abiding by rules that were completely unfair rising up to make her speak her thoughts aloud. 'Why can I not? I am also a woman.'

'You have a duty to your family name, to your brother…'

'Duty. Why is it all right for a man to take a lover and not all right for a woman?'

His expression held confusion and perhaps even a smidgeon of pity. 'One day you will wed. Your husband will expect, nay, demand, that you come to him untouched. It is the way of our world.'

'I suppose you would demand the same? And yet you have had mistresses. Lovers. You said you did.'

'I do not deny it,' he said stiffly. 'But my partners were not—'

She raised her voice, angered at his acceptance of rules. 'Were they not women?'

'Of course they were women. They were women who either had been married or women not of our class who had chosen not to wed.'

She knew exactly the sort of women he meant. Was she not one of them also? 'I told you before, I also choose not to wed.'

He hissed in a breath. 'Cynthia. Love. You do not know the temptation you offer. The consequences of doing any such thing would be disastrous. Of course you will wed. You are young. Beautiful. Titled. You have only to crook your finger to find yourself a husband.'

She reached up and grabbed him by the shoulders and shook him. It was like trying to shake a mountain. She flattened her palms on the fine fabric of his coat. Let his strength give her courage. 'Did you not hear what I said? I *choose* not to wed. I will not marry.'

He was staring into her face as if trying to understand her words. 'Why?'

The image of Cornelius floated across her mind. 'Because the man who should have married me wed another.' From him, she had learned that love was a fleeting thing, easily crushed. Her gaze slid to the head of the bed. The portrait was a lie.

Comprehension filled his gaze. 'He was your lover.'

Her stomach fell away. The truth uttered so starkly made the emotions she had experienced seem tawdry. She lifted her chin in defiance of his opinion.

But instead of rejection in his gaze there was sympathy. Something she had not expected.

Without thinking she leaned into him.

His arms came around her waist. He widened his stance to support her against his strong body as she rested her head upon his chest feeling safe, despite her dreadful admission.

'Oh, my dear,' he said softly. 'No man of worth would reject you for a youthful mistake.'

'Would they not?' She could not keep the dryness from her tone. 'Did you not just say it yourself? A man expects his wife to be pure when she comes to him.'

'Perhaps if it was explained beforehand...'

Her laugh sounded shaky. 'Surely you heard that I am a jilt?'

A silence ensued.

An uncomfortable silence.

'Well, in truth, it was not I who ended our engagement. When I told Drax the truth about my past, he demanded to be released from our engagement. The money I brought to the marriage was not enough to satisfy his pride, apparently. Instead, Thomas settled upon a sum for his silence.'

Perhaps it would have hurt her more if she had been in love with Drax. She had liked him a good deal, had respected him. His rejection had certainly humbled her pride. A feeling she had no wish to endure again.

'I see.'

She tried to pull out of his embrace, but he

tightened his arms, holding her fast. 'So, you decided you will never marry.'

She had decided she would never again accept an offer of marriage from a man who only cared for her money. Which likely meant she would never marry. 'Yes.'

'From my observation the life of a spinster can be a lonely one. You would deny yourself children. A home. A place in society.'

These were all the arguments put forth by Thomas. But what if she did marry and then her husband took a lover, like her grandfather had? There would be nothing she could say about it, having been accepted as used goods. How humiliating would that be? 'I have interests that will keep me busy. Until now, I have never thought I would feel lonely for the lack of a husband.'

'Until now?'

'I suppose there are some advantages a male in one's life can bring.'

His eyes widened. 'Advantages? You mean the advantages of a lover.'

She loved his instant understanding of what she alluded to. 'Indeed.'

'Are you by chance offering me the position?' He sounded incredulous, but also intrigued.

'I think you would do as well as any other. I believe you are an honourable man. That you would be discreet for Thomas's sake if not for mine.'

'I like your brother. Respect him. What honour would there be in taking his sister as my…?' He hesitated. 'Although I cannot deny the attraction between us.'

Was he throwing a sop to her pride or was he actually considering her suggestion? Perhaps he was worried that she might later demand marriage. 'I do not want to wed you, Marcus. We would not suit at all. You would want to rule the roost and I will not be constrained. I am four and twenty and quite on the shelf. Not to mention that I have been my own mistress for far too long to find the bonds of marriage to my liking. If you are not interested in becoming my lover, simply say so and let us continue as friends.'

An ultimatum. What was she thinking? She was giving him the perfect opportunity to reject her out of hand and no doubt this conversation of theirs would be reported throughout the *ton* in a heartbeat. 'It seems I was mistaken with regard to your feelings. Forget I ever spoke of this.' She pulled away.

He caught her arm and turned her back to

face him. 'Cynthia. Sweetheart.' He cupped her face in his hands, gazing intently into her face. 'You are not mistaken—of that I can assure you. If you are sure this is what you want?' He drew in a breath. 'I would be honoured to be your lover, but let us be clear. The arrangement would last only while I remain unwed. I have a duty to the title to marry and I would not dishonour a wife by keeping a mistress.'

A pang tightened her chest. A sharp little pain. Jealousy? Hurt? How foolish. She waved a dismissive hand. 'As far as I am concerned such an arrangement comes without strings attached.'

His expression heated.

As if by their own volition, her fingers unbuttoned his coat, then set to work on his waistcoat.

His mouth descended on hers and the delights of his kiss sent shivers of lust through her body.

This. This was what she wanted. Nothing more.

Of all the things Marcus had expected this day, making love to Cynthia had not been one of them.

As their lips melded, his body heated until his brain forgot it had any function other than to guide the physical action of his lips and tongue and hands.

Even so, a fraction of rationality warned him he trod down a dangerous path. Would he discover that despite her protestations of wishing to remain single it led straight to the parson's mousetrap? And if so, did he really care?

His family would care, Bess and her mother. Their objections would be loud.

Other men would be envious of his good fortune.

He stepped back and undid the knot in his cravat. It was always the thing women found most difficult about a man's attire.

Cynthia smiled softly, her lips plush and rosy from their kiss, her gaze hot with desire. Secure in the knowledge he could do no harm that was not already done, not if he was careful, he didn't actually give a damn about the future right now.

Desire swirled in the air. Heat blossomed in his body. He swept her up in his arms and carried her to the bed. Her sigh of satisfaction when he laid her down was a siren call.

He pulled his shirt free of his breeches and

stripped it off—at some point she must have undone the buttons. He leaned over her to drizzle kisses all over her face, loving the feel against his lips of her velvet-soft skin. Her eyelashes fluttered against his chin when he touched his lips to her forehead. Her breath whispered across his ear, sending shivers down his back when he kissed her jaw.

To his delight, her fingers burrowed into the waistband of his breeches. With the skill born of knowledge, she set any doubts he might have had about the truth of a lover in her past. The delicate yet firm touch as she caressed his bollocks nearly set him over the edge. He caught her hand in his and brought it to his lips.

'Slowly, love,' he murmured. 'Let us not be premature.'

She gave him a languid and utterly mysterious smile and opened her arms. 'Come to me.'

He lay down beside her, propping himself up on his elbow to gaze into her lovely face. Her lips parted on a little gasp when he pressed his knee against the juncture of her thighs. She arched into the pressure, moving rhythmically, and her eyes slid closed, an expression of hunger on her face.

A hunger he had no intention of denying.

As she moved against him, he carefully undid the frogs down the front of her riding habit and pushed the heavy fabric aside to reveal the fine lawn shirt beneath it. To his surprise, she was not wearing any stays, only a thin muslin chemise veiling the full glory of her small pert breasts and their rosy peaks.

The naughtiness of it caused his bollocks to tighten and the head of his cock to tingle. A warning jangled in the back of his mind. Was this a planned seduction? And, if so, why?

Olga had used his lust against him once— he was not about to let Cynthia try any such tricks. In this affair, he was in control. He left her side and went to the door, locking it with a flick of the key. There would be no visitors taking him by surprise. While Cynthia might be one of the most beautiful women in the world, his family, Bess and her mother, would be mortified if he was forced to marry a woman they considered their arch enemy. Not to mention that she was not the sort of woman he planned to marry.

He was looking for a peaceful life and a comfortable wife.

As he returned, she nodded her approval of his precaution, which allayed his concerns— somewhat. But until he was sure exactly what she was up to, he intended not to take any risks.

Laid out on the bed, her clothing in disarray, she tempted him as no other woman had for a very long time. Her body was slender, her skin pale, her cheeks flushed with passion, her nipples taut.

He gazed deep into her eyes. He stroked her cheek. 'Are you sure, Cynthia, that this is what you want?'

Confidence shone from her eyes. And heat. As if it was the reassurance she sought. She reached out and took his hand and pulled him towards her. 'I could not be more certain,' she murmured.

He lowered himself onto the bed to lie alongside her, kissing her deeply. Her mouth fitted his perfectly and the tangle of her tongue with his enflamed his desire to give her great pleasure.

He broke their kiss to slide achingly slowly down her body, taking as much as he could of the luscious swell of small breast into his mouth, biting gently with his teeth until she moaned her pleasure.

The kneading of his shoulders and back by her hands encouraged him to savour her other breast. Her body arched against his as he paid homage to her slender form with his hands and his tongue.

In a move that surprised him, she bucked him off and flipped him over onto his back. He laughed at the triumphant look on her face. 'What are you doing, darling?'

An enigmatic smile curved her lips. 'I appreciate you taking your time, Marcus, but...' she busied herself with buttons of his waistband '...we likely won't have a great deal of time.'

He lifted his hips and helped her pull down his breeches.

She sat back on her heels and regarded her prize.

He was as hard as a rock.

'Oh, my,' she murmured and licked her lips before settling her hips over him and her wet heat slid down his length. 'Next time, we will arrange things better, but I don't want Thomas worrying about our whereabouts and sending someone out to find us.'

'God, no.'

Her eyes closed and she leaned back a fraction. He guided her hands to support her weight against his bent legs.

He let out a soft groan and she rose up and sank down again. 'Next time.' His brain was having trouble comprehending this time. He pumped his hips and he altered the rhythm and position until her face registered extreme pleasure.

Gripping her waist, he drove hard into her tight silken heat. She cried out.

In a haze of painful pleasure, he warded off the threatening release. Leaving her to set the pace, he brought one hand to one tightly furled nipple to stroke and pet and the thumb of his other hand to the little nub at the apex of her thighs.

She cried out and her quim tightened around his shaft in a paroxysm of pleasure.

He held on, beating back the need to let go and fall with her. She tightened and came for him again. The third time, he could not hold back and he pulled free of her body. She collapsed onto his chest as he shuddered in mindless bliss.

A few moments later, awareness brought his eyes open. Her languid weight on his chest was a delightful warmth. The panting of her breath sang like music in his ears. He stroked and petted her back through the heavy weight of her wool riding dress. Such a hurried coupling was far less than she deserved, but more than he had expected when he arose this morning.

A knock sounded at the door.

He shot up to a sitting position, steadying her with a hand on her back.

The handle turned.

The lock held.

He had locked it, he recalled. A sigh of relief emptied his air-starved lungs.

'My lady?' The knock sounded again.

Cynthia eased away from him. 'What is it?' she called out. 'I am showing His Lordship some of my grandfather's treasures.'

Good god, what sort of euphemism was that? And he could not believe how calm her voice sounded.

'My lady, Lord Norton has sent a message.'

'Very well. I will be downstairs in a moment or two.'

She got up. He stood beside her and pulled up his breeches. He stripped off a pillow case and dried her off, then helped her dress. A few moments later he was shrugging into his coat.

She glanced into the mirror and smoothed her hair back, catching it with a few well-placed pins. She was so utterly calm. How many times had she run into this sort of situation with her previous lover?

He shoved the ungenerous thought aside. It did not matter. The good thing was that it seemed as if the housekeeper accepted the explanation for her halting footsteps faded as she returned downstairs.

They finished dressing.

She looked him up and down and nodded. 'Before we go.' She unlocked a dressing table drawer with a key she extracted from a trinket box on its surface.

She pulled out a carved wooden box and opened the lid. It was full to overflowing with jewellery of every kind. 'Grandfather's treasure. Only Mrs Frost and I know about them. And now you. They were hidden away by Lucy and she was unable to retrieve them before she was thrown out. If Grandmother had found them, she would have melted them down.'

'They belong to your brother now.'

'No. Grandfather left them to Lucy in his will. Mrs Frost said she had a daughter by a previous lover who came to visit from time to time, so if I can ever find Lucy, or perhaps even her daughter, I will pass them along. Please do not speak of this to anyone.'

Marcus stared at the glittering mass that must be worth a king's ransom. Did he believe that she would give them away? In the eyes of the law they belonged to her brother. But it was none of his business. He certainly wasn't going to discuss it with Norton.

His breathing stilled. She was trusting him to keep her secret. Was that because she trusted him? Or because she assumed him a fool who was under her spell? Or was it some sort of test?

'Are you ready?' he asked.

'As soon as I have returned these to their proper place I am.'

He watched her reverently return the jewels to their box and lock them away, then escorted her downstairs.

Chapter Ten

On the way down the stairs, Cynthia felt like giggling. She felt young and just a little bit giddy. She could only imagine Mrs Frost's face had she walked in on them. Thank goodness Marcus had had the presence of mind to lock the door.

It just went to show that he was far more experienced than she in such matters. And every time she looked at Marcus, which was far more often than she should, her heart seemed to tumble in her chest.

It was all nonsense, of course. Complete rubbish. She'd given away her deepest secrets and now relied on him to keep them. Why on earth did she think he was any different to any of the other men who had let her down?

She did not care. This feeling of reckless-ness simply would not be squashed. Besides, it was too late for regrets. What difference would it make to her life if he broadcast her outrageous behaviour far and wide? Indeed, perhaps dear Thomas would finally stop trying to marry her off to some hapless lord or other.

Mrs Frost was pacing the entrance hall when they reached it. She hobbled around to face them. Her glance skittered to Thorne and away. Clearly, she suspected something. Cynthia lifted her chin and Mrs Frost's hand smoothed her skirts.

'My lady,' she quavered. 'A messenger has come from His Lordship. Some sort of accident.'

Cynthia's stomach dipped. 'What has happened?'

'The messenger said he went to the lower pasture with the message for you and when he did not find you there, he came here, to ask if we had seen you. He is in the kitchen, taking refreshment.'

'I will speak to him at once,' Cynthia said.

'I'll have them bring the horses.' Thorne's calm voice steadied her nerves.

She appreciated his tact in leaving her alone to discover what problem might have occurred and turned to him with a grateful smile. 'I will see if the messenger can give me more information and be right out.'

'I will ask him to come to you, my lady.' Mrs Frost hurried off in one direction and Marcus sauntered out of the front door, having picked up his coat and hat from a chair where they were waiting.

A young farm labourer she did not recognise emerged from the back of the house. How very odd.

'You have a message for me from Lord Norton?'

The young man touched his forelock. 'Was the doctor that sent me, my lady. Me mam says he might have to cut off His Lordship's leg.'

For a moment the words made no sense. Then they did. She collapsed into the nearest chair. 'What happened?'

'Our Petal kicked him.'

'Petal?'

'Our cow, my lady. Smashed all the bones above the knee. His Lordship won't let the doctor use his saw.'

She felt ill. While she had been dallying with Marcus, Thomas had been injured and needing her. 'I will leave for Harrowglen at once.'

The man touched his forelock again. 'His Lordship is at my pa's farm. Mallock's. They can't move him.'

Heavens, this was a disaster. 'I see.' Mallock's was due north and closer than Harrowglen. 'The doctor is expecting me there?'

'Yes, my lady.'

'What is your name?'

'Ted Mallock, my lady.'

She nodded. The farmer had sent one of his sons. He looked like a bright young man. 'Very well, Ted Mallock. I need you to go at once to Harrowglen. Tell Lock what has occurred. Tell him to send two of our stable lads to your father's farm. Do you understand the message you are to deliver?'

The lad nodded. 'I does, my lady.'

'Good. After that, return home immediately. I may have more errands for you.'

She gathered her skirts and ran outside.

The horses were being led out accompanied by Marcus, who swiftly adjusted both girths and helped her to mount. 'The boy Jack says your brother is not at home, but at the farm where he went last night.'

'Yes.'

'In which direction does it lie?'

'North-west. We will go back to the main

road and turn off at the next crossroads. As the crow flies, it is not far, but there is no way to cross the river except at the road bridge. It will take a good thirty minutes to get there.'

They set off at an easy canter, when what she really wanted to do was gallop at breakneck speed. To do so would risk winding the horses and ultimately make their journey take longer.

Pepper seemed to sense her impatience and Cynthia worked to keep her under firm control.

It seemed like for ever, but it wasn't long before they reached the bridge. Cynthia swallowed the dryness in her mouth as they slowed to a walk to give the horses a chance to catch their breath.

The pause also allowed the worries to crowd in on her. What if Thomas died?

'I cannot believe Thomas was stupid enough to let a cow kick him.'

Marcus gave her a strange glance.

'Well, I can't.'

'He will be all right.'

The deep calm voice settled her nerves. She took a deep breath of crisp autumn air and prayed that Marcus was right. When the horses were ready, they urged them on and soon rode into the courtyard of Mallock's farm where a small gig with a pony stood with its nose stuck in a feedbag.

The farm was old but in a good state of repair, its thatch reasonably new and its out-buildings forming a quadrangle at the back of the farm as clean and tidy as was possible. A handful of chickens scattered in a flurry of feathers and squawks as the horses made straight for the water trough. A small lad came out of the barn to see what the noise was about.

'You go inside,' Marcus said. 'I will care for the horses.'

She had a terrible urge to ask him to go in with her. She gritted her teeth. She could do this.

The low back door to the house opened at her approach and a ruddy-faced woman in an apron and mob cap dipped a curtsy and gestured for her to enter. 'Mrs Mallock?' Cynthia said.

The woman beamed. 'Yes, milady. His Lordship is in the parlour.'

Thomas was laid out on the floor in a very small room at the front of the house that looked out to the road. Like the outside of the farm, it was as neat as a new pin, except for the large body stretched out in its centre and the man kneeling at his side. 'Baskin?'

The young vet looked up with an expression full of relief. 'Lady Cynthia.'

'I was told a surgeon was here,' she said, horrified.

Thomas hissed in a breath. 'Baskin is as good a surgeon as any other.'

For a horse, perhaps. She bit her tongue. 'What is the diagnosis?'

'The bone is broken. Provided it is a clean break, I can set it. If it heals well, then you will be up and about walking in six months.'

'Six months? Rubbish. I can't lie around for six months. Besides, what do you know? You are a veterinarian, not a doctor.'

'I know enough to know that if you don't follow orders you'll be losing that leg.'

The bald statement stole her breath.

'Damnation,' Thomas exclaimed. 'I don't care what happens, you are not taking my leg.'

If Baskin thought *she* could change her brother's mind when it was set upon a course of action, he did not know Thomas very well. 'Well, Thomas, I suppose it is better to be dead than lose a leg,' she said icily.

Thomas, his face grey and his breath coming in gasps of pain, glared at her. 'I won't die.'

'Saying it does not make it so,' she said.

Baskin pulled at his bottom lip. 'If you were a horse, my lord, I would be priming my pistol.'

Thomas chuckled weakly. 'So would I.'

'Do not be ridiculous,' Cynthia said.

She looked up at a sound. Marcus had arrived. 'Try to talk sense to my brother, Lord Thorne.'

Thorne grimaced. 'Let him do his work, Norton. Pray for a clean break. If it is not, then seek a second opinion.'

Thomas glanced at him blearily. 'From whom?'

'There is a surgeon I know who has saved more than one limb under the most difficult circumstances during the war.'

Baskin rose to his feet, his frown deepening. 'We do not have time to wait for a surgeon to come all the way from London. The wound—'

'He is not in London. He comes from this part of the world and I received a letter from him just the other day. He can be here this evening, I should think.'

'Then I should be grateful for a second opinion, should things not go well,' Baskin said. He turned to Thomas. 'Perhaps if you hear the same thing from two doctors, my lord, you will be convinced. In the meantime, I will need two more strong lads to hold His Lordship down while I try to set the leg.'

Mrs Mallock hurried out, presumably to get the help requested.

Baskin gave Cynthia a look of sympathy. 'It looks straightforward, my lady, as long as he stays off that leg for the prescribed length of time.'

'I will do my best to make him obey orders.'

'Good.'

Two burly farm lads tiptoed into the room. Had the situation not been so dire, she might have laughed.

'Why don't I make you a nice cup of tea, my lady?' Mrs Mallock suggested from the doorway.

Marcus gave her a glance that said he would do all in his power to make sure things went well and she believed he would.

Since the room was overcrowded and she could do nothing to help, she followed the farmer's wife into the kitchen.

Mrs Mallock set a mug of tea in front of Marcus, who was seated at her kitchen table.

'You look plumb wore out, my lord. Get this down you. It will help.'

He took a swig of the fortifying beverage. Exhausted was too mild a word. This was his third night of taking turns with Cynthia in caring for Norton, who had developed a fever on the second day after his accident.

They had not left the farm since they arrived.

The door to the parlour creaked open and Cynthia crept through it and closed it quietly behind her. If he looked worn out, she looked exhausted. Smudges beneath her eyes told the story of lack of sleep. For once her hair looked far from tidy. One long silver tendril hung down beside her cheek and her bun was askew at the back of her head. She'd been tireless in her care of her brother, snatching moments of sleep in the chair beside his bed.

The strain of it was taking its toll. He was beginning to fear for her health.

Marcus rose and offered her his seat at the scarred wooden table. She cast him a grateful glance. She cupped her hands around the mug of tea Mrs Mallock poured for her as if she needed its warmth. 'The fever has broken,' she said. 'He is sleeping.' The relief in her voice was palpable.

'Then you need to sleep, too,' Mrs Mallock said. 'Go home.'

'How can I leave him—?'

'You'll be no manner of use to him if you don't take care of yourself,' the kindly woman admonished.

She was right. It was something Marcus had thought, but he didn't feel he had the right to insist upon. But there was always more than one way to skin a cat.

'Go. I will send word to Bellavista if you are needed,' Mrs Mallock said. 'I'll send one of my lads on that fancy horse of His Lordship's hell for leather, I will.'

Cynthia had requested her things be moved into Bellavista when it became apparent Norton could not be moved, and Marcus had done the same, because he was the only one strong enough as well as gentle enough to move Norton as and when needed. The Mallocks' lads were of a rough-and-ready sort and, while they had tried to be careful, they handled him badly. Unfortunately, Norton's valet, despite his willingness, was too old and puny to be of much assistance.

'Mrs Mallock is right,' Marcus said. 'Both you and your brother will be laid up in a sick bed if you don't get some rest.'

Mrs Mallock nodded her agreement.

'When he wakes he'll need washing and—'

Marcus decided it was time to tell her of the plan he'd hatched with Mrs Mallock and Baskin the previous afternoon. 'Baskin has provided the name of a woman he highly recommends to assist your brother while you are resting. She is a skilled nurse with a good deal of experience with injuries such as this.'

Cynthia looked doubtful.

Marcus frowned at her. 'You are trusting your brother's health to Baskin's care so far and have not seen fit to call in a second opinion— why not trust him in this?'

'But if anything should happen...'

The anxiety in her face and voice made him want to fold her in his arms and protect her from all worry. Something he could not do. Not here. 'As Mrs Mallock said, she will send word for Baskin to come as well as let you know if there is any change. As much as we would like to believe we are indispensable here, there are others far more knowledgeable. Also, if you become so exhausted you cannot think, what help is that to your brother?'

She sipped her tea, then propped her chin in one palm. 'The thought of sleeping in a bed is irresistible.'

Thank heavens. She had given in.

'Then let me introduce you to Nurse Jolly.' He nodded at Mrs Mallock, who with a conspiratorial smile went off to fetch the nurse, whom she had installed in a small bedroom in the attic.

'She is here already?' Cynthia straightened in her seat, making a valiant attempt to look alert. 'You hired someone without consulting me?'

'I have not hired her. Baskin asked her to come so you could interview her.'

A heavily built young woman entered the kitchen. She had rosy cheeks, a large bosom covered by a pristine white apron and a martial look in her eye.

When her gaze took in Cynthia, her expression softened. She bobbed an awkward curtsy. 'My lady.'

A look of dismay crossed Cynthia's face. 'Surely she is too young?'

Nurse Jolly crossed her arms over her ample chest. 'I be older than you, I will bet a pound to a penny, my lady. I had six brothers, I did, all of them breaking things and me and mum taking care of them, as Mr Baskin well knows. It was he who suggested I hire out as a nurse when my pa became too ill to work and me not having prospects for marriage.'

'I see,' Cynthia said weakly, clearly over-whelmed by the young woman's forceful personality.

The woman's voice softened. 'Never you fear, my lady. I will take care of His Lordship as if he was my own.'

'Baskin says she comes highly recommended by a surgeon he knows,' Marcus added.

Cynthia looked at him, clearly torn.

'I think she will do fine,' he said.

Cynthia stood up and swayed on her feet. Nurse Jolly put out a steadying hand. 'There, there, lamby. Your brother will be safe with me. Never you fear.'

Cynthia's shoulders sagged and exhaustion claimed all the fight she had in her. 'I will go and sleep and return later.'

'If you have any sense, my lady, you will give yourself a day to recover. If there's any change, you will be the first to know.' She turned to Mrs Mallock. 'Now, I have brought some herbs for a restorative tea and I'll need a supply of hot water. That man will likely need a bath when he awakes.'

And just like that, Nurse Jolly took command.

'I think I should get you home,' Marcus said to Cynthia.

Nurse Jolly handed him a vial. 'If she has trouble sleeping, give her a drop of this in her tea. Mr Baskin's orders.'

Cynthia nodded. 'Yes. Let us go to Bellavista.'

'Our conveyance is waiting.' Hoping for the best, he had asked for it to be readied for them.

'Conveyance.'

'The Mallocks are loaning us their cart. I don't think either of us is in any shape to ride tonight.'

'Marcus,' she said sleepily, 'how thoughtful you are. How very good.'

His heart warmed at her praise.

It also pleased him that she trusted him enough to doze against his shoulder on the drive home.

Upon arrival at Bellavista, Cynthia climbed wearily down from the cart with the help of Jack, who then proceeded to help Marcus with unhitching the horses.

A footman opened the door to her and an irate-looking Mrs Frost met her just inside. 'My lady, it is not right. The two louts they sent from the main house are more trouble than help. I wish they would have sent a housemaid instead. They won't help with the fires nor make the beds. They stand around looking down their noses at me and Annie and are eating us out of house and home.' At the end of each sentence she stabbed her cane at the floor as if she was stabbing footmen's toes.

Cynthia, who had sent word to Harrowglen that Mrs Frost would need help since she and Marcus would need to reside at Bellavista until Thomas was recovered enough to move home, was too tired to listen to such grumbles. 'I will ask them to send a housemaid tomorrow. The footmen are here to get the covers off and move furniture as well as make sure you have enough wood for the fires in each room. Lord Thorne and I will take dinner in the breakfast room and then I need to retire. We can talk further in the morning.'

'Yes, my lady.' Mrs Frost limped away.

The footman, who had listened silently to the diatribe, bowed and took her coat. 'It isn't that we don't want to help, my lady, it's that she makes us take our boots off and—'

Cynthia put up a hand. 'We will sort it out tomorrow.'

'Yes, my lady.'

'Thank you, James. You will show Lord Thorne to the blue chamber, which I believe should be ready for him, and assist him to ready for dinner.'

She climbed the stairs to the room Lucy and her grandfather had used. She had always felt a special connection to this room. Now, after making love to Thorne here, it seemed to resonate with the warmth of his touch as well as the love shared by Lucy and her grandfather. Above all things, she wanted to claim this room as her own.

Would Thomas let her rent the house from him? It would likely break her heart if he did not. Break her heart? She didn't have one, though it did seem sometimes as if there might be a smidgeon of it left when she was around Thorne.

For a long time, she had not cared that her life was devoid of the choices she might once have made, but since meeting Marcus, they had once more surfaced as unattainable dreams. Becoming a wife. Becoming a mother. Both denied her by Cornelius and her own foolishness.

She pushed the maudlin thoughts aside. She had far more important things to think about.

The scullery maid was waiting to help her

out of her gown and had hot water in a jug ready for her to wash and Cynthia readied herself to go down for dinner.

Marcus was waiting for her in the breakfast room when she went down. He, too, had changed his clothes and as always looked remarkably handsome and exquisitely tailored in a suit that was far too informal for dinner in town, but perfect for the country.

He smiled at her entry. 'I have taken the liberty of pouring you a sherry.' He handed her a glass.

She sipped and sighed appreciatively. 'Thank you.' The man certainly had charm aplenty. But he had more than that. He was honourable through and through. His help this past few days had been a godsend.

'I am famished,' she said. 'Shall I ring the bell?'

'Food would be a welcome sight, no doubt about it.'

Cynthia rang the bell.

Mrs Frost, with the help of the two footmen she had decried, had as usual managed to prepare a wholesome if somewhat limited meal which arrived quickly after her summons.

There was a hearty game stew, a roast fowl

and an assortment of winter vegetables along with crusty bread and an apple tart. 'I apologise for the paucity of dishes,' Cynthia said as Marcus seated her. 'Hopefully things will improve as we go along.'

'This is perfect,' Marcus replied, sitting down.

She turned to the head footman. 'We do not require assistance, James. Go and eat.'

The footman bowed and signalled to his fellow to depart.

'I am so tired,' she said. 'I want to eat my dinner and go to bed.'

'Your brother is a lucky fellow to have a sister like you.' The deep voice was warm and comforting.

She looked at him in surprise. 'I think Thomas finds me a bit of a burden actually. A responsibility he hoped to be rid of long before now. A burden he would like some other man to take up.'

'Nonsense. Even on so short an acquaintance, I can see he relies greatly upon you. Even a little too much, perhaps.'

'At one time he did. But more recently he has forged ahead with his own plans and priorities. I am pleased that it is so.'

She was. And though in some ways she

would miss her current life, she was looking forward to being her own mistress. To commanding her own household, no matter how small it would be.

Wasn't she?

She had work to do. She would be busy. And she would not miss the parties and the politics of the *ton*.

Right now, what she really needed was sleep. Last night, she had stayed awake at Thomas's side all night, cooling his fever, making him as comfortable as she could, and again all day today, with a doze here and there when she was sure he was sleeping.

'It was very kind of the veterinarian to find Nurse Jolly. She impressed me a good deal.'

'An impressive woman overall, I would say.'

'Oh, goodness.' She chuckled. 'I could not quite believe my eyes when I saw her. But she will do very well with Thomas. I have no doubt.'

'And you will finally get some well-deserved rest.'

Marcus put down his knife and fork. 'My compliments to the cook. I haven't had such a comforting dinner since my mother was alive.

She was a farmer's daughter, you know. She made the best of dinners.'

She jerked her head up. Had she nodded off? 'Would you care for some pie?'

'Indeed I would. Let me help you to a slice.'

Chapter Eleven

Marcus realised he was speaking to himself. Cynthia's chin had dropped to her chest and she was close to falling sideways out of her chair.

In sleep she looked so young and so vulnerable.

What was he to do with her? He certainly could not leave her like that. He rose and gently cradled her in his arms. Her eyes popped open, but her eyelids looked heavy.

'Hush,' he murmured. 'You need to go to bed.'

'I know.' Her eyes drifted shut.

There was nothing else for it. He could either ring for a footman or do the task himself. He carried her up to her bed. There was no sign of any servant in her bedchamber. The little dressing room showed no signs of occupation. She must have used the scullery maid to help her dress.

He sat her on the bed and she managed to raise her head to look up at him. 'What are you doing?' Her voice was soft and husky and tentative as if she could not quite break the bonds of sleep.

When he released her, she fell sideways and snuggled into her pillow.

He contemplated throwing a cover over her and leaving her to sleep, but sleeping in her clothes would be uncomfortable. He searched the drawers and found a nightdress. It wasn't at all what he had expected. Instead of some frilly confection, it was the sort of thing young innocent girls wore to bed. A plain white cotton gown with a tiny ruffle high upon the throat and at the end of each long sleeve.

Virginal.

He bent over her and caught a whiff of her scent. Lily of the valley. A prosaic country-fresh smell that every time he caught a whiff of it reminded him of his youth.

He used to pick lily of the valley for his mother when he was very small.

What an odd contrast this woman was. Cold, sweet, strong, tender-hearted, wilful and self-centred. Which was truth and which was the lie? Gently he unlaced her gown and stripped her down to her stays and chemise. The stays would have to go. He took a deep breath and tried not to see her pretty breasts or the shape of her body beneath the fine lawn fabric of her shift. It was hard not to want to shape the curve of her waist or press the heel of his hand against the rise of her mons, so distinctly was her shape revealed.

Instead he removed her slippers and then her garters, gently rolling down her silk stockings until he could remove them over her feet. He caressed each ankle and the soft curve of her calf. Such lovely delicate limbs. How had she managed to work all night and day as she had? Determination. It resided in her expression and the angle of her jaw, and the jut of her chin.

He eased the nightgown over her head.

It did not require much effort to tuck her beneath the blankets.

It required great strength of will not to lie down beside her and hold her in his arms until she awoke.

To take advantage of her vulnerability would be dishonourable, because he had no doubt that if he stayed with her, the comfort he offered would lead to lovemaking. They were too attracted to each other for it not to be so.

Despite outer appearances, Cynthia was an extraordinarily passionate woman. His body ached to make love to her again.

Unable to resist, he leaned down and kissed the corner of her sweetly curved lips, the spot where her eyelashes fanned upon her pale skin and the tempting arch of her eyebrow.

She stirred and turned on her back.

He closed his mind against the vision of such temptation, pulled the covers up over her and, having doused the candles, tiptoed to his own chamber and his cool sheets.

Cosy, relaxed, Cynthia stretched.

And…sat bolt upright, looking around her. She could not recall readying for bed. She put a hand to her head and found her bun half down, instead of her hair brushed and braided.

She pulled out the rest of the pins and combed her fingers through the tangles.

A vague memory of being carried in strong arms and the beat of a steady heart in her ear… He had brought her upstairs and… Oh, goodness, was it he who had put her in her nightgown?

What time was it? She squinted at the clock on the mantel but all she could see was the glow from the fire. No light appeared at the window, so it must be late. What time had she fallen asleep? Early. Before nine perhaps.

And now she was wide awake. And not fully under the covers.

Pie. The last thing she remembered clearly was offering him pie. She must have fallen asleep at the table. And he'd popped her into bed and left.

Why had he not stayed? He could have. Perhaps he didn't think she would welcome him. Perhaps he was being kind because she was so tired. Perhaps he was concerned for her reputation. Well, that seemed a little far-fetched. Perhaps he had not enjoyed their lovemaking as much as she had and did not want to stay.

She wrapped her arms around her drawn-up legs and, resting her chin on her knees, considered the matter.

Should she be insulted that he hadn't stayed? Or…what?

She lay back down. Turned on one side. Turned on the other. Sat up.

She got up and held the clock close to the fire. Three in the morning. He would be sleeping.

She climbed the step to the bed and paused. It was hopeless. She would never sleep now. She needed to ask him.

She froze. She recalled herself as a girl, running out to Cornelius's cottage behind the stable block in the middle of the night. He'd teased her and mocked her until she hadn't been able to resist the challenge to show him she wasn't some little schoolgirl, but a real woman who knew what she wanted.

He'd only wanted one thing. Access to her money. He had never loved her or he would have waited until she was older and free to choose a husband.

What she felt now was nothing like those childish desires. She was a woman. She was free to decide if she wanted to take a lover... as long as she was discreet. She hoped. Surely Thomas would not interfere as long as she did not cause him any embarrassment.

Mrs Frost would say nothing, if she noticed anything at all. And the two footmen were housed in the servants' quarters, a small cottage separated from the main house by the walled garden.

She stepped down, lit a candle and pulled on her dressing gown. The distance from her chamber to the guest room meant crossing the landing into the south wing. The carpet muffled her steps and the candlelight flickered eerily on the wall. Silence filled the air along with the scent of beeswax and lemon. Mrs Frost had been cleaning and polishing in their absence. The mustiness she had noticed on their previous visit had been completely eliminated.

The guest apartments took up the whole of the south wing. Her grandfather and his paramour entertained few guests out of respect for her grandmother. But they had enjoyed the occasional visit from close friends, according to Mrs Frost. She said they were never happier than when they had no company but their own. Though as a scullery maid she might not have known terribly much.

Cynthia hesitated at the door. Did she knock or should she simply go in and see what happened? If the door was unlocked she would go in. If not, then... She turned the handle.

She stepped inside the sitting room and picked her way across the room to the bedchamber door, which stood ajar.

The rhythm of the deep even breaths of a

man fast asleep brought a smile to her lips. He, too, must have been exhausted after the days and nights they had endured at Mallock's farm. He had been so helpful. And so patient with Thomas, who had, at times, acted more like a ten-year-old than an adult man.

She stood watching Marcus sleep. He had thrown the covers back, revealing that he slept in nothing but his bare skin. The sight of the dark mat of hair on his wide chest sent a shiver down her back. He really was a beautifully formed man.

She suddenly wished she was not quite such a wraith, as she'd been called by some men. Perhaps he preferred more meat on a woman's bones.

Oh, goodness. His breathing had changed while she stood here hesitating.

He rolled on his side, facing her. 'Are you going to join me or not?' the deep sleepy voice asked, with a gentle teasing tone. 'Come, sweet.'

He made a welcoming gesture and she set her candle on the nightstand and jumped in beside him, snuggling up to his deliciously warm body.

'You are freezing,' he said. He brought the covers over them both.

'I didn't want to disturb you.'

'This sort of disturbance I will suffer at any time.'

She laughed, put her arms around his neck and kissed his lips.

He rolled on his back and brought her half across his chest, his arms wrapped around her, holding her close.

Their mouths melded in a mind-numbing kiss. His hands stroked and petted her. She felt treasured, even beloved. And for this moment, she would let herself believe it was true.

He rolled her completely over and sprawled across her. Though careful not to crush her with his full weight, he gave her a pleasurable sensation of being dominated as she sank into the mattress.

A man who was not afraid to take charge, yet who was respectful at the same time. How had she not known this was even possible?

The thought faded away as he gazed down into her face with a boyish smile. 'My beautiful girl. I must have been dreaming about you.'

He rocked his hips and the tip of his hard shaft pressed against her belly.

She made to reach down between them,

but he caught her hand in his and kissed the tips of her fingers.

'Let me love you, sweet.'

The words sent liquid heat through her body. Her limbs felt heavy and languid. She nodded her agreement.

He cradled her head in his large hands and kissed her so sweetly she thought she would cry, until he supported himself on one arm and his other hand and lips worked wonderful magic on her breasts.

Then there was no room for regret or tears, only sensation and stirrings and heat. Her body became his instrument of unbearable pleasurable torture. A string tightened to breaking point, a vibration pitched so high it hurt.

Her hands did a bit of exploration of their own, across the wide expanse of smooth back, the dip of his waist, the rise of firm buttocks. She cupped them and wrapped her legs high around him, cradling him within her thighs. She pulled him into her in one hard stroke when he would have entered her slowly. She moaned her approval.

The hiss of his indrawn breath sent a pulse of pleasure deep in her core.

He raised his head. 'You make me lose control. I find I cannot hold back.'

Yes, that was what she wanted. Him out of control. She arched her back, opening to him.

He drove into her hard and deep and she arched in counterpoint to his strokes, taking him deeper. He moved faster and his clever hands found her little nub at her entrance and bliss overwhelmed her. She fell apart. Heat rolled along her veins in a delicious tide.

A moment later, he withdrew from her and spilled his seed into the sheets. He sprawled out beside her and tucked her under his arm.

Sated, they lay together, the beat of his heart thundering against her ribs.

It felt so good to be in his arms, protected, well loved, together in their own little world. In her imaginings, she thought that this was how it must have been for Lucy.

It was why she had always loved this house. She had admired and respected her father and loved her mother, what she remembered of her, but their house had been full of duty, not love.

She pushed the past aside and let herself drift on a warm current of bliss.

It had been a while since Marcus had awoken with a sleeping woman curled up beside him, her breath cooling his chest each time she exhaled. The scent of lily of the valley filled his nostrils and made him want to bury his nose in the silky strands of her hair lying loose about her shoulders.

But he didn't want to disturb her, she was sleeping so sweetly, so trustingly in his arms.

After the most delightful lovemaking, he wanted her again. And likely again. But beneath the haze of pleasure at having discovered a most delightful bed partner lay a tinge of guilt. A prick of his conscience that he should not have taken advantage of her offer.

She was a lady. And single no less. Worn to the bone after the events of the last few days. A gentleman did not prey on a female's weakness. Nor did a man of honour.

It was all very well thinking he might see if he could dish up a bit of the heartache she had doled out to little Bess, but he had no wish to embroil her in a scandal, even if their affair was her idea.

Not that he had resisted to any great extent. It was a mutual coming together without a doubt. A rare and special mutual compatibility. At least from his perspective.

She sighed and snuggled closer.

A pang twisted in his heart. Painful, yet sweet. Did it have to be temporary? He had to take a wife. Would she not do as well as any other?

That was the trouble, wasn't it? She would not be like any other. She was society's darling. A diamond of the first water. A woman with a clutch of male followers. A woman who, by presenting a chilly untouchable, virtuous face to the world, lived a very different life behind closed doors.

And managed to get away with it.

Just like Olga.

He could not abide lies or the people who promulgated them. After his experience with Olga, who had hidden who she truly was behind a wall of lies, he would not go through that again. How could he trust a woman who did not trust him enough to tell him the truth? No, much as he enjoyed making love to Cynthia, she was not a woman he could see marrying. Could he?

She had many good qualities a man would want in a wife. She was lovely, that went without saying. She was also intelligent and an excellent housekeeper, not to mention her knowledge of running a stud, which for him would be an added advantage. Her loyalty and caring for her brother showed far more compassion than he had expected, as did her quest on behalf of climbing boys.

Was it possible that he was overreacting with regard to her treatment of Elizabeth? And what if she had a few little secrets? Everyone had things they preferred not to talk about. He never mentioned Olga.

No doubt, given enough time and opportunity, he would be able to change her mind about not wanting to marry, and convince her to marry him and that would solve Bess's problem also.

Cynthia would need careful wooing.

She made a slight sound and stirred and he realised he'd tightened his grip. He eased his hold. He had no wish to wake her.

Nevertheless, she raised her head a fraction. 'I must have fallen asleep,' she murmured.

'Rest,' he said. 'You had a long day and it will be the same again in a few short hours.'

The fingers of her hand wandered in lazy circles over his chest.

Yes. He wanted her again.

'I should go. With my luck Mrs Frost will send someone to make up an early fire in my chamber and discover me missing.' She slipped out of his grasp and off the bed. In the glow of the fire, the rise of her lovely curves and the shadowed hollows cast her as an ethereal nymph.

She slipped her nightgown over her head and shrugged into her robe.

He grabbed his dressing gown from the end of the bed. 'I will walk you back to your chamber.'

'Thank you, but, no. I would not want anyone to see us.'

She certainly seemed experienced in the art of deception. How many other lovers had she taken? He was startled by a little stab of... what, not jealousy surely? 'As you wish. But take care.'

She laughed. 'I will try not to trip on my way back. Do not worry, I am perfectly able to walk a few feet on my own.'

'Goodnight, then. Sweet dreams.'

She blew him a kiss and closed the door softly.

He lay back staring up at the canopy.

Now to change her mind about marriage. It would require a delicate hand. It was a challenge he realised he would enjoy. At least he would if he was ultimately successful.

The following morning was one of those perfect autumn days with trees glowing with hues of gold and bronze and the sky a pale shade of azure.

Marcus smiled at Cynthia as she entered the breakfast room. The smudges beneath her eyes had lessened, but she still looked tired.

'I did not expect to see you so early.'

'I woke up with a start, thinking of Thomas. I should go there as soon as I have eaten.'

He liked that she was so loyal to her brother. So caring. He pointed to a note beside her plate. 'Mrs Frost said it is a message from Mallock's farm.'

She snatched it up. 'Why didn't you send for me?' She scanned it quickly and then leaned back. 'It is from Mr Baskin. All is well. Thomas passed a good night and he and Nurse Jolly have looked after his dressings and so forth so there is no need for us to go. He suggests I rest today and come tomorrow. He promises to let me know if anything changes.'

'Can you bear to leave him that long?'

'Oh, dear. I have been fussing, haven't I?'

'I think you have been wonderful. Your brother is fortunate to have such a caring sister.' And he meant every word. 'Now eat. Gain some strength and be ready to step back into the fray tomorrow.'

'Thank you. Your words mean a great deal to me. Thomas has been a most caring brother. I would not for the world want him to feel neglected.'

'Nor would he want to see you completely done up from nursing him.'

'You are right, of course.'

'May I suggest a walk after breakfast. You can show me the grounds. I have been looking at that river from my window and wondering about the fishing.'

'The fishing is excellent. If you like we can take our rods and see if we can catch a trout or two. I am sure Thomas would appreciate it also.'

He stared at her in surprise. 'You fish?'

'I do.'

Likely he would spend his morning baiting up her hook and listening to her squeal if something took her line. Still, it would take her mind off her brother, so he was game.

'Very well. After breakfast, we will go fishing.'

'I think there is some gear you can borrow. My stuff will be far too small, but Grandfather's might fit, even if it is a bit old-fashioned.'

She had her own gear?

'Here they are,' Cynthia said, pulling out her boots from behind a stack of rakes and shovels in the gardener's shed behind the laundry. She threw them out into the courtyard, followed by Thomas's enormous boots and a pair used by her grandfather. 'See if either of those fit, Thorne.'

Mrs Frost, who was hovering at the shed door, eyed them askance. 'They are very dusty, my lady.'

'And soon they will be very muddy.'

She brought out a variety of fishing poles, a net and other gear they needed.

Marcus took them off her and set them down. 'Thomas's are too big, but your grandfather's might fit me.'

He sat on a bench and tried them on. 'They will do.'

'Excellent,' she said. 'Thomas and I used to fish here when we were children,' she said. 'Father didn't approve, but the fishing was always better than at Harrowglen and it is a nice ride out.' She smiled at the elderly housekeeper. 'And Mrs Frost was always ready to provide a sandwich and a jug of lemonade to make the day perfect.'

Mrs Frost beamed at the compliment. 'Take Leonard with you to help carry the gear. I have put up some food in this bag.' She held out a knapsack. Inside were sandwiches wrapped in napkins and two bottles of beer.

The footman, Leonard, who had ostensibly come to assist in the search for the boots and, after glancing into the shed, had said there was nothing in there but gardening tools, perked up.

Cynthia glanced at Marcus and they shook their heads. 'I am sure you have more important things that need doing around here,' Cynthia said. 'And once Lord Norton goes back to Harrowglen, you will not have the use of their services. You may as well make use of Martin and Lenny here, in the meantime. For one thing, the windows need a good cleaning.'

'I will ensure Lady Cynthia comes to no harm,' Marcus added.

Mrs Frost grinned. 'Come along, Leonard, let me show you where to find the rags and a bucket.' The tall young fellow's shoulders sagged. He followed in Mrs Frost's wake, the very picture of dejection.

'Oh, dear,' Cynthia said. 'I do hope he won't hold it against me.'

Marcus chuckled. 'I am sure he will never forgive you. But I would never have forgiven you, if you had agreed to his presence.'

She laughed. 'Right. Let us be off.'

He hoisted his basket onto his shoulder and reached for hers at the same time she did.

'I can manage.' She was used to carrying her own gear.

After a moment of hesitation, he grabbed one rod and left the other for her. He tucked a rolled oilskin blanket under his arm for them to sit on if need be.

As she had done so many times before, she slung the basket across her shoulders and they set off along the winding path that led from the outbuildings down to the river in the valley.

The track had become overgrown with lack of use and the grass was damp and here and there they ploughed through muddy puddles. Where once the shrubs and bushes growing alongside the path had been neatly trimmed, they now encroached across the track and, in spots, brambles caught at their clothing.

Marcus somehow always managed to get ahead of her and push these obstacles out of the way. She gave him a smile of thanks. After all, independence was one thing, common sense quite another and she appreciated his help.

A rotted wooden jetty projected out into the small swift-flowing river that cut across one corner of the property. A similar river running through Harrowglen joined it further downstream and then on into the larger river.

'I think we will be safer on the bank,' Marcus said, eyeing the jagged gaps in the platform.

'I will send word to our steward to see to its repair upon our return. I expect it got forgotten.'

They decided on a spot on the bank a little distant from the jetty and settled down to the business of fishing. It would be good to catch a fish for Thomas and for themselves, too, if there were enough.

Only the sound of the rush of water and the odd caw of rooks from their rookery in a nearby stand of tall trees broke the silence.

'Are you warm enough?' Marcus asked, digging in the soft earth beneath a willow tree with the small shovel brought for the purpose.

'Perfectly, thank you.' She picked up one of the worms his shovel had exposed and threaded it on her hook. 'Are you?'

She laughed at his startled expression. 'Marcus, I fish. I don't squeal at the sight of a worm and I remove the hooks from my catch. Thomas would never have let me go with him if I had been the least bit missish.'

'Thomas has a lot to answer for,' he grumbled, but then grinned as if he was only joking. She had the feeling something else lay beneath those jesting words. She decided to let it go. She wanted to enjoy this little bit of relaxation before jumping back into her duties in the sickroom.

He baited up his hook and they stood side by side watching their lines. The wind had a little bit of winter in it and it stung her cheeks and chilled her hands despite her gloves. But she wasn't going to complain. She was enjoying the respite too much.

He jerked on his line and began reeling in. He landed a nice-sized trout. She held the net for him and they hung it in the water.

'Another couple like that and we will be all set for dinner,' Marcus said.

'It will be a nice change from beef and chicken.'

Supplies of food had been sent over from Harrowglen along with the footmen, but fresh-caught fish would be a treat.

After about an hour, Marcus caught a second fish big enough for eating. Everything she had pulled from the water had been too small and had to go back.

'I really am not having much luck today,' she said. 'Are you ready for a bite to eat?'

'Famished.'

He put aside his rod and unrolled the oil-skin blanket. Somehow, he managed to arrange it so he used his body to shelter her from the breeze. A very gentlemanly thing to do and done without him drawing attention to his kindness. She really was going to miss him when they returned to their normal lives. She had the feeling she would remember this morning as a treasure to be hoarded among her store of memories.

They munched their ham sandwiches and swigged beer.

'I expect you will land something soon,' Marcus said.

'It doesn't matter. Really. As long as we go back with something worth cooking, I will be quite content.'

'You seem like a different person, out here in the country.'

'Different?'

He chuckled. 'I suppose we all do, really. I simply did not think of you as the sort of woman who would be happy tramping around with muddy hems and catching her own dinner.'

She leaned back on her elbows and lifted her face to the sun, absorbing the warmth into her skin. Not for too long, though, or she would burn badly.

'I grew up in the country. I think it is in my bones.'

'And the city? The balls and dancing and fashion?'

'Don't forget the politics.' She smiled. 'They are in my bones, too. And I see the same in you. A man who is elegant in the ballroom, who sits a horse well and who can move mountains like my brother if needed. We all have more than one dimension.'

'Anyone with half a brain does,' he said.

She sat up and looked at him. 'Now, that is a fine compliment to offer to a woman.'

He grinned cheerfully. 'My mother was the cleverest person I knew. My father did exactly as she told him. He was rather lost when she died.'

'How old were you?'

'I was twelve. He became rather reclusive. After that I spent most of my free time with the Dursts at Thorne Manor. I reminded him too much of what he had lost.'

'Oh, how awful.'

'I was lucky. I liked being with my uncle

and my cousin and they made me very welcome. Francis was like a brother.'

A pang of guilt hit her, when she had nothing to be guilty about. 'And Miss Elizabeth is as a sister.'

His expression did not change but his eyes darkened a fraction. 'She is.'

'Fortescue is not the right man for her, you know.'

'I don't think that is for anyone else to decide, do you?'

He might change his mind if he knew the truth. The thing was, ought she to tell him? She wanted to. A terrible urge came upon her that needed him to think well of her. And that was just foolish nonsense. Besides, she had no way to prove her knowledge and certainly did not want to say where she had learned it.

She shrugged. 'I suppose not, but it seems that Lord Fortescue made his own choice.'

The atmosphere changed from warm to cool in an instant. He was displeased with her answer. She repressed a shiver.

'Shall we see if we can catch one more before we leave?'

He helped her to rise and they returned to their fishing.

She finally added one to their haul and it was time to return to the house.

The moment Marcus had realised that his presence was needed here with the Finches, and that it would likely extend his stay for a few days, he had written to his aunt to let her and Bess know of his whereabouts should they need him. They were to expect his return later than planned.

Two mornings after their outing to the river, Marcus had left Cynthia to her slumbers and had been seated at the breakfast table when a reply arrived. His aunt's response merely thanked him for his courtesy and asked him to forewarn her of his new date of arrival.

Bess had included a note of her own.

You are as bad as all the rest. You have fallen under her spell. Do not dare write and tell us you have offered marriage. I will never, ever forgive you.

Dramatics. Though she wasn't entirely wrong. He had not fallen under the spell of society's darling, but rather he greatly admired the woman he had come to know these past few days.

Watching her deal with Norton's accident, he had wondered at her fortitude. She had been a pillar of strength for her brother, despite her rather sharp tongue, or perhaps because of it. She made Norton laugh despite his pain.

She made Marcus laugh, too.

He looked up at her entry. She smiled warmly. 'I seem to have slept in.'

'We were late getting home last night, I asked them not to disturb you.' They had feasted on the fish they had caught and Norton was looking very much more like himself, despite his irritability at being unable to get up and move around. Still, Baskin was very pleased with his progress and plans for returning to Harrowglen were in train.

'It looks as though it might rain today so I asked for our carriage and noble steed to be brought around in half an hour.'

He grinned at their ongoing joke about their current mode of travel. Their conveyance was the Mallocks' farm cart and their steed a rather old grey mare who ambled along at her own pace.

'I don't think I will ever get the smell of turnips and manure from my coat,' he said.

'Why would you want to, it is such a country-fresh aroma.'

'Perhaps I will see if one of London's perfumers can replicate the scent. We can wear it to balls and such.'

'If I wear it, no doubt it will become the rage.'

He chuckled at her mocking tone.

'Unfortunately, you could be right.'

'Good lord, do you think so? Dare I test your theory?'

'Please do not.'

She filled her plate from the buffet and sat down beside him. She had stopped sitting at the head of the table after the second morning they breakfasted together.

He poured her a cup of tea.

'Letters from home?' she asked.

He glanced at the folded missives. 'Yes. Everyone is well. No emergencies requiring my attention. My aunt sends her good wishes for your brother's speedy recovery.'

She raised an eyebrow. 'How very…generous. And Miss Elizabeth. She is in good spirits?'

'As well as can be expected.'

She sipped her tea. 'She will recover in time.'

'You do not seem to have recovered enough from your first love to contemplate marriage, so why would you assume she will? If I am not mistaken, your brother would like to see you enter the wedded state. Do you still hold a torch for this fellow, or perhaps you like your independence too well?'

Was that a pang of jealousy at the thought that she might still have feelings for the man who had deflowered her, or was he jealous that she, unlike him, could ignore society and avoid her duty to her family and live her life as she pleased? Or was he really challenging her to rethink her position? The latter would make most sense.

A slight stiffening of her shoulders indicated that whatever she said next would not be the truth. He'd learned to read the signs of her prevarication with unerring accuracy.

'You know why I cannot.'

Not a lie, but the avoidance of his question was not lost on him. He toyed with the idea of pressing her further. What was the point? If she did not want to reveal her innermost truths, let her keep her secrets. The fact that it widened the chasm of distrust between them meant nothing. They were lovers and would never be more.

* * *

After breakfast, when they boarded the cart, the clouds did indeed have an ominous cast. He urged their mighty steed into a trot.

At the crossroads, they met a pony cart coming the other way. It drew up at the sight of them. The equipage angling so as to block their path was driven by a handsome man of about forty, with brown hair pulled back in a queue and a set of magnificent whiskers. He beamed. 'Lady Cynthia, what a delight to run into you.' There was an unpleasant sort of familiarity in his greeting that set Marcus's teeth on edge.

'Mr Hart.' The chill in Cynthia's voice was as cold as the breeze sending leaves spinning and swirling in the lane. 'Lord Thorne,' she said icily, 'allow me to introduce Cornelius Hart to you. He used to be the riding master at Harrowglen.'

Hart's chuckle had a false ring to it, as if he was not pleased by the reminder. 'Many years ago now. A lot of water under the bridge since those days.' He inclined his head. 'A pleasure to meet you, Thorne.' The man raised his eyebrows. 'Village gossip reported you had come home with a bang-up-to-the-knocker gentleman in tow, my lady, and I see that it is so. Is it correct you have moved into Bellavista to be closer to your brother? How is Thomas? I hear he almost stuck his spoon in the wall?'

'Thomas is doing very well and will soon be able to return to Harrowglen.'

Hart cast her a sly look. 'I am sure you will be delighted.'

The hairs on the back of Marcus's neck rose at Cynthia's tension in the face of what was clearly innuendo.

He wanted to give the man a piece of his mind, but since Cynthia did not give him a set down, he opted for distant politeness and a terse nod. 'You will forgive our need to move along, Hart. Do you need assistance clearing the road?'

The oily smile widened. 'Well, if your business is so urgent you do not have time for an old friend—'

Marcus's hands curled into fists. The man was an ugly customer, to be sure.

Cynthia merely looked cross. 'Of course it is urgent, Cornelius. Thomas needs me at his bedside.'

'Of course, of course.' Hart shook his head sorrowfully. 'Dear Thomas was always one to go where angels feared to tread. Please give His Lordship our best wishes for a speedy recovery and a safe return home. I look forward to our next meeting. Perhaps at dinner, since the one planned was of necessity postponed.' Hart narrowed his eyes as if trying to gauge her reaction.

Cynthia smiled tightly. 'It will be a long time before Thomas is fit for entertaining.'

'Sad business. Very sad.' Hart picked up his reins and inched his horses over. 'My dear wife was so looking forward to catching up on all your news, Lady Cynthia,' he said. 'Perhaps, in the meantime, you will do us the honour of a call.'

Again there seemed to be an underlying threat to his words.

Lady Cynthia's lips thinned. 'I shall do my best. Give your dear wife my good wishes.'

Hart touched his hat as they passed, but his gaze was fixed on Marcus's face and his lips twisted in a mocking smile.

Marcus wanted to plant the man a facer.

He glanced at Cynthia. Her face was expressionless, but her eyes were full of shadows. There was something about this man Hart that made her unhappy.

'Was he a good instructor?' he asked in mild tones as they continued on their way.

The smile she gave him was stiff. 'Excellent. It was he who taught me to take that gate you were concerned about.'

'And now he has moved on to teach a new generation of children.'

She shook her head. 'He married well. He manages his father-in-law's property. The property his wife will inherit.'

Was that a bitter edge to her voice? Was he another of her conquests? And yet he did not seem like a man besotted. In fact, quite the reverse. He seemed overbearing. And he had been her riding master, no less.

When Marcus turned his head from the road to look at her face, she was staring at him with a stricken expression. He could not stop himself. Bunching the reins in one hand, he covered the hand that rested on her knee with the other. Even through his gloves, he felt the tremble.

'What troubles you, love?' The word slipped out without him thinking.

'He is the most despicable creature alive,' she said, her voice full of loathing. 'I do not know how his wife tolerates him. Or rather I do know. I just cannot believe she can be so foolish.' She pressed her lips together and pulled her hand free. 'I really do not want to talk about him.'

'There might be something I can do to help.'

'I do not need any help with the likes of Cornelius Hart.'

Another untruth. Mentally he shrugged. If she did not trust him enough to reveal the real reason for her troubled expression, there was no more he could say.

For Cynthia, the next few days sped by. She and Marcus spent every day assisting Thomas and, while Nurse Jolly took over their duties for Thomas, they spent every night enjoying each other's company and bodies.

To her relief, Marcus had not raised the issue of Cornelius again. Indeed, they had spoken very little of anything important. Likely because they were both too tired for sensible conversation. But the lovemaking had been wonderful.

Since their first night together in his room, he had joined her in her bed. She had made sure they would not receive unwelcome visitors by telling Mrs Frost that she did not want anyone waking her for any reason, because she was so exhausted after tending to her brother all day.

Mrs Frost had understood completely. Or

she had decided to turn a blind eye to her and Marcus, no doubt thinking she was aiding a romance that would lead to marriage.

Drifting on a languid tide of bliss in the aftermath of their passion, Cynthia let herself dream that it might be so. She could imagine the children they would have and the laughter they would enjoy together.

She forced herself to wakefulness. And reality.

It could not be. She would never be so foolish as to fall in love. It left one far too vulnerable to pain and hurt.

But she was certainly going to miss Marcus, who would go home on the morrow, since Thomas was to be transported to Harrowglen in the morning. Her heart ached.

Marcus rolled over and reached out to take her hand. 'Awake so early?' he asked in dark warm sleepy tones.

He always sensed when she was awake.

'I was thinking about my return to Harrowglen.'

'And planning my departure.' There was a teasing smile in his voice.

'That, too.' Her smile was forced as she did all in her power not to reveal her regret.

He rose up on one elbow and gazed into

her face. As was so often the case, his dark gaze was searching.

'This is the end, then? Of us?'

Did he also harbour regrets? The thought warmed her, though it should not. There was no future in it for either of them. He needed a wife. She needed to retire from society. She had come to this conclusion on the day after going fishing. Society no longer held any interest.

Instead, she would continue her work for the children by reaching out to local chimney sweeps with her message. The Norton influence was even greater in this part of the country than it was in London.

'I hope we may remain friends,' she said tentatively. The idea of completely losing him was painful.

'Is that what we are? Friends?'

He sounded disappointed. 'It is what we will become,' she said firmly. 'That is if you wish it.'

'What about marriage?'

She froze. A deep longing tore at her insides. Surely, he did not mean it? She laughed. 'I think I must have misunderstood you.'

He grimaced. 'I do not feel right about this affair, to be frank. We have taken advantage of your brother's illness. The honourable thing is for me to make you my wife.'

A feeling of hope welled in her chest. Her heart gave a little skip. But— 'You feel it is your duty to offer marriage?'

'Not entirely. We seem compatible enough, don't you think? And there are other advantages. You clearly know how to run a household, which would be extremely beneficial. As well as your knowledge of running a stud. There is the little matter of my family's likely disapproval to get over, but I am sure they can be brought around to my way of thinking and see the advantages of the match.'

An arrangement. He was offering her a cold-blooded arrangement, despite knowing she was besmirched. From the soaring heights of hope, her stomach plummeted in a sickening rush.

It was the sort of marriage her grandfather had entered into. And her father. And likely Thomas. A marriage of convenience with a mistress on the side.

Well, it was all she could expect, wasn't it? No doubt he thought she should be grateful he would even consider offering marriage to a fallen woman. Anger started to bubble.

No. She was wrong to be angry. None of

what had happened to her was his fault. She was the one who had acted like an idiot over Cornelius. Marcus was offering to do the honourable thing. Likely against his better judgement or wishes.

She must respect him for his generosity. But in marrying her out of duty, he would deny himself the chance of marrying a woman with whom he was in love. What if he met that woman later in life? Where would that leave them?

In the same boat as her grandfather, that was where.

And something else occurred to her. 'If we did wed, I suppose Bess would be delighted to resume her engagement with Fortescue.'

'Possibly.'

'He is not the right man for her.'

'Is he the right man for you?'

No man was the right man for her. 'I have not yet decided.'

He gave her a long look. 'Aren't you being a little bit of a dog in the manger, Cynthia? You say you do not want a husband, yet you will keep him dangling on a string to prevent him marrying anyone else.'

He really did have a high opinion of the

woman whose hand he'd just requested, didn't he?

She smiled sweetly. 'I thank you for your most flattering offer, but I am afraid I must decline.'

His lips flattened. He got out of bed and afforded her a glimpse of his beautiful strong body, the line of his flanks, the curve of his lovely bum, before shrugging into his dressing gown. 'Then there is no more to be said. I do not think we can be friends, my dear, but we will be acquaintances whose paths may or may not cross from time to time. I will depart as soon as your brother reaches home safely.'

Not friends. Of course not friends. She felt hollow inside. Scoured. Because of course in some small corner of her mind she had wanted this idyll to continue. Indefinitely. She fought back the hot burning sensation behind her eyes.

She nodded briskly. 'I will not see you at breakfast this morning. I plan to eat in my room.' At least they would be spared the awful situation of trying to make polite conversation over eggs.

Besides, it was going to take her an hour or more to stop crying and make herself look like her usual self. Cool, calm and collected.

He nodded slowly. 'I will meet you outside when you are ready.'

She inclined her head. 'In case I do not get an opportunity before you leave Harrowglen, I must express my sincere gratitude for your assistance to Thomas these past many days. I am sure much of his speedy recovery is due to you. If there is anything either of us can do to be of assistance in the future, I hope you will ask.'

'You owe me no debt, Cynthia, so you need not pretend that you do. I did no more than what any man worth his salt would do.'

'Then thank you for that. And you will stand by our agreement with regard to stud fees and so on?'

He made a sound of impatience. 'I do not go back on my word.' He walked out.

Chapter Twelve

Repressing a sense of boredom, Marcus waited for his aunt and his cousin to come down the stairs of their London town house.

Having got through the Christmas season and celebrated a quiet New Year with the family slowly coming to an end of their mourning, they had decided it was time to join society in London.

February in London was far from pleasant to say the least. Grey skies threatened snow. The smoke-filled air from coal fires was a poor exchange for the fresh air of the countryside he had left a few days before. But for a man in need of a wife, as Marcus was, there was no help for it but to attend the start of the main London Season that occurred after the Prince Regent opened Parliament after the Christmas holiday. He felt a remarkable lack of enthusiasm for the task.

If it was not for affairs of business that required his attention in town, he might have procrastinated until the following spring.

And, naturally, Bess and her mother had insisted they come along because Bess was also in search of a spouse and where else could one look?

Marcus glanced up at the sound of voices on the town-house stairs. Bess, looking more grown up than she had when he first arrived in England, glided down, followed by her mother.

He gave them a warm smile. 'I shall be the most envied man at Almack's with two such beautiful ladies in my company.'

Bess giggled and he caught a glimpse of the schoolgirl he had been so fond of, but then she offered him a very grown-up smile. 'Thank you, Thorne. May I say you are looking very dashing this evening?'

Almack's was one of the few places a man was still required to wear knee breeches. That and the Queen's annual levee.

He escorted the ladies out to his carriage and they set off in prime style, as Bess liked to say.

As usual, there was a long line-up of carriages outside Almack's and they waited patiently for their turn to alight at the door. There was no sense in walking the short distance, the ladies' skirts would be mired in short order.

'I am so looking forward to seeing my friends again,' Bess said. 'Mary Wilson will be here and the Carey girls.'

Her mother nodded. 'Yes, I am glad you will not be the only girl in her second Season.'

'La, Mama, you make me sound as if I am already on the shelf.'

'Certainly not, dearest.'

'No, indeed.' She smiled shyly at Marcus. 'I hope you will lead me out if no one asks me to dance.'

'For every dance, if I have to,' Marcus joked.

'Nonsense, Bess,' her mother said. 'You never lacked for dance partners last Season and will not do so now.'

The carriage drew up and Marcus jumped down. He escorted his ladies inside the lobby, where they changed into their dancing slippers and made their way up the stairs.

As expected, the assembly rooms were crowded, but it wasn't long before his aunt and cousin had met old acquaintances and were enjoying catching up on news. Duties discharged for now, Marcus took the time to take in the assembled company.

Almack's. The renowned marriage mart for members of the *ton*. Already, he could feel the hairs on the back of his neck rise as the mothers of hopeful daughters marked his arrival with interest.

And across the room, in the midst of her court, his gaze found what it had been seeking. Lady Cynthia. A vision in a gown of celestial blue he recalled all too well.

He had corresponded with her brother about the stud and once their business was completed there had been no further reason to communicate.

She looked as beautiful as he remembered, though at times he had half wondered if his memory was faulty. It was painful to realise it was not. Amid her court of admirers with a cool remote smile upon her lips, she looked untouchable.

When he knew it was all a lie?

Resolutely, he turned away.

She had made her feelings perfectly clear that last day. And he had been relieved when she turned down his offer. Had he not?

Somewhat, anyway.

A gasp from Bess made him look down.

She, too, was staring at the group across the room. 'My friends said she had not been in town for months.'

He didn't have to ask which *she* Bess referred to.

Bess's eyes widened and she glanced up. 'You know, Fortescue isn't nearly as handsome as I remembered. He looks older, too, and I think he is going bald. She is welcome to him.'

And right before his eyes, Bess seemed to grow an inch and along with it gain a healthy dose of confidence.

'Good for you,' he said.

She beamed.

A young man standing beside a lady talking to Bess's mother gazed at Bess with the look of a besotted calf. Bess fluttered her fan in his direction. Her mother must have seen the exchange of looks because she drew Bess forward and introduced her to the woman and the young man. The next moment the two young people were heading for the dance floor.

'He's a Maxwell,' his aunt whispered from behind her fan. 'Very good family. With full pockets, too.' She wandered off to chat to a turbaned lady a short distance away.

The scene he had been dreading, where Bess first saw Fortescue, had passed without tears or drama.

To his surprise, he realised that Cynthia was watching Bess closely and, for some reason, he thought she looked pleased. He also thought she looked strangely lonely despite her surrounding crowd of admirers.

And he could not help wondering about her brother. Had he recovered from his injury? He looked around, but did not see the towering Norton.

Very much as he had the first time he saw Cynthia, he had a sudden urge to ask her to dance.

If he asked her to join him in the next set, would she refuse him?

Why would he do that?

To prove to himself that he could be friendly and as unemotional about the past as she no doubt was, or just to enjoy her company?

A bit of both, perhaps. Besides, it had not sat well with him that they had parted on such bad terms. He had lost his temper when they spoke last, a rare occurrence for him. He wanted her to know that if she needed help she could rely on him—as a friend at least.

* * *

Thomas had insisted that Cynthia attend this Season as his hostess. She had tried to convince him that he could manage perfectly well without her and to let her retire to Bellavista, but he was quite adamant that until he found a bride he needed her help. Because he had also played on his lack of mobility she had reluctantly consented to accompany him to London. There were several young eligible ladies in this Season's crop of debutantes whom she had brought to his attention. To her great joy, it did seem there was one particular lady who had caught his eye. Perhaps Thomas's need of her would be over sooner than he expected.

Naturally, when she had agreed to come to town, she had braced herself for the possibility Marcus would be present. He, too, needed a wife. When he did not appear for the opening of Parliament or for the opening ball, she had told herself she was glad.

But he was here now and, as she had expected, seeing him across the ballroom, looking so handsome and rugged, was painful in the extreme.

And a secret pleasure. The fact that he was not yet married had nothing to do with the lift of her spirits and the warmth dashing along her veins.

She wasn't going to pretend that she did not like him anymore. But her feelings were not relevant.

More to the point, as she had hoped when she acted to save Bess last spring, the young woman had looked at Fortescue the way a girl looked when she was over her crush. Fortunately, the sweet young lady had not suffered any major harm.

If only she herself had been so lucky with regard to Cornelius.

Regret did not butter any bread.

But she could feel glad her experience had done another young lady a bit of good and her plan had worked.

'In case you have forgotten,' Fortescue announced to the group at large, 'your next dance is with Lamb, Lady Cynthia. I am down to take you driving in Hyde Park tomorrow. Lamb and I did an exchange.'

'Really?' she said.

'Indeed. I have an important question to ask you.' He stroked his moustache. 'I believe you have been expecting it. Indeed, I believe it is what you have been waiting to hear.'

His smug expression made the hairs on

her arms stand straight up. She gave him her chilliest smile. 'I am not going driving to-morrow.'

He started and looked at his notebook. 'I have it right. Let me show you.'

'No need.' She turned to her expectant dance partner. 'I am sorry, Mr Lamb, but I will not be dancing with you or anyone else this evening. And you may destroy your list, Lord Fortescue. It is no longer needed. I am returning to Harrowglen immediately. Good evening, gentlemen. Come along, dear Mrs Paxton, we are leaving.'

It was with a good deal of pleasure she left Almack's ballroom. She would never set foot in the place again. And she couldn't help a little chuckle at the look of shock on Fortescue's face.

Mrs Paxton trotted along beside her. 'Harrowglen, my dear Lady Cynthia? In February? You know I really do not do well in the country during the cold weather. Surely you are mistaken?'

'Not at all. I leave three days hence. I shall not be returning to London.'

'You mean you will miss the rest of the Season?'

'And every Season thereafter.' The words

were like music in her ears, even if it did mean she would never see Marcus again.

She had managed to convince Thomas in one of his few moments of weakness to let her rent Bellavista. She had been unable to finalise her arrangements because there were still loose ends. Now they were neatly tied off.

'Oh, no,' wailed Mrs Paxton. 'I couldn't live at Harrowglen year-round. I simply could not. You know I cannot bear the country in winter. You must reconsider—'

She took pity on the poor woman. 'I am not asking you to come with me. Thomas will remain in London for a month or two. He will be quite happy for you to remain with him until the little house he has bought for you is ready.' It was part of the agreement she had made with Thomas. She did not want Mrs Paxton underfoot, but she did not want her abandoned to some other relative.

'Bought? Did you say bought?' Tears welled in the woman's eyes. 'I never thought it…indeed, I never did expect…'

'But you hoped. And now it is yours. It is very small, but it is situated in a genteel part of town.'

'You are too kind,' she said. 'I am so grateful. Really, I am. If there is ever anything I can do—'

'Shall I call for your carriage, my lady?' the doorman asked.

'Please,' Cynthia said. 'Dearest, can you collect our coats?'

A lackey was duly sent in search of their vehicle and Mrs Paxton, still burbling thanks, went off to redeem their coats and shoes.

While Cynthia waited, she was surprised to see Marcus come down the stairs.

She did her best not to notice. Where had Mrs Paxton got to? The poor dear was in such a dither, she was probably looking for an article she'd forgotten at home and thought she'd brought.

'I didn't take you for a coward,' a deep, familiar voice said close to her ear.

She turned and arched an eyebrow. 'Lord Thorne, what can you mean?'

'Running off the moment you saw me.' He spoke in a low voice only she could hear.

'Nothing of the kind,' she scoffed. 'I have developed a headache and decided to go home.'

'I do not believe one word of it,' he said. 'You guessed I was going to ask you to dance.'

Her heart lurched and when she spoke she

sounded sharper than she intended. 'Why on earth would you do such a thing?'

'I thought we were to be friends.'

'Acquaintances, merely, you said.' She could still feel the pain of his words. 'And, yes, I did see you and Miss Elizabeth also. She looks ravishing, I must say.'

'Must you?'

Why was he being so…so difficult? 'My carriage will be here at any moment.' She glanced around for her companion.

'May I take you driving tomorrow?' he asked. 'As a mere acquaintance.'

'No.'

He chuckled and a chord low in her belly tightened and her core fluttered. She clenched her hands into fists at her sides, digging her nails into her palms.

'Is it someone else's turn, then?' he asked. 'Shall I bribe him to let me take his place?'

'Now you are being ridiculous. No one is driving me tomorrow. I am returning to Harrowglen.'

Mrs Paxton chose that moment to arrive. 'You cannot leave tomorrow, Lady Cynthia, you know you cannot. It will take at least three days to pack and you have ordered gowns from the dressmaker that must be fitted before we leave.'

Well, she could have stayed indoors so everyone thought she had left. She took a deep breath. 'I do not have time for driving out. As Mrs Paxton reminds me, there is a great deal to do and pack before we go.'

'Oh, do not worry about that, my dear Lady Cynthia. I can look after things while you are out.'

Now, after all these years of vagueness, the woman decided to do something useful? Exactly when it was not needed? Cynthia stared at her, astonished, and received a beaming smile in return.

Clearly, Cynthia would have to be rude to Marcus if she was going to refuse his invitation, yet she really did not want to give him a set down. She sighed. 'Very well, we can drive out tomorrow, weather permitting.'

'While you are praying for rain, I will pray for sunshine.' He bowed and made his way back upstairs.

'How very odd,' Mrs Paxton said, watching him climb the stairs.

How very dear, Cynthia thought. 'Yes, it was, wasn't it?'

Mrs Paxton clasped her hands at her bosom. 'Do you think he wants to make you an offer?'

He certainly wanted to speak to her alone. 'I doubt it. And I would not accept. We would not suit.' She would sooner live alone than enter into a loveless marriage with a man she adored. Meeting Marcus had made her realise that this was the only way she could be happy.

'Your carriage is here, Lady Cynthia,' the porter announced.

The lady at Marcus's side, snugly tucked up in a carriage blanket, had an aura of grimness about her this morning. As if she had been tasked with something unpleasant.

'I hope you do not think my request too much of an imposition,' he said as they wove their way through the traffic over London Bridge.

'Thomas tells me you want me to look at a filly you are considering purchasing for your stables?'

'Yes. If you would not mind? My stable master has rented a paddock across the river, so I can take a look at her. He heard that an Irish breeder was selling off his stock and thought we might get a better price if we bought before she went to market.'

'Why did you not mention this last evening?'

'I thought you might not agree. You did not seem particularly pleased to see me.'

'I was neither pleased nor displeased,' she said dispassionately.

Squashing his pretensions, no doubt. She'd had years of practice squashing the pretensions of young men. Only he wasn't one of her court. He wasn't in the least bit squashable.

He laughed.

She glanced over at him, lips pursed in disapproval. He pretended not to notice.

'How long will it take to look at this horse?' she asked. 'I have a great many things to accomplish before I leave for Harrowglen.'

Oh, she really did not want to be in his company. Perhaps he should abandon the venture. 'An hour there, an hour back. I also took the liberty of bespeaking a luncheon at a nearby inn, so all in all I would think about four hours.'

'I see.'

The silence between them became oppressive. 'If you are worried that I will repeat my earlier proposal, do not be. This really is strictly business.'

'Then there is no need for chatter.'

'No, indeed. However, please assure me you are warm enough. We are lucky to have sunshine, but the air is nevertheless chilly at this time of year. Not that anything could ever be as cold as Russia in winter.'

'I am quite warm, thank you.' After a short pause, she spoke again. 'Did you like Russia?'

'It was unlike anything I have ever experienced. It was interesting and exotic in the extreme, but I cannot say I liked it. The winters are beyond cold and the absolute power of the crown is exactly what led to such a bad end for France.'

'You believe the same thing will happen in Russia that happened in France? Revolution. Regicide?'

'It is hard to say. The peasants accept their lot in life, and yet…there is a new class of educated young people who talk of abuses and change… I suppose time will tell.'

They came to a crossroads. 'This is where we turn off.'

He eased the phaeton into a small road between high bare hedges with little clumps of old birds' nests clinging to the twigs. A carter with a load of manure coming the other way steered his vehicle close to the verge and tipped his hat as they passed by. Thorne acknowledged him with a wave of his whip.

'In such bucolic surroundings, it is hard to imagine that we are only a few miles from the City,' she said.

'It is, indeed.'

They turned at a wrought-iron gate with the words Ivy House worked into the design and drove up the driveway to a nicely appointed Tudor house with beams darkened by age with a freshly thatched roof. The thatchers had created a cockerel out of straw. It stood proudly on the roof's scalloped ridge.

Thorne drove around to the back of the house and drew up at the barn.

A dapper youngish man with a magnificent set of black whiskers running down his jawline emerged from the barn. 'My lord!'

'Parker,' Thorne said. 'I have brought Lady Cynthia along to look at the horse.'

Parker bowed low. 'I am honoured, Your Ladyship.'

Cynthia acknowledged his greeting with a dip of her chin, reverting to her usual chilly self. Had she taken some sort of dislike to the fellow or was this how she shielded herself from the world when she felt unsure?

He hadn't considered that before. Yet on

several occasions in the past he had sensed her feeling vulnerable. She had no reason to feel that way with him at her side.

Parker went to the horses' heads while Thorne helped her down.

'Is she in the paddock?' Marcus asked.

'As you requested, my lord,' Parker said, rubbing his hands together with a dry rasping sound.

'Excellent.' He held out his arm and Cynthia rested her hand on his sleeve.

Parker strode ahead.

The filly, a long-legged beast, pricked up its ears at the sight of them. Its halter was tied to the fence rail. It watched them approach with flicks of the ears and twitches of its tail.

As they drew close it showed the whites of its eyes and jerked away.

'What is her pedigree? Cynthia asked.

'Her great-grandsire was Bartlett's Childers,' Parker said with obvious pride.

'Impressive,' Cynthia said.

'So I told His Lordship.'

'And on the dam's side?'

'She can trace her lineage all the way back to the Darley Arabian.'

'A lineage to be envied,' Cynthia said drily.

Parker shot her a sharp look. 'I have the documents to prove it, my lady.'

'Walk her for us,' Marcus requested.

Parker led the filly around in a circle.

'I find her a little straight in the shoulder,' Cynthia said. 'Apart from that, she looks very nice.'

Parker led her back to the fence. 'Her sire did well and was similarly conformed, my lord. What she loses in length of stride she makes up for in strength and stamina.'

'Her ancestry is good, but buyers like to see a few ribbons on the dam before they buy any foals.'

Parker gave her a look of irritation. 'I can assure you, my lord, you won't find a finer filly this side of Ireland.'

Cynthia gave him a sweet smile and he blushed. 'That is a great reassurance, Mr Parker. It was you who advised Lord Francis Thorne on the purchase of his horses, was it not? Tell me, who was your employer before you were employed by Lord Thorne? Perhaps I know him. A great many of my brother's friends breed horses.'

Parker gave her a winning smile. 'I worked for Lord Pettigrew's stud and before that in the Duke of Beauville's stables.'

'They gave Parker excellent references,' Marcus said. 'I found them among my cousin's papers.'

She nodded. 'Both men had great reputations in my father's day. One doesn't hear much of them any more.'

'Getting a bit long in the tooth,' Parker said. 'Starting to sell off the best of their stock. It was why I moved on.'

Thorne ran a hand down the filly's withers. It shied away.

Parker shortened the halter rope. 'She's still a bit skittish after the journey.'

'Let me see her paces,' Thorne said.

Parker trotted her around in a circle, then a canter.

Cynthia narrowed her eyes. 'Is it my imagination or is she winging that left hind foot in?'

Thorne squinted. 'So she is.'

'It is very slight. She might grow out of it.'

'Do you think so?'

'It is hard to tell at this age, but it is more likely to get worse. We had a colt with the same problem when I was young. He was as fast as the wind, but more often than not he'd clip the other hoof and stumble. He was much better suited to carriage work. Personally, I would not advise purchasing this animal for breeding.'

'Should Parker not have noticed this fault?'

'It is minor. And yet…yes, I believe a man with his professed experience should have seen it.'

Marcus frowned. He did not like the sound of this. 'You seem to doubt his qualifications. My cousin purchased several horses upon his recommendation.'

'Oh, dear.'

'You think Francis might have been misled?'

'I would suggest you contact Parker's previous employers because I honestly cannot believe either one of them would give a reference for an unqualified man.'

Parker ran back to the fence. 'What do you think, my lord?'

Marcus shook his head. 'Why did you not mention that she wings out?'

Parker's jaw dropped a fraction. 'A small thing, my lord, nothing to be concerned about. It runs in her lineage in her distaff side. All the way back.'

Cynthia's eyes widened. 'All the same you should have mentioned it, I would have thought. Also, I have never heard that the Darley Arabian had any such flaw or that it was found in any offspring.'

Parker's expression was sullen. 'My lady, I have spent years training racehorses. I know whereof I speak.'

The fellow sounded defensive. A bad feeling churned in Marcus's gut.

'For such a sum as the seller is asking, the horse should be nigh on perfect,' Cynthia said. 'Who is the seller? Perhaps I know him.'

Parker shuffled his feet and Marcus's suspicions were confirmed. Something was not right. 'An Irish gentleman by the name of O'Toole. Sir Seamus O'Toole.'

Cynthia shook her head. 'I have never heard of him.'

'Like His Lordship, Sir Seamus has been abroad for many years. Came back to Ireland recently. A friend of mine let me know he was selling off stock. I think you will be sorry later, my lord, when you see this girl walking off with a Newmarket purse.'

'More likely to break a leg and trip the whole field,' Cynthia said.

Horrified, Parker stared at Marcus. 'My lord, animals with this sort of pedigree don't show up every day of the week.'

Parker's eagerness struck a sour note. 'I will think about it.'

'I would advise making an offer right away, my lord. I—'

'You will have my answer by the end of the week, Parker. Lady Cynthia, I think we should eat lunch and then set out on the return journey.'

He took Cynthia's arm and they headed back for their carriage.

'I have a great deal of doubt about the filly's lineage,' Cynthia said.

She glanced at the house. 'Is this one of your properties?'

'No. Parker was told about a likely filly being for sale at a horse fair nearby and arranged to take a look. He convinced the animal's owner to rent stabling here until I had a chance to look her over. He actually asked me to give him *carte blanche* to make the purchase, but I wanted the benefit of your greater knowledge.'

He glanced back at where Parker stood with hands on his hips watching them leave.

He looked decidedly unhappy.

Seated beside Marcus on the way to the inn where they would lunch, Cynthia could not help but be flattered by him seeking her opinion of the little filly. Naturally, if Thomas had been up and about, Marcus would have deferred to her brother. But Thomas, while he was able to get around using a cane, found long journeys by carriage arduous. The drive to London had been taxing for them all, and he certainly could not yet sit on a horse. Still, she was gratified by the way Marcus had deferred to her greater knowledge, particularly in the face of a man who had declared himself an expert.

And she felt happier than she had felt in weeks. Being with Marcus did that to her.

She quelled the thought with a frown.

'Your man seems almost desperate for you to make the purchase,' she mused. 'It is almost as if he has some sort of personal interest in the sale.'

'I thought so also. I will check with his previous employers as you suggest.'

'And ask around about this O'Toole individual while you are at it. If he ran a decent stable, someone will know of him.'

'Indeed I will.'

The inn they drew up at was not far from the farm they had visited, in a small village with a duck pond in the middle of the village green.

The innkeeper led them to a private parlour overlooking the green.

'It will be pretty simple fare, I am afraid,' Marcus said. He looked at the menu and ordered an assortment of cheeses, a loaf of bread, along with sliced ham and an apple tart.

'I will take a tankard of your best ale,' he said to the innkeeper.

'A glass of mulled wine for me.' She rubbed her hands together and went to stand by the fire while the innkeeper and his waiter bustled about preparing the table and delivering the food.

'You are chilled. I should have brought the closed carriage,' he said.

'Then we would have had to endure my dear Mrs Paxton for the drive. You would have been treated to a thorough inventory of every ill that has beset her for the past fifty years. You may not have minded, but it is old news for me.'

'It does not sound as if I have missed a treat. However, I will have them heat a couple of bricks for you for the return journey and please keep your hands under the blanket. You do not need to hold on, I will not overset you, I can assure you.'

Her smile did things to his blood he did not like to think about.

He helped her to sit at the table and waved off the waiter when he came to pour the wine. He fully intended that during this lunch he would have her cards on the table and he didn't want hovering servants listening to their conversation.

He served her some bread and cheese. 'It reminds me of our picnic by the river.'

She visibly relaxed. 'It was a good day.'

'Tell me about your committee. How are plans coming along?'

She buttered another slice of crusty bread and bit into it, clearly thinking about her answer.

'It is not going as well as we had hoped, quite honestly.'

'Why is that?'

'Many of the sweeps are claiming the brush does not clean nearly as well as the little boys do. And it gets stuck in the flue more frequently. It does not navigate the bends as easily as do the boys.'

He frowned. 'So they are going back to using boys.'

'Not all. But some. And if homeowners become suspicious about the cleanliness of their chimneys using brushes, they will refuse to use sweeps unless they use boys. The cruelty of it makes me feel quite ill.

'I didn't say anything when we were at Bellavista but Jack, the boy who works in the stables, was employed by one of the worst master sweeps in London. He was burnt and beaten and thoroughly cowed. And so very little when I found him in my living room in a panic because he had taken a wrong turn.'

Anger vibrated in her every word.

This was the woman behind the cool mask. The same passion she'd shown in their lovemaking exuded from every pore in her body as she spoke. Her depth of caring for the plight of these children made him ashamed he had taken the need for climbing boys for granted.

'You are right. Something needs to be done.'

'It will take years to get acceptance of the use of brushes, unless a law is passed to stop the use of children. Only Parliament can solve the problem and they have no appetite for change.'

'Because it is their chimneys that need cleaning.'

Her gaze turned hard. 'Exactly.'

'And the brush does not work very well.'

'It is adequate, but some sort of improvement would help. We need a champion in Parliament to take up the cause.'

'Your brother?'

'Because of me, Thomas only uses sweeps who use brushes, but grumbles all the time about the risk of fire. It is hard to be a champion for something you do not believe in.'

'I would like to see this brush in action.'

'You would?' She looked astonished. 'That I can arrange before I leave.'

'Never to return.'

'Indeed.'

'And you will give up this crusade of yours?'

'Certainly not. I will start a branch of the Committee in our local town and work just as effectively from there.'

But it was London and Parliament that held the power to make the change. It didn't make sense to him that she would leave town at this juncture.

'You will be living at Harrowglen, then?'

'No. I have leased Bellavista from Thomas. It is time he took a wife and while I have been there making his life easy, he has procrastinated. Therefore, it is better if I set up an establishment on my own.'

And did she have another lover standing in the wings?

'Tell me about Hart.'

Cynthia froze. Her stomach dipped. Why was he asking about him? 'I do not know what you mean?'

'The way he spoke to you. His innuendo you purposefully ignored. He has some sort of hold over you. I would know if I can be of some assistance?'

She felt ill. Ashamed that he had seen what no one else had. And once he knew the full truth he would likely never want to speak to her again. And this after she had received the first real promise of help for her Committee from a peer.

He would despise her.

Perhaps it was better if he did. She would never have to see him again and be reminded of what she could never have because she had been so wilfully stupid as a girl.

'You are right. Hart was my lover.' She lifted her chin. 'My only lover, apart from you, as it happens.'

She half expected him to rise from the table

and leave. Indeed, she was sure of it when he moved. But it was only to refill her glass.

'When?'

'When what?'

'When was he your lover?'

'What does it matter when?'

'How old were you?'

She shrugged. 'Seventeen when we made love the first time, but he'd kissed me and petted me many times before.'

He looked grim. 'Seventeen. My god! Barely out of the schoolroom. He debauched you.'

'I am not so sure. I threw myself at him. I was convinced I was in love with him. When it was time for me to attend my first Season in London, I told my father I did not wish to go. That I wished to marry him. That I would marry no one, if I could not marry him.'

'I expect your father took that well.'

'He was already ill at the time. I think the shock nigh on killed him, though he never knew the full extent of our affair. Neither I nor Cornelius had the courage to tell him we had made love.'

She sighed. 'I wonder if things might have turned out differently if he had known? In hindsight, I am grateful that he refused to countenance the match.

'Instead, unbeknownst to me, he bought Cornelius off and as part of the settlement my father made with him, Cornelius convinced me to go to London for my Season. To put my father off the scent, Cornelius said. Within three weeks he had married my best friend.'

She shook her head. 'Poor girl. On my return home from London, for Papa's funeral, he told me that since my father had blighted all of his hopes for marriage to a titled lady, he would make sure that no one else married me. Any man to whom I became engaged would be informed of my lack of maidenhood. I could not have been more shocked. Or hurt.

'Naturally, I told him that any future husband would be informed by me of the mistakes in my past, because that was the honourable thing to do. Not because of his threats. I suppose I was naive enough to hope it wouldn't matter so very much.'

'I am surprised your brother didn't call the dastard out.'

'I never told Thomas it was Cornelius. He assumed it was one of the young men who were sniffing around me in my first Season. I let him believe that and refused to give him a name. What was I to do? I could not let Thomas become a murderer.

'So we see Cornelius socially when we are at Harrowglen and I grit my teeth, smile and pray he continues to keep my secret. I believe Hart sees Thomas's affability towards him as a mark of his advancement in the world, something he would lose were he to speak out, so I say nothing.'

'Blackmail.'

'Of a sort.'

'The blackguard.'

'There is nothing to be done about it. The truth will ruin me and put a black mark on the Norton name. And that I will not do. Worse yet, Thomas told me yesterday that Cornelius and Felicity are coming to London. He received a note announcing their arrival. He wants Thomas to take him to Tattershall's. I was so pleased when I saw Miss Elizabeth no longer hankered after Fortescue and I could leave London and return home. The last person I want to see smirking at me over the dinner table is Cornelius.'

'Hart is a cur. A dog.'

She was shocked by his vehemence. 'He only did what men will do when offered a plum ripe for the picking and financial advancement is in the offing.'

'You are wrong, Cynthia. No gentleman

would take advantage of such a young and impressionable girl.'

Marcus would not, of that she was certain.

She waved a hand. 'It is too late for regrets. I am willing to pay the price for my foolish behaviour provided it does not drag my family name into the mire.'

She hoped she sounded more accepting than she felt.

He sighed. 'And Fortescue?'

'What?'

'Why did you lure him away from Bess?'

'I told you, I did not lure him. He simply switched his affections.'

'Do not lie. You deliberately wooed him away.'

'Believe what you will.'

'Cynthia, from the moment we met you have been telling me half-truths and outright lies. I would have the whole truth now.'

'I doubt you would believe the truth.'

'Try me.'

'Very well. If you must know. I tried to warn Lady Elizabeth about Fortescue. I told her the man's character was not of the best. She refused to listen as did her mother when I dropped a hint.'

'Why would you do that?'

'After what Hart did to me? I would not have Elizabeth fall into the same trap given what I heard about Fortescue.'

A grim look of satisfaction crossed his face. 'I am glad to see you acknowledge that Hart was at fault.'

Astonished, she stared at him. 'You are right. I do blame him, but in my heart, I fear that I was the one who did wrong.'

'No. You did not. He was a man ten years older than you and with a great deal of experience of the world. He knew exactly what he was doing. He made you fall in love.'

The assurance made her heart seem twice its normal size. 'Thank you. You do not know how much that means to me to hear you say so.'

She hesitated. 'From what I hear, Fortescue is worse than Hart. I learned through a member of my Committee that he associates with ladies of the night and beats them nigh unto death. There is a rumour that one did die after a night with him. I do not want that for Elizabeth. She was my friend. But once married, what could anyone do to save her?'

'Then she *was* right. You did lure him away from her.'

'I did, but don't you see—'

He reached out and took her hand across the table. 'I see perfectly well, Cynthia. You ruined your friendship with my cousin to save her from disaster. You have my gratitude.'

She closed her eyes briefly, let the warmth of his hand comfort her, though of course his gratitude would be all she would ever have.

Somewhere a clock struck two. 'It is time we returned to town,' she said briskly. 'The hot brick you offered sounds like a very good idea.'

He frowned, but nodded and went off to carry out his errand.

By the time he returned from his mission she was perfectly composed and held a lively conversation with him all the way home, yet could not remember one word of it when she sat in her drawing room sipping her tea.

She took a deep cleansing breath.

Tomorrow would be a new day. And a new life.

Albeit a lonely one.

Sitting in his study, Marcus drummed a rhythm on his desktop with his fingertips and glanced at the ormolu clock on the mantel.

His visitor should arrive at any moment and hopefully another loose end would be tied up.

The first had been Parker. Cynthia had been right about the stable master. The man was a fraud who had disappeared the day after Marcus and Cynthia visited the horse he was trying to convince Marcus to buy.

Upon further enquiry it was clear that neither of the men Parker had used as references had ever heard of him. Now Marcus was left with a stable full of animals whose pedigree he could not trust.

Thank goodness Cynthia had been knowledgeable enough to see right through the man or he might have sent good money after bad, the way Francis had.

Now the more difficult loose ends remained. Firstly, Hart.

If he'd learned one thing in the diplomatic corps, it was to use rumour and gossip to his advantage. And the rumour that he might be thinking of making Cynthia an offer of marriage brought a worm out of the dark and into the sunlight.

His butler scratched on the door and opened it to admit the gentleman in question. 'Mr Cornelius Hart, Your Lordship.'

Hart strode in with the air of a man with important news. 'My lord, we met a few months ago, as I hope you recall.'

Marcus rose and gestured to a chair. 'I do indeed, Mr Hart. Please be seated.'

Hart flipped his tails aside and sat down, crossing one leg over the other and leaning back with the air of a man used to moving in exalted circles.

Marcus sat. 'And how may I be of service today?'

'Oh, dear me, no, my lord,' Hart said with an ingratiating smile. 'I plan to be of service to you. It is naturally a matter of utmost confidentiality. Although, yes, there may be some small token of appreciation I would desire, but for a man in your position it would be a mere bagatelle.' He snapped his fingers.

Marcus released the clench of his jaw. He inhaled a deep breath and smiled. 'How is it you can be of service to me, Mr Hart?'

Hart leaned forward, confidentially. 'A little bird tweeted that you are soon to be married.'

Marcus feigned a frown. 'What little bird?'

Hart waved airy fingers. 'It is of no import. However, I must tell you, the lady in question, the woman…' he made a face of distaste '…is actually no lady at all.'

Marcus shook his head as if puzzled. 'I honestly have no idea what you are talking about.'

'You are thinking of getting married, are you not?'

'What business is it of yours?' He did not want to make this too easy for Hart. He didn't want him becoming suspicious.

Hart swallowed. 'If the lady in question is Lady Cynthia, you should be wary, my lord.'

'Why?'

His eyes darted around the room and back to Marcus. 'This is difficult for me to say. I have known the family for many years. But Lady Cynthia will not come to the marriage bed pure.'

Anger filled Marcus. Blood ran hot in his veins. 'You know this to be a fact?'

Hart must have interpreted the anger as directed at Cynthia because his expression became sly. 'Oh, indeed, my lord. One would only have to look at the letters I have in my possession to see the truth of what I say.'

Cynthia had mentioned nothing about letters. 'I would see these letters.'

Hart brought forth from a breast pocket three or four folded notes of pink paper addressed in a rounded childish hand. He placed them on the desk in a little pile.

Marcus wanted to choke the breath from the fellow, but that would not help Cynthia. He picked up the top one, opened it and looked at the signature, before folding it again. 'I see.' He tapped it against his fingers. 'You mentioned some token of my appreciation.'

Hart twirled his moustache. 'I do not ask for much. My wife would dearly like an introduction into society.'

The servant's door to the right of Marcus's desk, well-disguised by the wallpaper, swung open. Norton stumped in, leaning heavily on a walking cane with a silver handle. 'My father already paid for your silence, did he not?'

'I… Well…' Hart spluttered. 'It is criminal that you are letting this gentleman marry soiled goods without saying a word.'

Marcus's good friend Caulfield stepped into the room. 'As a justice of the peace, I would say that the crime in progress is slander, for which I would impose a heavy sentence. Let me call a constable, Thorne, and have him arrested.'

Hart turned a pale shade of green. 'I have done nothing wrong. Is it a crime to inform a man he is being hoodwinked by a conniving female?'

Marcus glared at him. 'If you repeat your false accusations one more time, I shall eviscerate you.'

Hart wrung his hands 'They are not false. I have proof.'

'Do you?' Caulfield asked. He picked up the letters and cast them onto the fire without as much as a glance at their contents. The fire flared up, then died. 'What proof?'

Hart looked at the ashes in the grate and shook his head.

Caulfield glared at him. 'Blackmail is a hanging offence. Be glad I do not charge you with that.'

Hart shrivelled like a deflated pig's bladder. 'I—'

Marcus put up a hand and he ceased speaking. 'May I suggest a trip to India? I hear they are always looking for hard-working fellows there. A riding master should not have too much trouble finding work. I will pay for your ticket.'

'India?' he gasped. 'But my wife…'

'She can go or stay,' Norton said. 'You should return in about twenty years. Or perhaps you would prefer a convict ship to Australia.'

Hart wrung his hands. 'India,' he whispered.

'Good,' Caulfield said. 'One of my constables is waiting outside. He will escort you on board.'

Marcus bared his teeth in a wolfish smile. 'Oh, and by the way, another gentleman will be joining you. A Lord Fortescue, a gentleman also seeking his fortune abroad. He will be somewhat unwell for the first few days. Too much laudanum. I am sure you will take good care of him until he feels better.'

'Fortescue?' Hart squeaked.

'Yes. Tell him there is a warrant sworn out against him for murder.'

'Murder?'

'Do you have to repeat everything I say?' Marcus growled.

Hart swallowed and shook his head.

'Do not worry, old chap,' Norton said. 'I will inform your wife of your whereabouts. If she decides to join you, I will be more than glad to buy her a ticket for a later sailing.'

'And if one word of these false accusations is heard from this day forth I shall find you and gut you like a fish,' Marcus added.

Caulfield escorted Hart out of the door, leaving Marcus and Norton alone.

'Blackguard,' Norton said. 'I would prefer to see him swinging on the end of a rope.'

'But that would necessitate a trial and a great deal of scandal,' Marcus reminded him.

Norton sank into the chair vacated by Hart.

'Poor little Cynthia. I cannot believe it. Why did she say nothing to me? I would have—'

'You would have done what I was very tempted to do.' Indeed, he had wanted to strangle the fellow with his bare hands. 'Your sister knew this and feared it would result in a hangman's noose around your neck. So we will not negate all her years of suffering by going against her wishes now. Instead, we have dealt with it in the best way possible.' Marcus poked at the fire. 'It has ended. Now we deliver the other scoundrel to the ship.'

'Fortescue.'

'Indeed.'

Cynthia glanced out of the drawing room window. She had moved into Bellavista two months ago with Thomas's blessing. In the pouring rain, the view across the valley had a mystical quality, but the peaceful scene did little to lift her spirits. Not a good day to go for her usual walk.

She glanced at her writing desk. She had not yet replied to Thomas's last missive. She had been procrastinating over sending him a reply for two days now.

Unfortunately, her brother could not write to her without mentioning Marcus, gleefully informing her of meeting him at every ball and rout that London had to offer. According to Thomas, Marcus escorted his little cousin everywhere and she had taken London society by storm. She was the darling of the fickle *ton* and Cynthia could not have been more pleased.

She had not seen Marcus again after their ride out to view the filly he was thinking of purchasing. Before she left London, he had written a brief formal note of thanks for her assistance and to tell her that her suspicions about Parker had been correct. She was grateful he had let her know. It was kind of him, but then she would not have expected otherwise. He was ever the gentleman and, heaven help her, she missed him terribly.

No. She must not think that way. She had everything she ever wanted. Her independence, the house she loved, her work with the Committee. She was even starting a chapter of the Society.

She needed something to stop her mind wandering back to thoughts of Marcus and lowering her spirits. An embroidered footstool in the corner caught her eye. Yes. The very thing.

She rang the bell for Mrs Frost.

The old lady arrived, leaning heavily on her cane. 'My lady?'

'I am going to pay a visit to the attic.'

Mrs Frost paled. 'You wish me to go with you?'

Cynthia repressed a smile. 'Not at all. I would like the key.'

The housekeeper sorted through her chatelaine and handed over a large iron key. 'I hope it works. No one has been up there for a long time.'

'I will let you know if I have a problem.' With a lantern in hand, Cynthia climbed the back stairs to the fourth floor. After a bit of jiggling of the key, the small door creaked open. Cobwebs hung from the open rafters and boxes and rolled-up carpets were piled neatly in one corner.

Cynthia lifted the lid of a green-painted trunk and knelt down. Ah, here was what she sought. Scraps of fabric, skeins of silk and neatly rolled linen tied with ribbon. She unrolled one of the smaller pieces.

How charming. The half-finished rendition of an eye. She looked at it this way and that and tried to recall the portrait of her grandfather. She would have to compare the two, but she was almost certain the iris was the same colour as the one in the picture She could only assume it was that of her grandfather.

She sorted through the threads, trying to match the colour Lucy had chosen for the iris, a bright sky-blue, much like the colour of her own eyes. She imagined Lucy working away in her grandfather's absence. Perhaps it was intended as a gift. How sad that she hadn't finished it.

Heavy footsteps on the stairs. Who would have followed her up here? She rose to her feet at the knock on the door.

And started.

There was Marcus on the threshold, rain glistening in his hair. 'Marcus?'

She almost rushed forward, but at the last moment dipped a curtsy instead. 'Goodness me, what can Mrs Frost be thinking? I would have come down.'

'Mrs Frost sent me up,' he said stepping into the room. 'She is sending tea along to the drawing room, if you would care to come down.'

'Oh, dear. I am sorry she sent you with her message. What must you think?'

He looked a bit shamefaced. 'To be honest, I was concerned that you might not want to see me, so I offered to find you. What treasures did you discover?'

'Oh, it is a piece of work Lucy started.' She held it up for him to see. 'I thought I might finish it, as a thank you to her and my grandfather for the house.' She gave an awkward laugh. 'A bit of foolishness really, but something to do on a rainy day.'

'I apologise for arriving unannounced. I didn't actually plan this visit. I was on my way home and I simply kept going when I should have turned off miles back for Thorne Manor.'

'I see.' She didn't really. 'Perhaps we should go downstairs or Mrs Frost will wonder where we have got to.' She wouldn't, but Cynthia had an urgent need for a bracing cup of tea. Why had he come? Her heart picked up speed. What did he mean, he had not intended to call?

He glanced around the attic. 'Since there is nowhere to sit, I think the drawing room would be more comfortable.'

She smiled. 'If I had known to expect a visit in the attic, I would have had some chairs brought up.'

He laughed. And all at once she felt perfectly comfortable. This was Marcus. And she was pleased to see him, no matter the circumstances.

She rolled the silks inside the needlework and led the way downstairs.

A silver tea tray on a table in front of the sofa awaited them. Cynthia sat behind it, then added water to the teapot.

'I know your brother intends to write to you about Hart, but I wanted to tell you.'

Her heart stopped. Her stomach dipped. He had betrayed what she told him in the utmost confidence. 'You told him? How—?'

He put up a hand. 'When you left London in such a hurry he came to me, asking why things had gone wrong between us. I told him you did not want to marry and he told me that he did not believe it. That you would make some man, I think he meant me, a perfect wife.' He took the cup of tea she handed him and sat down beside her. 'Your brother cares for you deeply and will always be concerned for your welfare. I decided that it was not right that Hart should get away with what he did to you.'

'You have no right—'

'I have no right to interfere, but your brother does. Until you are twenty-five, he is your guardian.'

Terrified for Thomas, she leapt to her feet. 'It is water under the bridge. I am as much to blame as Hart—'

'Hart has been suitably punished.'

Her heart seemed to stop beating. 'What? You cannot have—'

'He is on a ship to India with instructions not to return for twenty years or repeat any more of his lies, unless he wishes to find himself incarcerated.'

'But they were not lies.' She swallowed her embarrassment. 'He has letters—'

'The letters are burnt. Faced with the prospect of being brought up on trial for blackmail, Hart decided to find employment in India where a man who works hard can make himself a fortune.'

She sank onto the sofa. 'You mean it is over. He can no longer create a scandal.'

He took her trembling hand in his. 'It is over. He is gone. As is Fortescue. They left on the same ship.'

'Fortescue, too?' She was having trouble taking it all in. 'I do not know how to thank you.'

He passed her a cup of tea. She sipped it and her heart lifted. 'This is wonderful news. Now Thomas can find a bride without any fear of my scandal rearing its head and spoiling things.'

He tilted his head with a puzzled expression. 'I did not understand it before, but now I realise that you always put the happiness of others before your own.'

She felt heat rise in her cheeks. 'Not always. If I had been a little more caring about my father's happiness, I would never have behaved the way I did with Hart and my father might not have died quite so young.'

'You were not to blame for a man like Hart setting his sights on a girl half his age. To be honest, your father should have spotted what was happening long before it bloomed into an affair. We men know exactly what other men are like.'

'It is kind of you to exonerate me, but I cannot think of myself as blameless.'

'Well, it is over and you should think of your needs.'

She raised her chin. 'I think I am being very selfish, taking this lovely house for myself. It is what I have wanted for a very long time.'

Marcus gave her an intent look. 'Is this house all that you want, then?'

It was all that she could have. Just because

Hart had been disposed of didn't make her any less of a wanton. She wasn't going to pretend she hadn't had an affair. Indeed, now she had enjoyed a second with Marcus, she was definitely beyond the pale. 'It is enough.'

'I am sorry to hear it. I believe you deserve so much more.'

'We do not always get what we deserve.' She poured him a cup of tea and handed it to him.

He was looking at her with a very odd expression. Was he thinking they should resume their relationship? Heat flushed her cheeks.

And the rest of her body.

Her heart raced.

Was she actually thinking of agreeing? Thomas would not be pleased.

'I don't think it is a good idea,' she said.

He frowned. 'Why not?'

'To begin with, Thomas would be most upset.'

'No, he would not. I asked him.'

'You asked him if he would mind if I became your mistress and he agreed?'

'My— Of course not. Silly goose. I asked him if he would mind if I asked for your hand in marriage.'

Her jaw dropped. She could not comprehend what he was saying. 'After all that has happened, you want to marry me?'

'I love you. I have loved you for quite some time.'

'It is not possible.'

His expression became unreadable. 'I see.'

'I mean, it is very kind of you, but you could do so much better for yourself.'

'Let me be the judge of that. I have to admit I have had my doubts, despite how very attractive you are to me. The falsehoods you tripped out at every turn troubled me a great deal. I thought you were like a woman I knew a long time ago. A woman who lied to me about everything for her own selfish ends.'

'A woman?'

Regret filled his expression. 'A woman I thought I loved when I was very young and very green. She made me distrustful. But in spite of the lies you told me, I kept finding myself trusting you. And I was right. I realise now that you were trying to protect everyone around you rather than protecting yourself. I find that very dear, if somewhat misguided.'

Her heart tumbled over. 'I don't know what to say.'

'You could say yes.'

She seemed to be trembling from head to

toe. She swallowed. Tried to think. 'What if Hart returns to make trouble?'

'He will not dare. I have witnesses to his perfidy.'

'What if—?'

'Cynthia, we will stand together. The only thing I ask is that you trust me the way I trust you and never tell me anything but the truth. Is that too much to ask?'

'Not if you make me the same promise.'

'I always have and I always will.'

A stab of uncertainty caught her breath in her throat. 'You really do love me?'

'I do. With all my heart.'

And since she knew he would never lie to her, she believed him.

'I love you, too. Oh, I do. But I thought it impossible. And after you spoke of doing your duty...'

'Yes. I apologise for that. I was not being entirely honest at that particular moment. But I don't think I knew it.'

He put down his cup and stood in front of her, reaching for her hand. He kissed the tip of each finger and the inside of her wrist. Thrills ran along every vein in her body.

He dropped to one knee with a smile. 'Lady

Cynthia Finch, will you do me the very great honour of becoming my wife?'

'Yes. Just let anyone try to stop me.' She threw her arms around his neck and kissed him.

Somehow during that kiss, he managed to lift her up, sit on the sofa and settle her on his lap.

They kissed and they kissed. His hand wandered down her thigh and teased at the hem of her gown. She snuggled closer and parted her thighs—

And the door crashed opened. 'Cynthia,' Thomas said, then stopped, staring at them mouth agape. He put his hands on his hips and glared at them. 'I come all this way post haste to tell you that Thorne wants to make you an offer and that I insist you receive him, and I find the fellow has beaten me to it.'

Marcus seemed unperturbed and gently prevented her attempt to leap to her feet. 'Norton, you are the first to know. Your sister has accepted my hand in marriage.'

Thomas blinked. 'I should dashed well think so, if you are going to be carrying on like that.'

Cynthia laughed. 'Thomas dear, don't you think you should be offering us your congratulations?'

Thomas marched to the bell and pulled it.

Mrs Frost must have been hovering outside the door, because it did not take her above a moment to answer the summons.

'Mrs Frost,' Thomas said. 'Break out some of that champagne my grandfather put down. We have some nuptials to celebrate.'

Mrs Frost beamed. 'See. I knew it.' She scurried off.

Epilogue

Whereas Cynthia and Marcus would have settled for a marriage in Harrowglen's drawing room, Thomas had wanted them to mark their wedding in grand style at St George's in Mayfair. They had compromised with a small wedding in the family chapel in the grounds of Harrowglen. Marcus had obtained a special licence so they had only had to wait a week for the ceremony and they planned to spend the two weeks of their honeymoon at Bellavista.

Millie pinned a small pearl and emerald brooch fashioned in the shape of a spray of lily of the valley to Cynthia's lapel. It was one of the items from Lucy's collection. It represented something borrowed, since Marcus had agreed they would do their best to discover what had happened to Lucy and return her jewels to her or her family if at all possible.

Millie stepped back. 'You look beautiful, my lady.'

Cynthia had chosen to wear the pale blue she loved so much and, given the time of year, she had selected a long-sleeved velvet spencer to wear over her gown.

'She does look lovely,' Bess said from where she sat on the end of the bed. She had come to help Cynthia dress and, because the day was fine, if a little chilly, they and Thomas would walk together to the chapel.

Cynthia smiled at Bess. 'Thank you. I only hope Marcus feels the same way.'

Bess grinned. 'Of course he does. He is marrying the most beautiful bride in England.'

Cynthia smiled at her soon-to-be cousin-in-law. 'I am so happy you and your mother agreed to attend our wedding and I know Marcus is, too.'

'I love Marcus like a brother,' Bess said. 'And you have made him the happiest of men. He told me this.' She jumped up from the bed. 'I want nothing more than for him to be happy.' She hesitated. 'Also, he told me I should thank you for preventing me making a huge mistake in marrying Algernon. I was very angry at the time. But when I saw him with you in London, I realised I had been mistaken in my feelings towards him. And I do thank you.'

Cynthia breathed a sigh of relief. She had been worried that Bess would continue to harbour resentment towards her and the last thing she wanted was for Marcus to lose the affections of his family.

She gave Bess a hug. 'Thank you for telling me. I hope that we can be more like sisters than cousins. And I will look forward to celebrating your nuptials when it is time. I hear there is a young man who is showing you very particular attentions.'

Bess blushed. 'I—'

Cynthia gave her a quick hug. 'I know. It is far too soon to be talking of engagements and such. Make the most of your Season. The rest will come in due course. Let us go down, I am sure Thomas will be getting impatient.'

They walked downstairs together where they were met by Thomas and one of his friends, who walked them the few yards to the chapel door. To Cynthia, the day seemed especially bright and, although the air was cool, Cynthia could only feel the warmth of happiness.

The small chapel was brimming with well-wishers, family and friends and neighbours, all of whom turned at her entry, but the only person she had eyes for was Marcus, who was waiting at the altar with a smile on his lips and a look of admiration in his eyes.

And Cynthia knew without any doubt at all—this was the culmination of all her hopes and dreams. She would have the love in her marriage that her grandfather and Lucy had found in each other.

When Thomas placed her hand in Marcus's and their gazes met, it was the happiest moment in her life. Without a doubt, there were going to be many more such happy moments to come for her and Marcus.

* * * * *

COMING
SOON!

We really hope you enjoyed reading this book.
If you're looking for more romance, be sure to
head to the shops when new books are
available on

Thursday 28th
October

To see which titles are coming soon, please visit
millsandboon.co.uk/nextmonth

MILLS & BOON

THE HEART OF ROMANCE

A ROMANCE FOR EVERY READER

MODERN

Prepare to be swept off your feet by sophisticated, sexy and seductive heroes, in some of the world's most glamourous and romantic locations, where power and passion collide.

HISTORICAL

Escape with historical heroes from time gone by. Whether your passion is for wicked Regency Rakes, muscled Vikings or rugged Highlanders, awake the romance of the past.

MEDICAL

Set your pulse racing with dedicated, delectable doctors in the high-pressure world of medicine, where emotions run high and passion, comfort and love are the best medicine.

True Love

Celebrate true love with tender stories of heartfelt romance, from the rush of falling in love to the joy a new baby can bring, and a focus on the emotional heart of a relationship.

Desire

Indulge in secrets and scandal, intense drama and plenty of sizzling hot action with powerful and passionate heroes who have it all: wealth, status, good looks…everything but the right woman.

HEROES

Experience all the excitement of a gripping thriller, with an intense romance at its heart. Resourceful, true-to-life women and strong, fearless men face danger and desire - a killer combination!

To see which titles are coming soon, please visit

millsandboon.co.uk/nextmonth

MILLS & BOON

Coming next month

UNWRAPPED BY HER ITALIAN BOSS
Michelle Smart

'I know how important this maiden voyage is, so I'll give it my best shot.'

What choice did Meredith have? Accept the last-minute secondment or lose her job. Those were the only choices. If she lost her job, what would happen to her? She'd be forced to return to England while she sought another job. Forced to live in the bleak, unhappy home of her childhood. All the joy and light she'd experienced these past three years would be gone and she'd return to grey.

'What role do you play in it all?' she asked into the silence.

He raised a thick black eyebrow.

'Are you part of Cannavaro Travel?' she queried. 'Sorry, my mind went blank when we were introduced.'

The other eyebrow rose.

A tiny dart of amusement at his expression—it was definitely the expression of someone outragedly thinking, *How can you not know who I am?*—cut through Merry's guilt and anguish. The guilt came from having spent two months praying for the forthcoming trip home to be cancelled. The anguish came from her having to be the one to do it, and with just two days' notice. The early Christmas dinner her sister-in-law had spent weeks and weeks planning had all been for nothing.

The only good thing she had to hold on to was that she hadn't clobbered an actual guest with the Christmas tree, although, judging by the cut of his suit, Cheekbones was on a huge salary, so must be high up in Cannavaro Travel, and all the signs were that he had an ego to match that salary.

long while, her gaze studying him. 'The offer is very…
generous,' she said at last.

'I don't care if it's generous, Miss Peverett. Is it
tempting?'

He wanted her to say yes, despite the voice inside
whispering a warning, *you are tempting fate.*

She nodded, but her words were wary. 'Yes, it is.'
She was still suspicious.

That voice inside was more insistent now. *As well
she should be—you are concealing your true purpose
from her.*

Ferris refilled their glasses, ignoring her suspicion
and his twinge of conscience. 'A toast, then, to a new
partnership.' The idea of having her here should not
please him as much as it did, nor should the thought of
his undisclosed agenda sit so poorly with him. He didn't
like the feeling that he was misleading her.

Anne had summed up his offer correctly. He did want
to keep an eye on her and she needed the space. There
was just more that he'd omitted telling her. Perhaps the
omission wouldn't matter in the long run. They both had
what they wanted and people would be served by the
arrangement. But the 'ends justifying the means'
reasoning didn't quite assuage his conscience as well in
practice as it had in theory.

'To teamwork.'

Continue reading
LORD TRESHAM'S TEMPTING RIVAL
Bronwyn Scott

Available next month
www.millsandboon.co.uk

LET'S TALK
Romance

For exclusive extracts, competitions
and special offers, find us online: